PRAISE FOR FLETCHER MICHAEL'S

Glass Bottle Season

"Fletcher Michael's *Glass Bottle Season* is a closely observed coming-of-age tale set against the backdrop of the insular culture of Newport Beach royalty. This boozy, immersive novel will resonate with anyone who has ever felt like an outsider or has experienced that painful passage between the last gasps of childhood and beginnings of adulthood. It's a terrific beach read, and just like summer, you won't want it to end."

—Michelle Brafman, author of
Washing the Dead and *Bertrand Court*

"This boozy coming-of-age novel is a great read for anyone who's felt out-of-place in their own home, or clung too hard to that one last carefree summer."

—Tyler McMahon, author of *One Potato*

GLASS BOTTLE SEASON

ALSO BY FLETCHER MICHAEL

Vulture

GLASS BOTTLE SEASON

A NOVEL

FLETCHER MICHAEL

KEYLIGHT BOOKS
AN IMPRINT OF TURNER PUBLISHING

KEYLIGHT BOOKS
AN IMPRINT OF TURNER PUBLISHING COMPANY
Nashville, Tennessee
www.turnerpublishing.com

Glass Bottle Season
Copyright © 2023 by Fletcher Michael. All rights reserved.

This book or any part thereof may not be reproduced or transmitted in any form or by any means, electronic or mechanical, including photocopying, recording, or by any information storage and retrieval system, without permission in writing from the publisher.

This is a work of fiction. All the characters and events portrayed in this book are either products of the author's imagination or are used fictitiously.

Cover and book design by William Ruoto

Library of Congress Cataloging-in-Publication Data

Names: Michael, Fletcher, author.
Title: Glass bottle season / by Fletcher Michael.
Description: Nashville, Tennessee : Turner Publishing Company, [2023]
Identifiers: LCCN 2022027197 (print) | LCCN 2022027198 (ebook) | ISBN 9781684429424 (hardcover) | ISBN 9781684429417 (paperback) | ISBN 9781684429431 (epub)
Subjects: LCGFT: Bildungsromans. | Novels.
Classification: LCC PS3613.I34255 G57 2023 (print) | LCC PS3613.I34255 (ebook) | DDC 813/.6—dc23/eng/20220819
LC record available at https://lccn.loc.gov/2022027197
LC ebook record available at https://lccn.loc.gov/2022027198

Printed in the United States of America

FOR JULES

PART I

JUNE

It is better to be a young June-bug than an old bird of paradise.
—MARK TWAIN

CHAPTER 1

An Interview in Boston

Sweat coated Ray's palms, leaving faint streaks on the steering wheel. Cool air sputtered from the battered AC vents, and the fraying seat belt seared his neck each time he turned his head. The ice at the bottom of the plastic Dunkin' Donuts coffee cup lodged in the cupholder had long ago melted into a sludgy mixture of cheap sugar and dairy residue. After circling the block twice, a parking spot appeared. Ray reversed into the tight space. Checking the dashboard's clock, which he'd set ten minutes fast to counteract his persistent tardiness, he cursed and flung open the car door. Steaming city air and the smell of fresh asphalt accosted his lungs as he jogged in the direction of the address he'd been given.

The rectangular gray building squatted obstinately on its cement foundation, the brutalist edifice casting a long shadow several blocks up Beacon Street. Gold letters spelled out Williams, Fisk & Boggs, Esq., over the entrance. Ray paused before entering the lobby, retucking his shirt and adjusting the stiff necktie that bit into his collar, which the humidity had rendered limp as a dishrag. He hadn't worn a tie since high school, swearing off such formal garments after enduring four years of a strictly enforced dress code. Using the reflection of the dark glass door, he dabbed at the sweat on his forehead with his sleeve. Despite Ray's explicit instructions, the haircut his brother had given him the day before exposed his remarkably large ears, which he usually kept concealed behind a curtain of dark hair. He shrugged at his reflection and yanked on the heavy glass door. Climate-controlled air washed over him as he entered the building, seeping through his damp shirt and raising goose bumps on the back of his freshly shorn neck.

When the sharply dressed secretary with long, tapered fingernails ushered him into the office, Ray already knew everything he'd be expected to say—when to nod and when to laugh; when to lie and when to tell the truth. Mentioning the tightly rolled spliff currently jammed in the back of his glove compartment, for instance, would likely be poorly received in an interview of this kind. Old-school Boston lawyers—who tended to be aging white guys who thought wistfully of the bygone era when men wore hats—would be far more interested in where he'd gone to school, what sports he'd played, how he knotted his tie, who he'd met or hoped to meet, whether his politics were liberal (tolerable so long as he noted his fiscal conservatism), and how he planned to make a good American of himself.

Ray rarely left the island and often regretted it when he did, especially in the summer. Just last night, he'd been sipping rich brandy out of a crystal tumbler to ward off a sudden chill that had blown in from the east. The breeze had nearly spoiled the sunset cruise through Narragansett Bay, which he and the rest of the party had been enjoying from the bow of a friend's catamaran.

Rhode Island summers could be as fickle as house cats—sunny and pleasant all morning before onerous gray clouds would trundle across the sky in the late afternoon. Residents of America's northeasterly region are never allowed to forget that winter is always lurking around the corner, ready to spring out in full force as soon as the first October leaf hits the ground and maintaining its bitter, cold dominion until the last pebble of ice salt has been scourged from the street by the late-spring rains. Still, the brandy last night had been good.

Boston had been pulling at his friends like a magnet ever since graduation, but Ray resisted the compulsion that they all deemed natural—life's logical next step. So even as his peers clamored over salaries and got fitted for suits, Ray pushed all thoughts of cover letters and résumés far from his mind. If Finch's father hadn't gone out of his way to set up the interview, Ray never would have given up a perfectly viable beach day to drive two hours through traffic up Route 24 with what was beginning to feel like a terminal hangover. He popped an Advil, his third of the day.

The interviewer greeted Ray gregariously. He was a tallish man who looked to be in his late forties. Ray guessed that the man was neither Williams nor Fisk nor Boggs—they were probably testing out their new putters somewhere on the Cape on a glorious afternoon like this—but rather one of their aspirational acolytes. He gave his name as Phil and he wore a trim blue suit that didn't quite hide his paunch. He sat on a leather rolling chair, his legs sprawled beneath a sturdy oak desk. His steel cuff links clattered against the grandiose face of his watch when he shook Ray's hand. Several framed degrees were pinned to the wall behind the desk, each one proudly bearing an Ivy League crest. A bronze telescope positioned by the window (which pointed, for some reason, *into* the room) seemed to be a component part of a meticulously cultivated nautical theme. Among the leather-bound tomes that lined the floor-to-ceiling bookcases were old sextants, ornate compasses, a brass ship's clock, and artfully frayed ropes scattered at carefully placed intervals along the shelves. A massive iron anchor rested in the corner by the door.

"Maritime law," Phil said, noticing Ray's furtive glances. "We do all kinds of things here at WF and B, but maritime law is what we've become known for, you know."

Phil gestured casually at the rigid wooden chair opposite the desk and Ray seated himself, doing his best to look earnest and impressed. But all he could think about was whether the snug blazer he hadn't donned since high school was dark enough to hide the half-moons of sweat he felt forming on the fabric pinched under his armpits.

The interviewer squared up the résumé in front of him with a practiced tap of his fingers.

"So . . . Raymond Wilson-Domingo. Sounds like a law firm itself, doesn't it? Ha! All you're missing is the esquire. Now, Domingo . . . is that . . ." The interviewer waited for Ray to finish the sentence.

"Cuban," Ray said. "Only on my mother's side, though."

He'd meant to change it before hitting Print. But he'd been running late, snatching the warm document from the printer tray and peeling a tangerine with his teeth on his way out the door. He hadn't even had time to type up the details of the internship he'd been intending to fabricate. It seemed that each time he'd sit down at his desk, his hands hovering over his laptop's keyboard and either his sophomoric résumé or the blank document that might one day feature an impressive cover letter filling the screen, he'd receive a text from Kirley (typically a photo of a just-purchased handle of dark rum unaccompanied by words but implying volumes) or else a slurred call from Finch beckoning him to some happy hour. Declining such invitations never felt like much of an option to Ray; it would've been like trying to ignore the pull of a strong undertow. Boston's June humidity seeped through the office walls, smothering the central air and painting shiny patches beneath Ray's eyes. Last night's brandy was army-crawling down his back in a platoon of sweat droplets.

He had a sudden urge to stand up and leave without a word, to peel off his blazer on his way out the door and to drive back to Aquidneck Island with the radio blaring. He'd felt this way before, as a child, when he would become gripped by a strong notion to climb a tree and hide among the upper branches when the school bus would appear at the corner of his block. If he were to leave now, there might still be a little daylight to be salvaged by the time he got home. The muscles in his legs tensed, preparing to stand. But the roaring impulse quickly passed, subsiding to a dull ache in his stomach.

Phil perched Ray's résumé on the ledge created by his protruding midsection as he relaxed back into the plush chair, his thin lips parting to reveal milk-white veneers.

"Ah," Phil said. He nodded sagely before adding, "You know, I smoked a real Cuban once." A conspiratorial expression glazed his face.

"Really? Even I haven't done that," Ray said, feigning incredulity. Ray pictured Phil wearing a colorful Hawaiian shirt and Rainbow flip-flops, expensive sunglasses perched on his sunburned nose. An easy mark for some savvy caballero pedaling counterfeit cigars to tourists cologned with sunscreen and ambling along Miami's Calle Ocho in their sensible walking shoes.

"Down in Miami, yeah. It was unbelievable," Phil replied. He glanced down at Ray's résumé. "You're from Newport? Beautiful area. Me and the wife try to get down there at least once a summer. You ever eat at 22 Bowen's?"

Ray used to bus tables at 22 Bowen's during his summer vacations back in high school. The version of Newport that Phil was picturing as he fiddled with his kempt beard, Ray knew, was the quaint seaside town prominently featured in gift shop postcards: the Gilded Age mansions with spectacular ocean views, the kitschy little shops selling glassware and coffee-table books, the historic cobblestone roads, the beaming blond families holding overstuffed lobster rolls up to the camera. He certainly wasn't thinking of the ramshackle houses deep in the city's Fifth Ward neighborhood, or of the underfunded public high school nestled (hidden, really) along one of the many curving roads that led to some of the country's most opulent homes, or of the budget condominiums that sprawled in the shadow of the island's sole Walmart, or of the Portuguese fishermen who made daily predawn sojourns to the edges of the rocky outcroppings that jut out into the sea like tusks at violent angles along Ocean Drive.

"It's great in the summer," Ray said. He straightened in his chair, displaying his most hirable spine.

"Isn't there some big wedding happening down there this summer? Some rich Newport people?" Phil asked, sliding Ray's résumé to the side and folding his hands over his belly.

Ray wasn't surprised that news of the Campbell–Doheny wedding had pricked ears in Boston. New England's old-money circles were close-knit, entrenched in nearly every scenic coastal pocket along the East Coast stretching from Manhattan's Upper East Side and New Canaan to the south and up through Newport to Boston and on to Bar Harbor in the north. And this wedding wasn't just "some big wedding." Wealthy betrothed couples had lavish seaside weddings in Newport nearly every weekend in the summer. The city's socialites and arch gossips had fanned the Campbell–Doheny wedding's intrigue (through an artful combination of secrecy, rumor, and leaked detail) that all but guaranteed the event's enviable grandeur and haughty exclusivity.

It was only June, and already the wedding had taken on a fascination generally reserved for royal weddings of the Buckingham variety—not that the Queen herself could've gotten an invitation at this point. Just as their British forebears had stamped themselves with hierarchical imprimaturs of class through anointing ceremonies and swords touched meaningfully upon shoulders, Americans of the Gilded Age had compelled societal status into a commodity to be purchased and displayed—in the form of mansions, world's fairs, transatlantic vessels, and the like—before being handed down to the next generation, reducing their fringe relations with barons and duchesses across the Atlantic to amusing anecdotes to be politely (*almost* self-deprecatingly) bragged about at cocktail parties.

Even Ray, who took pride in maintaining an amused distance from Newport's elitist doings, admitted (though only to himself) to a definite interest in the wedding. Olivia Doheny, progeny of the Pan American Petroleum & Transport Co.—drillers of fine oil and practitioners of corporate corruption since 1916—had replied in the affirmative to Wayne Campbell's (as in, the makers of canned soup since 1869) proposal of marriage, continuing the aristocratic tradition of securing power through bloodline. Anybody driving a Land Rover en route to Montauk or practicing knots on the catamarans moored in Buzzards Bay would be talking about little else this summer, the gossip slipping past their blocky patrician teeth and out the sides of their dour Anglo-Saxon mouths. Of course, the ceremony wouldn't actually take place until late August.

Phil picked up Ray's résumé again. His eyes roved up and down the page.

"Anthropology major, eh? Okay, no problem. We don't get a lot of anthropology majors interviewing here, but different is not always bad . . . I suppose the anthropology industry isn't exactly booming these days, is it?" Phil chortled.

"Right," Ray said, forcing a laugh.

Phil ran a hand through his thinning hair and puffed his chest, gathering his legs underneath him from their previously sprawled state like a puppeteer rectifying a collapsed doll. Too vain to wear reading glasses, he squinted down at Ray's résumé. He asked the usual questions about strengths and weaknesses, past jobs and future goals, and Ray gave the expected answers.

They stood up together, and Phil shook Ray's hand. It was a firm, practiced handshake—probably something Phil was proud of having mastered, Ray thought.

"We'll let you know! Thanks so much for coming by, Ray," he said. "And give my best to Finchy, won't you? Tell him he owes me a bottle of Laphroaig."

Ray thanked him and walked out the door, past the benignly smiling secretary. A boy with a smart haircut and a tailored suit almost bumped into Ray as he was exiting the waiting area. A cloud of cologne and aftershave followed the boy into the office, not fully obliterating the rank smell of cigarette smoke embedded in his clothes.

"Bertie! How's the old man, huh?" Phil bellowed, clapping the boy on the shoulder.

Ray figured Bertie's dad was a friend of one of the partners, and Bertie was probably short for Bertrand or Alberticus or something. Maybe he and Phil had met once at a golf outing or a company retreat or some other place where they used *network* as a verb. As soon as Ray stepped out of the suffocating building and into the metropolitan streets of Boston, he loosened his tie and tore his damp shirttails out from his belted waist. Men and women in dark suits strode past him in both directions, their arms fixed like fins as they clutched their cell phones to their ears. Sweat glistened on their furrowed brows. Their dark shoes scuffed against the grime-coated sidewalk, and their pant legs swished against each other as they walked with purpose toward uptown train stations or downtown happy hours.

Ray clambered into the old Volvo and let the tepid AC blast over him. The Red Hot Chili Peppers crooned from the car's boxy speakers as he pulled out of the cramped parking spot. Fishing his hand into the back of the glove compartment, he watched as Boston's angular skyline receded in his rearview mirror.

CHAPTER 2

A Rendezvous in Middletown

Coyne's parents' house was the kind of home you might draw with crayons as a child: a big two-story square with symmetrical windows, a bright-red door, a perfectly trimmed green lawn, and a two-car garage with a basketball hoop sticking out over the driveway. Two Labradors bounded toward Ray as he traversed the flagstone walkway, huffing protectively until they'd appeased themselves with a sniff of his sneakers. Coyne appeared from under one of the partially raised garage doors and ushered the dogs back inside. A half-eaten granola bar protruded from the side of his mouth. He jerked his head toward the house.

"My mom wants to say hi. I told her it had to be quick."

Ray followed Coyne into the kitchen. The house smelled of grilled salmon and chopped chives harvested from Mrs. Coyne's lush garden. A few thick tomato slices bathed in a puddle of balsamic vinegar on a large ceramic plate, pebbles of salt clinging to their pink flesh.

"Ray, honey! Come on in," Mrs. Coyne said. "Did you eat? Are you hungry? I'll fix you a plate."

Coyne rolled his eyes and grimaced at the time displayed on his Apple watch as Mrs. Coyne pulled Ray's lanky frame down into a tight embrace. The Labradors wriggled figure eights through their legs, nearly knocking them over in a tumble of human and canine limbs.

"I'm okay, thanks. I just ate," Ray said.

No matter the weather, a mug of hot tea was perennially clasped in Mrs. Coyne's hands. Her ruby-lacquered fingernails drummed against the ceramic cup.

"Your mom tells me you're thinking about moving up to Boston," Mrs. Coyne said. "Any idea what you'll do up there?"

Though Ray and his friends had been fielding this same question (posed always with a mixture of curiosity and parental concern) for several months now, few of them had a very satisfying answer yet. While true adulthood would be postponed for a few sunny months, he and his pals would be moving out by summer's end, presumably to an eastern metropolis of some kind. Perhaps New York or Boston or Philadelphia or Washington or some other place where serious people went to live and work. Never, it should be noted, was Los Angeles deemed a legitimate place to take one's business. There was simply too much glitz in L.A., all flavor and no substance—a floating, glittering sprawl unmoored from any respectably historic antecedents. California hadn't even become a state until 1850, by which time Rhode Island was a proud septuagenarian. Among Ray's crowd, Boston was the ideal post-college metropole: far enough away to claim independence, but close enough to come home for every holiday and every other weekend to do laundry and eat from a refrigerator stocked with more than loose White Claw Hard Seltzers, flaccid soy sauce packets, and calcified onion rings. But these were September thoughts, and this was a promising June evening.

"No, not really," Ray responded with a shrug. "I just have a lot of friends living up there right now. I'm thinking about it, I guess."

Mrs. Coyne smiled and nodded her head sincerely, her fingers still tapping against the mug. "Yes, that would be fun. Lots to do up there in Boston."

"Yep, anyways, Mom, I think we're gonna head out," Coyne said, slinging his backpack over one shoulder. His leather flip-flops thwacked against the kitchen tiles as he stepped purposefully toward the door.

"So you boys will be carousing around Jamestown tonight?" Mrs. Coyne asked, her tone playfully disapproving. Coyne sighed and rolled his eyes again.

As he grew older, Ray had found that he could make riskier jokes, be more puckishly flippant than he would have dared when his gawky, fifteen-year-old limbs had been squished into the back seat of Mrs. Coyne's BMW. The parents seemed to enjoy this light testing of the boundaries these days, too, a sportive reminder that they'd been young once and that their children would one day be old. It was an opportunity to embody their caricatures more fully, to be the shrugging, head-shaking parents and the brash, rebellious kids; a pantomime of a remembered, not-so-distant reality tinged with nostalgia and relief, which both parties now and then enacted out of a sense of melancholic duty.

"Oh, you know me. I like a nice quiet night with a paperback," Ray replied, his dimpled cheeks belying the mock seriousness of his tone.

A hoot of laughter erupted from Mrs. Coyne's rouged lips just as Mr. Coyne made a rare appearance indoors. He ducked into the kitchen from the backyard, where he was eternally tinkering away at his boat. The bill of his faded Red Sox cap swiveled back and forth as he shook his head, chortling ruefully as he rinsed engine grease off his hands. By way of greeting, he lifted an empty beer bottle in Ray's direction before dropping it into the recycling bin under the sink.

"Oh!" Mrs. Coyne yelped, as though she'd just remembered something terribly important. "Ray, honey, did I hear correctly that you're catering the wine for the Campbell–Doheny wedding?"

No doubt she'd heard it from Ray's mother, who was equally excited about the wedding and her son's fringe association with the ceremony. Coyne groaned and looked longingly out the window, just as his Labradors might upon seeing a squirrel scurrying across the lawn. Mrs. Coyne ignored her son's ill-concealed displeasure, keeping her eyes trained on Ray.

"Not me personally," Ray replied, laughing. "But yeah, the store is handling *all* the booze for the wedding, actually."

Out of the corner of his eye, Ray could see Coyne popping up and down on the balls of his feet, jingling the car keys in his pocket.

"Oh my! So then, are *you* delivering it?" Mrs. Coyne asked, her eyes widening and her fingertips ceasing their rhythmic beat against the mug. Even Mr. Coyne paused at the fridge after procuring another Harpoon IPA.

"Mom! Quit interrogating him. He probably doesn't even know yet," Coyne harrumphed. He placed his hand declaratively on the doorknob as he spoke.

"Well, that is really *something*, anyway," Mrs. Coyne said, repositioning her hands on the mug. Her unblinking eyes held on Ray's face as though willing him to say more, to divulge any glamorous details about the Campbell–Doheny wedding that he might be withholding.

Ray nodded, bending to stroke one of the dogs when the silence stretched beyond comfort. Mrs. Coyne opened her mouth as though to speak but her son broke in before she could articulate whatever she'd been about to say.

"Yeah, well, this is fun and all but we should really get going," Coyne said, shifting from one foot to the other.

His parents leaned against the granite countertop. It was clear that they would have loved to linger on like this, to spend some time with these two adults who had at some point replaced their husky son and his gangly friend. Ray half wanted to indulge them, maybe pop open a decent bottle of cabernet and ask Mr. Coyne how the boat was coming along. But Coyne had seized on the momentary lull in conversation like an osprey striking an unsuspecting bass, yanking open the door to punctuate his parting words. The dogs hurtled out into the yard in a blur of dark fur and whipping tails.

"You boys have fun. And give our best to Maya's parents!" Mrs. Coyne called out. "And get those dogs back in here before you leave. I saw a skunk wandering around my tulips a few nights ago."

Mrs. Coyne clutched Ray in a parting hug, mentioning something about his height. Ray turned to give Mr. Coyne the most trustworthy, responsible, college-educated handshake he could muster before heading out the door, but he realized too late that the elder Coyne had already slipped back outside to his boat. A drill whirred from somewhere inside the boat's sloping hull.

The bronze Lincoln Continental had been Coyne's sixteenth birthday gift, and Ray heaved the large parcel that he removed from his own car into the Lincoln's trunk before sliding down into the cushy passenger seat. The ocher June sky turned to slits of dappled light as it filtered through the branches of the beech trees that rose up on either side of Wapping Road. They passed house after house decorated with wooden anchor door ornaments or artsy lobster mailboxes.

"I swear she'd just keep talking like that all night," Coyne mumbled. Because he was deaf in one ear (the result of an incident at his ninth birthday party involving a ne'er-do-well cousin and a paintball gun), Coyne always cocked his head to one side when he spoke, angling his functioning ear toward the conversation in a way that often made him look somewhat skeptical of whatever was being said.

"My mom's the same, man, it's all good," Ray replied.

"How was the interview?" Coyne asked. "Nice haircut, by the way."

"Thanks, Tony did it. The interview was . . . you know, fine. First one, so."

Coyne nodded and poked at the radio tuner, landing on a classic rock station playing Nirvana's "All Apologies." The men who had waited all afternoon for the worst of the day's heat to dissipate revved their expensive lawn mowers, filling the neighborhood with a droning hum as they tended to their square green empires. Labradors barked from every other porch, and more than a few driveways reserved space for a sleek boat resting high on its trailer. Laughing children pumped their skinny legs on bicycles, racing each other around the safe blocks, where speed limits never exceeded twenty-five, pricking their ears for the song of the ice-cream truck.

CHAPTER 3

A Get-Together in Jamestown

Cool dusk air blew in through the window that Ray had lowered on the passenger side, draping his arm over the door and letting the soft breeze ripple through his fingers. Coyne's head bobbed to the music as the car belted westward. A contented silence settled between them as they drove, broken now and then by occasional remarks about where some restaurant seemed to have moved or how the road closure attending the construction of some new hotel would likely affect seasonal traffic. Summers provided ample opportunity to slacken the pace of conversation, progressing from one topic to the next as unhurriedly as the overlong daylight hours that slipped gradually into night and freeing them from the necessity of engaging in the burdensome catch-up chats that characterized the intermittent hangouts of school breaks.

Ray sank deeper into the luxury sedan's plush seat as Coyne munched absently on a toothpick, a habit he'd picked up as a means of quitting the Juul pods he'd become addicted to in college. The toothpick was now a permanent fixture between Coyne's teeth, jutting out like a brief tusk from the corner of his mouth.

"Allllllll right ladles and jungle-men, that was, of course, Nirvana with 'All Apologies.' Now let's settle in, shall we? Sink into that easy chair, top off that cocktail, and light up that cigarette because up next we have a little band you might've heard about called the Talking Heads with 'This Must Be the Place.' You're listening to Rhode Island's home for classic and alternative rock: 95.5 WBRU."

The disc jockey's rasping voice faded into silence as David Byrne's reedy, soaring vocals filled the car. Ray pictured the disc jockey, imagining him in a cramped studio somewhere in East Providence with a cigarette perched on his lip, wearing some faded black Pink Floyd T-shirt he'd picked up at a concert in the '80s and would never dream of throwing out, his long gray hair falling to shoulder length. The man sounded content to Ray, cozied up behind his desk with a pair of boxy headphones dangling from one ear as he scrolled placidly through some infinite database of albums and tracks. Ray turned up the volume a touch.

"You know the Talking Heads formed at RISD back in the seventies?" he said.

"Yeah, I think I heard that once," Coyne said.

Coyne took a sharp left down Van Zandt Avenue.

"Why don't you just take Broadway up to West Main?" Ray asked.

Coyne just rolled his eyes and ignored Ray's comment. A lifetime Aquidneck local, he took pride in knowing every back road and uncharted shortcut. His fingers drummed against the steering wheel in sync with the song's rhythm as he puttered down a narrow one-way and maneuvered onto the Newport Bridge. Lowering his window further, salt air poured into the car, and Ray looked down at the blue-green sea churning far below, peppered here and there with triangular white sails and rusting lobster boats. Seagulls perched along the bridge's turquoise railing. The cloudless sky had taken on a brilliant peach hue, and the ebbing whitecaps glimmered in the golden light. They came to the end of the bridge and the car drifted noiselessly onto Conanicut Island.

Old lighthouses stood at resolute intervals along the rocky granite coastline. The dairy farms and goat pastures that lined the unmarked roads granted the island a certain bucolic sublimity. Conanicut was the second-largest island in Narragansett Bay, after Aquidneck, and was occupied only by the sleepy village of Jamestown. Enormous waterfront mansions that could be seen only from the sea loomed at the end of long, sloping driveways. The only reason that Ray knew these mansions were there at all was because he'd driven for Uber during his Christmas vacation one year to save up enough money to join his friends on a spring break trip to New Orleans. He'd routinely accepted the rides that would take him from Newport to Jamestown, knowing that each trip could yield an opportunity to breach the elaborate private entrances and glimpse the magnificent homes where his drunken passengers spent their nights.

Coyne slowed toward the end of East Shore Road to watch several deer grazing in a grassy lot. Their long, tapered ears were silhouetted in the pinkish light. Sensing the humming car engine's presence, their tails pricked skyward, and then they bounded toward the trees in long, athletic strides.

The car fought to accelerate up the steep driveway that led to Maya's house. In the winter, with an inch-thick sheet of ice coating the ground, the severe incline of the driveway challenged even the staunchest of vehicles. Sitting on an abrupt hilltop, the enormous three-story home formed the highest point on the island. From the third-floor bedroom, one could see all the way to Portsmouth and, occasionally, when the fog lifted off the bay, all the way to Block Island. It hunched on its foundation, unfinished in places but comporting itself with a rambling dignity. Despite the clapboards and shingles missing here and there, there was nothing impoverished about the house's aspect—especially considering that it could have fit three regular-sized homes comfortably within its walls. Rather, it exuded a simple unpretentiousness, the prideful austerity favored by lifetime New Englanders (certain Puritan sensibilities were hard to kick, even four centuries later). It was a masterpiece of schizophrenic architecture, as though three Civil War–era frigates had at one point collided, and rather than separating them, the architects had simply done their best to fit the disjointed planks into one massive wooden juggernaut of a home. The numerous rooms of the disjointed estate were connected by circuitous stairwells and winding, narrow hallways. Owners had added and subtracted amendments to the house in the decades since its ill-fated construction, optimistically hiring contractors and unveiling pristine blueprints, though all of their efforts had been vanquished by the peculiarity of the house's dimensions. Each renovation attempt would unearth heretofore unknown rooms or hallways (remnants of previous such attempts), maddening designers and owners alike and compelling them to foist the gargantuan mess onto the next quixotic buyer.

Maya's parents had never felt the need to impose changes on the defiantly illogical home. They'd simply accepted its inherent irreconcilability and raised their entirely functional family within its dysfunctional walls. None of the doors locked properly, balconies jutted at sharp angles off all sides of the house, and windows appeared at odd intervals along the facade, cut seemingly at random into the tired wooden beams. Four different doors could be mistaken for the front entrance.

"I'll be honest, I've always found this place creepy," Coyne said.

His eyes roamed over the chaotic collage of planks and shingles. The toothpick rolled back and forth across his lips. Ray paused to admire the house's stately ramshackle appearance. There was something admirable about a house that wore its flaws with a self-aware shrug, he thought.

Coyne pulled a twelve-pack of Newport Storm Summer Ale and a handle of Tanqueray gin from his trunk. He scanned the receipt to make sure he hadn't been overcharged before crumpling the flimsy paper and stuffing it into his pocket.

They knew that knocks would go unnoticed in a house that constantly made mysterious creaks, squeaks, and knocks of its own. And the doorbell had been broken for years. The slightest touch would set it off, tolling relentlessly until Maya's mother could unjam the button with a slim butter knife. The door was ajar as usual, and they pushed their way over the threshold and into the sweet must of the foyer. There was little fear of crime in Jamestown and, it seemed, little worry of much at all. The only businesses on the sleepy island were a few seafood restaurants, a couple of tourist shops selling shell key chains and sea glass necklaces, a bakery, a weekly distributed town paper, a post office, a town museum, a local bar, an overpriced grocery store, and two marinas, all of which were collectively referred to as the "town." A coyote yipped somewhere in the distance, and Ray glanced at the iridescent gibbous moon, just now becoming visible against the tangerine sky.

"You made it! I was getting worried," Maya cried, sliding gracefully down the railing of a nearby stairwell.

"My mom trapped us at the door," Coyne sighed, shaking his head and rolling his toothpick impatiently.

"It wasn't that bad, dude," Ray said, laughing as he gave Maya a hug.

They followed Maya through a series of hallways and down a brief flight of stairs into a cramped parlor. Maya seated herself on the arm of a sagging green loveseat and resumed mixing a Dark and Stormy cocktail on the coffee table beside her perch. Round bubbles of condensation coated the tin cup, and the sharp scent of ginger and lime mixed with the spice of the rum, perfuming the humid air.

Ray glanced around the parlor. He couldn't be sure, but he didn't think he'd ever been in this particular room before. No matter how many times he'd been to the house, the staircases and hallways and false doors and dumbwaiters that linked one room to the next remained navigable only to Maya, her parents, and her three older brothers. Amid the piles that coated every surface of the room were various tide charts, nautical maps of indeterminate age, novels with yellow pages, and faded Polaroid photographs. A broken piano squatted in one corner, topped with a collection of ashtrays and melted candles. It was half hidden by a stack of antique chairs, a pile of mud-caked shoes, and a bundle of hockey sticks, golf clubs, lacrosse helmets, and soccer cleats. Ray's family had moved so many times that none of the houses in which he'd grown up had ever had a chance to accumulate this archival evidence of familial history.

"You guys want one? There should be more cups in the kitchen," Maya said, squeezing a lime into her cocktail. She wiped her hands on her romper before pulling her mass of dark, curly hair up into a bulbous bun atop her head.

"Thanks. We brought stuff too," Ray said. Coyne held up the sixer and the handle.

"Oh, good. My brothers were back in town for Memorial Day and I swear they drank everything in the house," Maya said, rolling her eyes. She crossed her willowy legs and raised her drink in a brief toast toward Coyne and Ray before taking a sip.

"Should be a fun little party here tonight," Coyne said. Using a lighter he found wedged among the collection of melted candles, he managed to pry open two beers, passing one to Ray. Ray was grateful for something to hold. The condensation coating the bottle soaked his palm. They dropped their backpacks to the floor and seated themselves on the piano bench, the six-pack and the bottle of gin nestled between them.

"Don't call it a party. If my mom asks, it's just a 'get-together.'" Maya used a dish towel to wipe the coffee table clear of moisture. Coyne and Ray clinked their beers before taking a long swig. The cold bubbles burst down Ray's throat and sent a pleasant throb of warmth to his fingertips and toes.

"Anyone remember that kid who got expelled on the second day of school sophomore year? I forget his name, but I think I saw him at Dunkin' the other day," Coyne said.

Conversation came easily. As they lazily reminisced about eccentric teachers, sadistic coaches, particularly creepy monks, inedible dining hall meals, endless church services, the cruelest upperclassmen, puritanically policed coed dances, the bizarrely robotic headmaster, the glum lizards in the biology lab, and memorable suspension cases, Ray pictured himself back on the sagging dormitory couches at St. Bede's. The nostalgia hit him like a drug, and he yielded himself to the feeling.

Coyne passed Ray the last beer and Ray beheld it for a moment before taking a sip. The glassware felt satisfying in his hand in a way that aluminum could never replicate. The bottles, tumblers, steins, flutes, and snifters that he and his pals had taken to using of late had a pleasant heft in his palm. And when coupled with the inherent fragility of the glassware, these vessels bestowed a touch of responsibility—intention, even—to the act of imbibing. A strong cocktail poured into an attractive glass was nothing less than controlled chaos, equally liable to facilitate amusing conversations over the course of a pleasant evening as it was to shatter against the ground in a drunken slip of the fingers, dependent upon the steadiness of the hand in which it was held.

"The AC is kicked, by the way," Maya said, fanning herself with an old issue of the *Jamestown Press*.

Humidity hung thick in the room, sagging the piles of paper on the office desk, rendering the cheaply upholstered furniture sticky, and giving every object a look of wilted lethargy.

"Now that the sun's set, we might catch an ocean breeze," Coyne said. He drained his beer and peered through a grimy window over his shoulder.

Ray stood up, subtly pulling at his T-shirt to unstick it from his back as he did so. Making his way back outside to the driveway, he hoisted the large cardboard wine box from the trunk of Coyne's car, its heavy contents clanking against each other as he carried it back inside. Making turns at random (as he liked to do when visiting Maya's house), it wasn't long before he discovered a small kitchen. He carefully emptied the contents of the heavy parcel into the refrigerator. Coyne appeared out of a crooked hallway and set his beer on the stovetop to help Ray unpack the box.

"So they really just let you take whatever you want?" he asked.

"No, not really. Only if it's something that we can't sell anymore, like a six-pack with only five beers in it or a bottle with the seal broken. They let me take things like that," Ray said.

Coyne nodded, rummaging through the box and inspecting each item before stowing it in the refrigerator. Together they lingered in the fridge's cool glow, cracking open two Yuenglings and lapping up the foam that had accumulated under the bottle caps over the course of the drive from Middletown.

"Are you assholes just gonna stand in front of my fridge all night?" Maya's voice surprised them. She approached on her tanned, bare feet from out of yet another dimly lit hallway. Smiling, she reached past them for the chilled bottle of spiced rum.

"Hey, look at that! It finally came!" Coyne said, pointing at the crisply starched white lab coat draped over a chair in the corner.

"Yep! Starting to feel real," Maya said.

"Try it on!" Ray exclaimed, holding the coat up behind her.

She slipped her long arms into the sleeves and smoothed the coat over her torso.

"Look at that! Dr. Maya, as I live and breathe," Ray said.

"Not quite yet. Still got plenty of schooling to get through."

An irrepressible smile worked its way across her face, but she quickly peeled off the unblemished white coat and hung it neatly back over the chair. Though her mother had framed her acceptance letter to Boston University School of Medicine when she'd first been accepted, it had since gone missing among the house's impenetrable clutter.

"Sorry it's so fucking hot in here," she said, still beaming.

The F-word was the preferred garnish of the New England dialect, irrespective of tax bracket. There was nothing especially crude about its deployment in a conversation. It simply linked one word to the next as naturally as a breath.

"Don't worry about it," Coyne said.

"Actually, it is pretty rude that you'd have a party while your AC is busted," Ray joked.

"Okay, ha ha, fuck you, Ray. And it's a get-together, not a party, remember? Or are you already blackout?"

Maya punched Ray on the shoulder, and together the trio left the pleasant chill of the fridge, the boys tailing Maya through a series of hallways back to the parlor. Coyne had just collapsed onto his seat when he shot back up to his feet. He pulled frantically at his clothes, his eyes darting from one limb to the next.

"Oh shit. Oh shit. Oh shit . . ." The curses streamed past Coyne's lips as he yanked off his shirt and began unzipping his pants.

"Dude, what the hell's going on?" Ray asked. He got to his feet with the intention of helping but found he wasn't sure how to be of use, so he stood awkwardly next to Coyne, who was now tugging off his shoes, his pants pooled around his ankles.

"I just saw a tick crawl down my shirt, and now I can't find it!" Coyne cried out.

Maya jumped up next to Ray and, standing on each side of Coyne, they perused his body for any sign of the minuscule insect.

"I don't see a bull's-eye rash anywhere . . ." Maya offered.

"Thanks, doc." Coyne grumbled. "It must've crawled up my leg at McShane's bonfire last night. If I get Lyme disease, I'm gonna be so pissed."

A plum-colored haze descended over the ocean, staving off the true black of night. Headlights from a jet-black Jeep that looked like it had just been driven off the dealership lot weaved up the driveway. Clark Bane stepped gingerly down from the car, triple-checked that he'd locked the doors, and strode up the creaking steps of the porch. He wore Vineyard Vines shorts and a consciously casual shirt that made him look like an executive on vacation. A pair of Ray-Ban sunglasses dangled from a strap around his neck. It was always something of an effort to get him to come to these get-togethers. His domineering father rarely let him out of his sight. A few stiff drinks would usually quell Bane's anxieties enough for him to put the interrogation with which his father would accost him the following morning temporarily out of mind.

"Hey there, Bane!" Ray hooted, clapping him clumsily on the shoulder as he entered the parlor. His sandy-blond hair never seemed to grow, chopped at sharp angles around his noble face and combed flawlessly to one side. His bright, blue eyes darted around the room, and he accepted the hugs of greeting with a smile that showcased a perfect set of blunt white teeth.

Everyone called him Bane, never Clark. Almost all of the guys went exclusively by their last names, in fact. Perhaps it was a habit born of years playing on teams together. Or perhaps it was because if they didn't, coherence would quickly deteriorate into a confusing Anglo-Celtic jumble of Michaels, Andrews, Seans, and Peters. Bane paused at the threshold of the parlor, staring quizzically at the sight of Coyne standing in the middle of the room wearing nothing but his boxer briefs.

"And here I was worried that we wouldn't have enough booze for tonight," Bane said, finally.

"Coyne saw a tick crawling down his shirt. And shut up, it's a get-together," Maya said, suppressing a giggle.

Never one to show up empty-handed, Bane cradled two twelve-packs of Sierra Nevada Pale Ale and a handle of Captain Morgan in his thick arms. Already they had accumulated far too much alcohol for their scant numbers. Ray led Bane into the nearest kitchen to refrigerate the beers.

"And how is father Bane dealing with his son's gallivanting this evening?" Ray asked, handing Bane a bottle opener.

"You know, he's up my ass. What the fuck else is new, right?" Bane grumbled.

"A shot?" Ray suggested.

Nodding, Bane grabbed the bottle of rum and snapped the cap free of its plastic seal with a quick twist of his beefy palms. Though the room had cooled off somewhat, Bane often got sweaty when he drank. Beads of moisture were already beginning to form on his poreless brow. The richly spiced liquid left a pleasant burn in their chests. Back in the parlor, Maya continued searching Coyne's body for the tick. Their voices crescendoed and fell to muffled warbles in the cavernous hallway that separated them from the kitchen. After a while, the sound of leather flip-flops slapping against the floor announced Coyne's presence in the kitchen, his thin brows knitted in suspicion as he tugged his Patagonia T-shirt over his head. Maya followed, giggling when she made eye contact with Ray and Bane.

"Did you guys just do a shot?" Coyne asked, his eyes narrowed, head cocked to one side.

"Did you find the tick?" Ray asked.

"No. But I don't want to think about it anymore."

"I got Lyme once. Got bit at lacrosse camp. Back in 2012, I think? Yeah, summer going into senior year at Bede's," Bane said. "But honestly, dude? Getting Lyme disease is sort of a New England rite of passage, you know?"

"Whoopee," Coyne said. "Now, did you bastards do a shot without me or what?"

Bane and Ray smiled conspiratorially.

"It better not have been my Tanqueray," Coyne muttered. The toothpick rolled peevishly about his lips.

"Relax, man. Nobody touched your gin. Another?" Ray held up the bottle of rum to Coyne's face.

They circulated the bottle in silence. Any edge they'd shouldered over the bridge into Jamestown disappeared in the rich, dark taste of the rum.

CHAPTER 4

Full Swing

Moths fluttered in the pale light cast by the naked bulb of the lamp that hung over the patio adjoining the parlor, and small bats careened past the windows in furious bursts. The moon bathed the island in a glimmering, silver opalescence. Every so often, one of the bright stars that pierced the cloudless indigo sky exhaled, succumbing to the weight of itself, and collapsed earthward in a short ellipse marked only by a brief, shimmering tail.

Turning from the window, Ray inched his stool closer to the cluster of sagging furniture where Coyne, Bane, and Maya had seated themselves.

Coyne leaned back in a wicker chair, using his toothpick to stir a gin and tonic.

"You guys hear about Moon View?" he asked.

"Yeah, my dad's company is doing the restoration. He says it's a huge project. Basically a rebuild," Bane replied, wiping sweat from his brow with his shirtsleeve.

"What the hell is Moon View?" Ray asked.

"You know it. It's that huge abandoned mansion—" Coyne began.

"Abandoned until recently," Bane interjected.

"Right," Coyne continued. "The 'abandoned until recently' mansion. It's the one up on that crest right before Brenton Point. I always point it out to you on Ocean Drive."

Ray's pitiful knowledge of Aquidneck Island real estate bewildered Coyne to no end. That Ray could spend nearly a decade of his life in Newport and yet somehow not know the names and locations of the island's more noteworthy estates offended Coyne on a cellular level. The houses that so preoccupied Coyne and the rest of the island's real estate junkies were built to such size and splendor that they had at some point transcended the numerical addresses of the masses, instead being christened with names like firstborn children.

"So do you know who's moving in there?" Coyne asked, returning his attention to Bane.

"Nope. But people are saying it's some blond lady. Moving in there alone," Bane replied.

People in Newport talked about estates changing hands the way high school students discussed prom, and the bigger the place, the more pitiless the rumors. The way Bane had spat the words *blond lady* made it sound as though it were a fault to be either. But he was probably just parroting his dad.

"Alone!" Coyne yelped.

His widened eyes made his face appear even rounder than usual, and he sat bolt upright on his chair, nearly knocking over the cocktail perched between his legs.

"That's what I heard," Bane said, shrugging.

As he drank, Bane's broad shoulders gradually sank away from their tense position crowded about his ears, receding back into the comfort of the pink armchair he'd commandeered for the evening.

An engine coughed up the driveway, followed by two loud clunks as the doors of Kirley's old Saab were slammed shut. Moments later, boisterous voices echoed through the cavernous foyer.

"Kirley! We're in here, man!" Ray shouted.

"Where the fuck . . . I can never find . . . oh, there you all are. Jesus, what a maze, huh?"

Kirley stumbled into the parlor, tripping over his unlaced Converse low-tops. His footwear clashed with the rest of his garb—the pinstriped suit he'd donned for his summer internship at BankNewport. A long, ancient-looking case of some kind was slung from a strap across his shoulder. Were it not for the hugs that greeted him at the threshold, he would likely have tumbled right to the floor. McShane cackled as Kirley was passed from one set of arms to the next, accepting his own hugs once Kirley had been dumped onto a nearby couch.

"Dear god, McShane, please tell me you drove," Coyne sighed.

"You know Kirley doesn't let anyone else drive the Saab," McShane chortled.

"Jesus, where are his keys?" Maya asked, fighting off Kirley's weak, drunken flails and fishing through his pockets. Finally, she held up a triumphant fist, the Saab's keys clutched between her fingers. She disappeared up a staircase, jangling the keys over her shoulder.

"Good luck finding those, Kirley," Coyne said, patting him on the head.

"Oh, come on, I'm not even that bad," Kirley groaned, propping himself up on his elbows.

"Would you please drink some water, kid?" Ray said. He grabbed the YETI water bottle from the side pocket of Coyne's backpack and thrust it toward Kirley, who took a long glug, spilling water down his chin.

"Really? Did it have to be my water?" Coyne whined.

"Have a heart, man, he needs it more than you do," McShane said.

Finding his balance again, Kirley got to his feet. A hand-rolled cigarette poked out from behind his right ear, having somehow survived his chaotic entrance. His tie hung in a loose knot about his neck, and the American flag pin he'd taken to sporting on his lapel (he intended to run for Congress one day, he'd explained) was affixed upside down on his sleeve.

"I'm a victim of circumstance, okay?" he slurred. "Me and some of the other interns got drinks after work. Happy hour. At Diego's."

"Jesus," Bane said, chuckling and shaking his head. "You're an animal, dude."

"Oh, shut the fuck up, Bane, you sweaty bastard! What are you, some kind of saint?" Kirley howled, smiling like a jack-o'-lantern.

He made a fist as though to punch Bane but then he plunged his small hand into the battered leather briefcase he chose to use instead of a backpack. When his hand reappeared, it was holding a half-empty bottle of cheap vodka, to which his friends responded with mild boos. Hoisting the plastic bottle over his head, he shook its contents into a froth with dramatic thrusts of his skinny arms. The mischievous glint never left his bloodshot eyes, which shifted from side to side in rapid jerks beneath a messy crop of brown hair that fell over his pockmarked forehead. No matter what Kirley said, it always sounded like he was lying or joking or both, the words seeping through the wry grin that never left his face.

"And we didn't want to show up sober," he said through the corner of his mouth, his crinkled eyes jumping around the room.

"Mission accomplished, kid," McShane said, giving Kirley a high five.

"Seriously, Kirley? A plastic bottle of vodka? Are you trying to give us all a hangover circa freshman year?" Coyne asked. "And McShane, you're an enabler, you know that?"

"Sorry mom," McShane replied, grinning.

Cackling, he revealed a six-pack of Budweiser from behind his back, reveling in the further groans it elicited from the room. In calculated defiance against the unspoken group ethos, he'd brought cans. Three of the plastic rings surrounding the lids were conspicuously empty. The fraternity he'd joined at the southern school he'd attended had soured his allegiance to the self-important demeanor of the New England elite and inspired in him a desire to cosplay as a white trash douchebag whenever the masque might prove entertainingly provocative. However, a few drinks were usually all it took for him to drop the act and revert to his country club origins. Nearly to a person, the rest of his peers—including those gathered tonight—had matriculated to the elite East Coast colleges and universities that accepted students from the small but significant pipeline of tier-one New England boarding schools with clockwork regularity every spring.

St. Bede's Preparatory School's brick buildings, grassy quads, and exorbitant tuition had prepared them well for the brick buildings, grassy quads, and exorbitant tuitions of their respective undergraduate institutions. In some ways, they had been predestined to attend these private liberal arts schools, the ones with recognizable names that often appeared in the upper sections of the *U.S. News & World Report* ranking list—the only acceptable institutions from which to receive a bachelor's degree should the progeny of the East Coast's highest tax bracket fall short of the Ivy League. After all, hadn't it been the guaranteed progression to an elite college, one complete with an appropriately aristocratic school crest, that St. Bede's had promised parents when they'd enrolled their gawky sons and coltish daughters at the end of their eighth-grade years? Though Ray had been accepted to several of these prestigious schools, none had offered enough financial aid, and he'd ended up commuting to a small college on the island.

"Jesus, Cubano, it's only June. Save a little tan for the rest of us," McShane hooted. He grabbed the vodka bottle from Kirley and thrust it into Ray's chest.

Ray laughed and flipped him off, taking a long swig from the bottle. The room felt loud and warm. Music (if it could be called that) plinked from the untuned piano where Kirley was beating upon the ivory keys. The tie that had formerly been strewn around his neck was now knotted in a Rambo-style headband across his brow.

"You've been down in Louisiana while we've been buried in snow up here for the past seven months. What's your excuse, bro?" Ray asked, passing the bottle to Coyne.

"This Scottish skin doesn't like the sun, buddy," McShane replied, rolling up a sleeve to reveal a thick shoulder the complexion of candle wax.

The vodka passed from hand to hand, each reluctant imbiber grimacing at the chemical lemon flavoring. Peacocking for the small crowd, McShane took a long, purposeful pull and passed the bottle without so much as blinking at the vile taste. Like the dark sunglasses perched atop his head, this playful pompousness in him was new. It had replaced the polite, tennis-playing, occasional cigarette-smoking, fastidious hair-brushing, burgeoning Europhile they'd all met back at St. Bede's. There was nothing regrettable or offensive about the change; he was still the same McShane behind those sunglasses, after all, as any conversation about Premier League soccer or oysters on the half shell would quickly reveal.

"Hey, where's Finch?" McShane asked.

"He couldn't make it tonight. I think he's working a shift at the Pearl," Maya said.

"Didn't he get some tech job in Somerville?" Coyne asked.

"Yeah, but he didn't want to start until September. The Pearl is a good summer gig, though. Good tips. The waitresses there are always super hot chicks. Plus the chowder is dope," McShane responded.

Everyone nodded approvingly in recognition of the veracity of this final claim. Some time after the interminable vodka bottle had finished its third circumnavigation of the room, Josh shuffled into the parlor, a yellow acoustic guitar slung across his back. Nobody had even noticed his car pull into the driveway. The drunken group summoned the energy to spring off their respective seats to grip him in a tight hug.

Josh's last name was Anwar, but the Middle Eastern shape of his surname didn't trip off the tongue quite as readily as the Anglican names of his friends, so everyone just called him Josh. It was the same reason that Ray was Ray rather than Domingo or Wilson-Domingo. For a while, he had tried to get Wilson to catch on, but it had never stuck. His and Josh's warm-climate names never quite fit the piney New England setting.

With a wan smile, Josh's bloodshot eyes lazed around the room. He smelled of the half-smoked joint that poked out from the dark, thickly coiled mass of hair over his right ear. A small pile of ash rested on the shoulder of his flannel shirt, and a few gray flakes lingered in the curls of his sideburns.

An obsessive personality is somewhat difficult to imagine in the abstract, but to know Josh was to become intimately acquainted with the manifestation of the concept. In high school, it had been NBA basketball—the Celtics, specifically. His face an inch from the TV screen, he would shout commands and expletives at Paul Pierce until his voice went hoarse or a basket was made, whichever came first. Then there was the brief cinephile turn, which occurred sometime around junior year. He and Ray had snuck sips of Dr. Anwar's bourbon while watching Tarantino movies on a projector in his basement, Josh rattling off which of the IMDb movie rankings he approved of and which ones he deemed shamefully ludicrous. The summer before college, it had been psychedelics. According to Josh's estimation, he had dropped acid seventeen times and tried every upper, downer, and in-betweener under the sun.

He'd mellowed out considerably since then, consumed by his geology studies. In September, he would begin graduate school at UMass Amherst. This semi-recent fascination with rocks was received with much chagrin on the part of his father, who'd hoped his son would pursue anesthesiology like himself—an arena in which Josh had dabbled briefly, though he hadn't cared for the sleepiness that accompanied the high enough to embrace it as a career. To be sure, the obsession with rocks was better for his health, though the anecdotes that accompanied the sober academic realm of geology weren't nearly as captivating as those that resulted from Josh's earlier predilections.

But the acoustic guitar awkwardly hanging from his shoulder signaled an even more recent obsession: bluegrass folk music. He had taught himself the necessary chords and plucks in just a few weeks, and now he played in jam bands at dive bars around Amherst with old white dudes who had tobacco-stained beards and wore suspenders on their dungarees. And while he knew that the private concerts he played for his friends on evenings such as this weren't necessarily welcomed in the early hours of the gathering, the performance would be tolerated after a certain number of drinks and a critically timed joint had rendered his audience docile.

"I thought I heard some idiots back here," he mumbled sardonically, a grin curling one cheek.

Sensing that the new arrival called for some kind of celebration, Bane rose from the couch and bounded into the kitchen, returning with the bottle of Captain Morgan and sending the mustachioed captain on a doomed journey around the room. The drunken voices crescendoed and melted into one another as the boozy sociability reached its zenith, and they laughed hard at stories they'd heard a thousand times. Outside, the night sky had settled firmly into darkness, and the salty breeze Coyne had predicted drifted in through the open windows. A mosquito droned near Ray's ear and fireflies bobbed laconically in the darkness beyond the patio.

Ray joined Coyne outside, positioning himself strategically on his friend's left side. They shared a cigarette. A pleasant buzz spread through Ray's chest with each inhalation.

"You nab this off McShane?" Ray asked, the slim tube smoldering between his lips.

"Nah, I bought it."

Raising his eyebrows, Ray passed the cigarette back to Coyne.

"Since when are we buying cigarettes?"

"A few months, I guess," Coyne said, shrugging.

"So you're trying to quit the toothpicks, then?" Ray joked.

"Something like that," Coyne said, chuckling softly. He took a long drag and exhaled smoke through his nose. "Kind of seems like a phase we should go through though, don't you think?"

"Sure," Ray said. He tried to exhale through his nose, but it made him hack up a cough, and he handed the cigarette back to Coyne. "But when does that end, you know? When do you stop being a guy who smokes as a character choice and start just being a guy who smokes?"

Smoke poured in a controlled river from Coyne's lips. After a final puff, he used his toe to stub out the cigarette on the creaking floorboards of the deck. Then he buried it among the years of secreted butts and joint roaches in the fallow herb garden under the window.

"Are you trying to sound deep?" Coyne asked. "Because that sounded deep to me."

"Really? Just sounded drunk to me," Ray said. Laughing, he added, "I was starting to get embarrassed when you didn't respond at first."

Coyne laughed and slapped him on the shoulder, jamming a fresh toothpick between his teeth.

"Let's go back inside."

Returning to the parlor, they saw that Ella had arrived, twirling a long lock of blond hair between her thin fingers as she talked. Her audience moaned and chuckled at intervals as she regaled them with the drama of her latest boyfriend. Pausing only to pick at tangles in her hair or slap at the mosquitoes that hovered around her bare shoulders, she stared intently upward at the slowly turning ceiling fan as she spoke. Joining the conversation late, Ray caught something about a broken marriage and a gallant fellow from the Naval War College. The revelation that he was a quadragenarian elicited another loud groan, followed by spurts of laughter.

"Stop that! He's nice!" Ella cried, though a knowing smile creased her lips.

"Yeah, nice and old!" Bane crowed.

Ray squatted on his heels to greet Ella's dog, a black puggle named Rosie who accompanied Ella wherever she went. The small dog seemed more skittish than usual tonight. To her, the room must have felt like a maze of legs and chairs, all begging for the individualized attention of her quivering black nose.

"Hey, Kirley, what the hell have you got in this old case?" Bane asked, hoisting the long wooden box up from the floor where it had dropped during Kirley's tumultuous entrance.

"Open it up," Kirley said, smirking.

Bane unclasped the brass locks and lifted the lid. The case emitted a whining creak as it opened.

"Are you fucking kidding me, dude?"

"Oh, shit," McShane said, laughing and putting a hand to his forehead. "I forgot you brought that thing, you psycho."

"What is it? Hold it up!" Coyne commanded.

With both hands, Bane lifted an old musket out of the case. It looked like something a minuteman would have used. The heavy wooden butt of the gun had lost its luster to time, and the steel barrel was flecked with rust.

"Jesus Christ, Kirley, you brought a gun to my house?" Maya yelled, though she was laughing incredulously as she spoke.

"It's from the Revolutionary War. My dad just bought it. At this flea market. In Saunderstown. I wanted to show you guys," Kirley snickered, taking the musket from Bane's hands and carefully placing it back in the case. "It still functions too."

"Put that thing away!" Maya shouted, punching Kirley on the shoulder. "You're nuts, you know that? This is not normal behavior, Kirley."

"Who wants to be fucking normal?" Kirley retorted, snapping the clasps closed.

A limp body occupied every available surface in the room, and, over time, the group split off into separate conversations. Words drifted from the patio to the parlor as people alternated between sitting and drinking inside and standing and smoking outside. The conversations were easy to join and easy to leave. The flick of a lighter or the abrupt whisper of a bottle being opened cut easily through the cool night air.

Snippets of phrases floated above the room for brief moments of pure coherence before descending back down into the fervent cacophony of rambling, drunken speech:

"I really want to do dermatology, but I've heard it's really competitive."

"Wait, so how long have you guys been dating?"

"No, okay, but, so listen, man, just listen. The sediments, right? Okay, so the sediments shift, right? This is where it gets interesting . . ."

"Are you going to the Campbell wedding?"

"Am I passionate about consulting? Fuck no. Of course not. But I'm only gonna work there for a year or two. Plus the money is pretty great. But what I really want to get into is wealth management . . . Right, like my dad."

"Can we not talk about Trump? Like, Jesus, I need a night off from that shit, you know?"

"Moon View? Yeah, my dad's doing the renovation, actually."

"Finch is working. He couldn't make it tonight. I think he's having a party this weekend, though. Should be fun."

"Nah, Joe Rogan's a fucking idiot. But he does have some interesting guests sometimes, so . . ."

"Law school is the plan right now, but we'll see."

"I feel so fucking old, dude. Can you believe that this time next year we'll be celebrating our five-year reunion? Bro, do the math: We're class of 2013, and, brace yourself, Kirley, it's 2017 now, so . . ."

"Stop calling it a party, jackass. It's a get-together. If my mom hears, she'll flip."

"Right, but what are you going to do after this summer? Like, for a job, I mean."

This last question seemed to be the evening's central preoccupation, the prism through which all other topics were transmitted. The fascination was understandable enough. Freshly released from the reliable nest of schooling, they were now expected to take up a career, pay their own phone bills and rents, begin dating the people who could eventually become their spouses, figure out when the recycling was scheduled for pickup, and read books for pleasure and personal improvement rather than SparkNotes-ing the novels assigned by a syllabus. But the discussion lent a grim finality to the summer at hand, Ray felt. Summer break, as a concept, would not exist in this new phase of their lives. It was already over, in fact, having ended back in May with the conferral of their degrees.

Of course, Ray had heard many of his friends' parents use the word *summer* as a verb when it suited their purposes. Perhaps that could be his fate too, he thought. Maybe he too could regularly return to Aquidneck for the summers, to summer among other people summering.

CHAPTER 5

Afterglow

As the late hour began to burden their eyelids, the dispersed parties drifted back to the parlor, collapsing onto the sagging couches and overstuffed chairs. Someone closed the screen door to keep the mosquitoes from taking up residence inside. A pile of playing cards lay scattered across the sticky surface of a coffee table. A few cards were jammed under the oval metal tab that one used to crack open a beer can. Nursing final drinks, the group reminisced about St. Bede's and summers past. Bits of gossip passed through their tired lips: this teacher had been fired, and that alum had embarrassed himself at a reunion. Occasionally someone would summon the energy to tell a story in animated detail, jumping to their feet to reenact a particularly comical anecdote. Laughter left their throats in wheezes, and each story flowed into another. Their faces were coated in places with shiny patches of sweat. A pleasant heaviness settled in Ray's limbs.

The vigor that had hours ago pulsated throughout the parlor had waned. Somehow it had become two o'clock in the morning. Ella was asleep on the love seat, and Rosie licked her fingers where they dangled near the floor. The cardboard wine box brimmed with empty glass bottles. Coyne followed Ray's eyes.

"Thinking what I'm thinking?" he said, almost whispering.

With a wordless nod, Ray grabbed the box, and they made their way out to the street. McShane, Kirley, and Maya followed. The sour smell of pot slowed their purposeful steps. The bright orange embers of a joint revealed Josh's slim form leaning against the porch rail. Thick darkness shrouded him to the point of obscurity but for the hazy white smoke that drifted from his mouth when he exhaled. Bob Dylan played softly through the retro headphones dangling around his neck. His hand rose in a weak wave of greeting as his friends passed by.

"Wanna join?" Coyne asked.

"No, thanks," Josh mumbled, yawning. "But toss one for me, would you?"

The bottles clinked in the cardboard box as they walked up the street, away from Maya's house. A cool breeze enlivened their steps, and the inky night blanketed the houses they passed. They didn't stop until they'd reached the silent, sloping road by the chicken farm.

One bottle at a time, they hurled the glass vessels down the lane. Each crash was greeted with a primal whoop of joy as the bottle collided with the unseen pavement beyond. The senseless tradition had begun back at St. Bede's, after a winter semiformal dance, though none of them could remember which year or why. They hadn't indulged in the practice of this youthful rite in some time. Back then, they had thrown the bottles simply out of an adolescent delight in destruction. Now it was nostalgia that animated their limbs, throwing the bottles in high arcs that crashed spectacularly against the street.

A creaking whine followed the thud of old buckles unclasping, and they looked down to see Kirley removing the musket from the case. They'd been too distracted or too buzzed to notice him grab it on the way out the door.

"Oh, god. Please don't tell me you're going to shoot that thing, are you?" Maya groaned.

"McShane, go set up some bottles down there," Kirley said, ignoring Maya.

Nodding enthusiastically, McShane grabbed a handful of bottles and placed them in a line a few meters from where Kirley stood. Pulling a small leather sack from the case, Kirley procured a lead ball the size of a grape and loaded it awkwardly into the musket.

"I'm standing over here," Coyne said, stepping back several paces. "I've already lost hearing in one ear."

Kirley took aim, let out a short breath, and pulled back on the trigger. McShane, Ray, Maya, and Coyne clasped their hands over their ears as a thunderous crack shouted forth from the barrel, followed by a burst of shattering glass.

"Holy shit, my turn!" McShane called. "I can't believe this thing still works."

"Worked against the British too," Coyne giggled.

Kirley loaded another pellet into the musket, and McShane shot down a bottle with another loud crack. They each took turns—even Maya—until they'd exhausted Kirley's supply of pellets, at which point they returned to throwing the bottles down the street into the darkness. Finally, the box was empty. The group laughed weakly, panting as they trudged back to Maya's house.

"There must have been, like, thirty bottles in there," Kirley breathed.

"What a mess. I feel kinda bad," Coyne said.

"Don't feel bad," Maya snapped. "Nobody even uses that road anymore. It was built in the colonial times or something. That's why it's only wide enough for a horse carriage. Plus, that chicken farmer is a total dick. He has a 'Make America Great Again' sticker on his car."

Back inside, Josh had passed out on the piano bench, snoring softly. The big headphones sat askew on his brow, partially encircling his head like a laurel crown. "Like a Rolling Stone" issued softly from the padded earpieces. Already he looked the part of the frumpy geology professor, slumped at his desk during office hours after a long night spent hunched over a microscope.

Bane was asleep on the couch, his arm awkwardly bent into a shield over his eyes. The members of the group who remained awake, ignoring their exhaustion so as to keep the night going a little longer, arranged themselves on the uncomfortable patio furniture bathed in the weak light of the porch lamp. The cushions that sat askew on the iron chairs were damp with dew. A joint was rolled and passed around—this one pinched with tobacco to kick a little life into the somnambulant group. The ripe smell of the burning pot and tobacco hung in the air and clung to their clothes. Feeble conversation leaked through mouths too tired to move.

"We won't be able to do this much more," Kirley murmured, stirring.

"Still got a few good months left," Ray quickly replied.

Heads seemed to nod in the darkness beside him, though he couldn't coax his neck into turning to check for sure. An abrupt snore burst from McShane's sprawled form. His head was tilted back over the edge of the chair as though he were about to receive a hot towel shave, and his arms hung loose at his sides. Kirley roused himself to pen a mustache on McShane's face—revenge for an incident a few weeks earlier in which McShane had Picassoed Kirley's face with a Sharpie, unaware of the job interview that Kirley had scheduled for the next morning. Despite his heroic efforts with hand soap and hot water, a crude outline of the male anatomy's most distinguishing feature remained faintly visible on Kirley's forehead for several days afterward. He hadn't landed the job, and McShane had been sincerely apologetic.

Just before the first rays of sunrise began to poke through the graying night sky, the stragglers gathered themselves to their feet and forced their numb legs to carry them in the direction of a surface on which to succumb to sleep. Through the butler's pantry and up a staircase, Coyne found an unclaimed four-poster bed, falling asleep after prying off just one of his shoes. Maya disappeared into the maze of hallways and staircases to her childhood bedroom.

Following the stairs up to the top floor, Ray found a large hammock strung between two sturdy columns. He collapsed clumsily into the hammock's coarse netting, nearly concussing himself on the floor. In a buzzed half-stupor, Ray thought of his family, of how they'd spent their respective evenings while he'd been here, doing what he'd been doing. He pictured his mom reclined on the love seat back home, flipping through channels; his dad stabbing at a bowl of steamed rice with chopsticks in the mess hall of the Naval base in Okinawa; and his brother, Tony, sweeping up the hair in the barbershop at the end of his shift. The images, lurching through his stupefied mind like a series of lagging YouTube clips, sent a faint twinge of guilt through his stomach.

Sleep took him quickly, and soon his soft breathing echoed the creaks of the gently swaying hammock. In dreaming wakefulness, his thoughts turned to the network of red diamonds that would tattoo his back come morning.

CHAPTER 6

A Hangover in Jamestown

The window blinds that had collapsed in a dusty heap to the floor at some point in the house's chaotic history left Ray exposed to the first warm beams of dawn. They pierced through the glass and cooked his groggy brain. Rubbing at his swollen eyelids with numb fingers, he rolled to one side and managed to hoist himself up into a seated position. Sweat coated his face like a thin veil. A dull but constant pain throbbed in his skull. Running his dry tongue around his mouth, he felt a film coating his teeth like a fine layer of moss. When he managed to stand up, his back groaned in protest, aching from the rigid ropes of the hammock. A wriggle of his toes detected the socks he'd neglected to remove last night, which now felt like they'd been painted to his feet. The hangovers were expected, though their severity always came as a surprise.

On stumbling feet, he walked outside to the balcony. The sweet smell of damp grass rose from the lawn and he inhaled gratefully. He closed his eyes and a warm crimson curtain blotted his vision. When the sun got too warm, he trudged back downstairs to the kitchen. His back spasmed briefly when he bent to position his face under the faucet. He let the cool water wash over his skin and flow into his mouth. He drank greedily, feeling each mouthful splash into his stomach.

The parlor looked only slightly more disheveled than it had when they'd arrived the night before. The chairs and couches that had been dragged into a wobbly circle in the middle of the room were still there, and a few foggy glasses stained with wine were accumulated on top of the piano. Empty, dented beer cans had been arranged into a precarious pyramid atop the coffee table. Ella's petite form was still curled up on the couch. Rosie wriggled out of the nest she'd made between Ella's legs and bounded to the floor to sniff at Ray's ankles.

Moving chairs and stools back to their original locations, Ray managed to organize the room and the patio into a rough semblance of order. He paused to wipe sweat from the gutters under his eyes and took another long drink from the faucet. Despite his efforts to move the furniture quietly, the stools landed hard on the glossy wooden floors and the ancient couches groaned at the slightest provocation. The screen door slapped against its frame each time he passed from the kitchen to the patio.

Before the others awakened, Ray walked down to the end of the road by the chicken farm to survey the damage from last night's bottle smashing escapade. It was early but already hot, the sun burning white in the cloudless sky. The thick, reedy forest that lined both sides of the defunct road pulsated with a living charge. Cicadas droned from the trees, and the verdant greenery nearly blotted out the sky overhead. Rather than widening the road to accommodate the cars that had replaced the carriages and buggies for which it had been created originally, the township had abandoned the narrow lane to the encroaching forces of nature.

Tiny spiders of sweat crawled from the pores on Ray's scalp and back. Hearing a sharp crunch under the soles of his sneakers, he paused. A blanket of broken glass littered the cracked asphalt. He tried halfheartedly to kick some of the shards off the road and into the dirt embankment on the side.

Back in the house, he roused Coyne. It had taken Ray nearly twenty minutes to find the right room. Pulling back the curtains of the canopied bed, he discovered his friend slumbering beneath a richly textured quilt. Coyne did not stir even when Ray removed the toothpick that hung limply from his friend's lower lip. A thin trail of drool had seeped into the pillow beneath his jaw. Ray pawed his shoulder gently at first before giving him a solid shove. Through slitted eyelids, Coyne peered up at Ray. After a moment, he rose to his elbows and, yawning, wiped the drool from his chin with the wadded sleeve of his T-shirt.

"Breakfast?" Ray asked, cocking one eyebrow.

"Atlantic Grille?" Coyne grunted in response.

His words sounded brittle, like the gears of an old freight elevator churning after centuries of disuse.

"Duh," Ray said.

Most Aquidneck locals of a certain age would agree that Atlantic Grille was the only logical choice when contemplating where to eat breakfast following a night of excessive alcohol consumption. It might have been a great place for breakfast regardless of the headaches and somersaulting stomachs that summoned Ray and his friends to its doors, but they had only ever patronized the restaurant when caught in the jaws of a vicious hangover. Plodding through the endless curving hallways of Maya's house and poking their heads into unlocked rooms, Ray and Coyne eventually managed to wake the rest of the party with unceremonious shoves and jostles. They were restless to reignite last night's festive mood. The radiant day begged to be enjoyed.

Ella woke easily and picked contentedly at the chipping paint on her fingernails, Rosie licking at her leather flip-flops. When his first efforts to wake Maya failed, Ray collected the small dog and placed her on the bed near Maya's face. Rosie's pink tongue lapped at Maya's cheek, and soon enough Maya groaned and rolled herself up into a seated position.

"Jesus, okay. Well played. Very creative. I'll be down in a sec. But do know that I hate you," she grumbled.

"I know you don't mean that," Ray said, swatting her with a pillow.

"At least tell me we're going to Atlantic," she said, yawning and stroking Rosie's velvety ears.

"Where else?" he replied.

Bane sat at the patio table, sipping a glass of ice water and swiping placidly through Bumble profiles on his phone. He looked only slightly disheveled, having missed a button on his shirt, though his hair lay smooth and neat across his scalp. A flimsy bandage clung to his earlobe, and a few maroon specks stained his collar. Sometime after midnight, he'd asked Maya to pierce his ear. But he'd changed his mind as soon as the sewing needle had drawn blood. He held an ice cube against the tender lobe with his free hand.

"My dad's gonna kick my ass when he sees this," Bane said, laughing weakly. The melting ice cube sent rivulets down the side of his neck.

Bane's father, the square-jawed founder of the massively successful Bane Concepts construction corporation, could often be heard before he was seen. The company was an empire that the younger Bane was one day expected to helm, though the likelihood of this peaceful transfer of power shifted in tandem with the day-to-day swings in Mr. Bane's mood. Whether directed at his offspring, insubordinate employees, the liberal news media, or the family's incontinent spaniel, his vitriolic meltdowns and brash declarations had garnered the elder Bane a level of infamy throughout New England that was generally reserved for Yankees fans and people who preferred Starbucks to Dunkin' Donuts. At the same barbecue where Mr. Bane had explained to Ray that 62 percent of American vegans were illegal immigrants, he'd claimed to have told Whitey Bulger to quote, unquote, "go fuck himself" when the notorious Boston gangster had double-parked his car at a Bane Concepts work site in 1979. Three decades of shaping corrugated steel and liquid cement into sprawling multilevel malls and brutalist parking garages seemed to have led Mr. Bane to the conclusion that his son was yet another flexible material to be shaped—by a sustained combination of heat, pressure, and time—into a rigid, unbreakable structure.

Waking up on separate ends of the same long leather couch, their bare feet touching, Kirley and McShane rolled onto the floor to yank on their shoes and socks. Their wrinkled clothes were stained with sweat and spilled drinks, and the rank smell of cigarettes and stale beer followed them like a shadow. Finding an unopened beer jammed under the couch, McShane hoisted it triumphantly into the air as though he'd caught a foul ball at Fenway Park. Wordlessly, he cracked the seal and took a swig.

"Oh god, McShane, why?" Ella cried.

"He's an animal!" Ray shouted gleefully.

"I'm nauseous just watching that," Bane said, grimacing.

For a moment, McShane looked as though he was about to vomit, his eyes straining and his hand flying to his mouth. But then he smiled and gulped loudly as though he'd just drained a cup of coffee. With an exultant grin, he passed the can to Kirley, who hesitated for only a moment before snickering and obliging. No doubt the flat, warm beer ranked low on the list of things Kirley would prefer to ingest first thing in the morning, but he delighted in the groans and retches of his audience.

The piano bench where Josh had slept was empty save for a few scattered crumbs of pot. Ray figured he'd taken off early to beat the traffic on his way back up to Amherst. Maya finally appeared on the porch, still rubbing the sleep out of her eyes and carrying Rosie's squirming form in her arms. Placing the writhing dog in Ella's lap, she gathered her long, unruly hair into a riotous ponytail. She paused at the top of the stairs, smiling at her jocular guests, before joining them in the driveway. Though multiple cars were available, all seven of them piled into Bane's Jeep, sitting on each other's laps once all the seats had been filled. Rosie huddled in Ella's arms, her soft ears flailing about as the doorless vehicle took off. Wind roared around them as they crossed over the bridge, heading toward Aquidneck Island. None of them felt particularly hungry, but they soldiered on in the name of tradition.

◊◊◊◊◊◊◊◊◊◊◊◊◊◊◊◊◊◊◊◊◊◊◊◊◊

The waiters and waitresses employed by Atlantic Grille must gird themselves when they see the cars parking haphazardly in the lot, wincing at the sight of the parties who stumbled out of these vehicles, stretching and yawning in their wrinkled evening wear and shielding their eyes from the sun. Groups of this kind frequented the restaurant on weekend mornings, weary revelers washing up to their door like beached refuse after a long night at sea. Late on weekend mornings, the fatigued carousers would claim the booths in the corner and drag chairs up to accommodate their numbers (forgetting that reservations could be made in advance, which the host would gently remind them). Though these boisterous groups generally behaved politely enough, the server would have to muster a congenial smile when the bedraggled party inevitably asked for separate checks.

"Can I start you off with some waters? Coffee, maybe?" the waitress asked.

She cocked a knowing brow over one eye, and the lips she'd rushed to rouge early this morning pulled into a cheery smirk. When all seven of them ordered mimosas, her face betrayed no sign of surprise. With a curt nod and a subtle wink, she turned from the table and hustled purposefully in the direction of the kitchen. Maya passed out Advil capsules from her purse.

"Am I dead? Is this heaven?" Coyne asked, lolling his head back against the plush booth.

"Not if McShane's here," Maya cracked.

"I need water," Bane gasped, clutching his head.

"And coffee," Ray droned.

Coyne took a keen interest in everyone's order, either nodding approvingly or giving a condescending shake of his head with a sharp intake of breath. He'd been a patron of Atlantic Grille since the days when he'd been propped up in a high chair with a fistful of crayons at the edge of the table, and he claimed the menu hadn't changed one iota in all that time. Pancake and waffle combo platters were named after the island's various local beaches.

Ella slipped morsels of toast and sausage under the table to Rosie. Between mouthfuls of pancakes and impassioned abuse of the restaurant's bottomless coffee policy, there was talk of a beach trip.

"Forget the beaches. Let's go to Beavertail," Maya declared, slicing neatly into her eggs Benedict and using her phone to capture a video of the oozing yellow yolk. "Think about it—the tourists don't know about the coves. It'll be totally private."

"So . . . we could drink there?" McShane asked, draining his second mimosa and signaling to the waitress for a refill.

"Yeah, that's exactly my point!" Maya said.

After finishing breakfast, Kirley dry heaved in the parking lot for a few troubling minutes before they piled back into the Jeep. With backslaps and disingenuously effusive gratitude, they thanked Bane for picking up the tab, as they all knew that the heavy black card he'd brandished belonged to his father. Such grand gestures were not uncommon from Bane. On Coyne's twenty-first birthday last year, for example, Bane had purchased and distributed a bottle of champagne at each of the five bars they'd visited that night.

Only once they'd left the restaurant did Coyne inform McShane about the thick mustache inked under his nose.

"Are you fucking kidding me? The whole time we were at breakfast? That waitress didn't even say anything! And neither did you assholes!" he yelled, laughing as he grabbed hold of Kirley's collar, figuring him to be the culprit.

Again they crossed the Newport Bridge to Jamestown. Laughter and conversation issued off their tongues with renewed spirit, the mimosas, coffee, waffles, eggs, and bacon energizing their fatigued brains. Sitting in the passenger seat beside Bane, Ray stared down at the bay over the bridge's slitted railing. The water was a dark shade of blue, interrupted only by the occasional whitecap and a few red barges that looked like toys from this height. Driving over the bridge as a child, Ray had imagined the lobstermen on their dingy crafts waving up at him from their perches on the bow. Today, he wondered if they enjoyed their work, or if the monotonous raising and lowering of lobster traps had ground them into the same bitterness that he imagined plagued the average nine-to-fiver.

Beavertail Cove was hidden in the back recesses of Conanicut Island. A crescent of granite crags partially enclosed a pool of green sea. From above, it looked as though a giant pair of dentures had taken a great half-moon bite out of the shoreline. Waves rolled in from the far reaches of the bay and crashed into the cove, pounding up the chute formed by a gap in the slate rock and smacking against the shore with relentless regularity. The rocks in the waves' path had been rolled smooth by eons of this churning process. Beneath their bare feet, the pebbles felt loose and solid all at once.

Shooing away squawking gulls, they clambered down the steep shale to a place where they could sit close to the water. Each of them found their own rocky shelf to lean against while sea-foam flecked their sweating skin. Cool ocean breezes spat salt into their hair, solidifying their locks into a mess of windblown angles and rogue tufts. It would have been easy enough for them to drive into Middletown to one of the three beautiful state beaches that were often featured in Google Image searches of the island, but that would have meant maneuvering through crowds of mainlanders and risking reprimand from a self-important lifeguard. These impromptu weekend reunions seemed to call for maximal intimacy and privacy—and that was exactly what the cove's sloping igneous walls provided as morning stretched into afternoon.

"Good call on Beavertail," McShane said to Maya, bumping her fist with his own.

The sunbathers nodded in agreement, their eyes closed. The quick dispatch of the warm dark cherry White Claw Hard Seltzers that Kirley had discovered in the trunk of Bane's Jeep rendered the party sleepy and content. Coyne draped a towel over his head like a tent in order to light the joint he'd rolled under the table at breakfast. Ella kept a watchful eye on Rosie, who was busily sniffing after a rock crab. Maya napped on a beach towel she'd stretched across a flat slab of limestone.

"Last night was fun," Bane said softly.

Ray smiled but said nothing. Earlier that morning, Ray had overheard Bane receiving a call from his father. The hollering voice could be heard blaring through the receiver even from the short distance down the driveway where Bane had taken refuge. But then Bane had hung up, silencing the shouts mid-rant and rejoining his friends on the patio without mentioning a word of the conversation. Ray had never seen him hang up on his dad like that before.

Together they recounted the events of the previous night, contriving a patchy mental timeline so as not to forget any remotely memorable moments. Each anecdote was answered with appreciative laughs or embarrassed groans or simply nods of acknowledgment. There were petitions for elaboration by those who had been out of the room at the time, smoking a joint with Josh on the back deck or falling asleep too early. One story after another was added to their communal zeitgeist, to be called upon whenever it might be useful or pleasurable to rekindle in the future.

Ray dove beneath a rising swell, washing off the previous night's stink. The churning salt waves made his body feel like an Alka-Seltzer tablet dropped in a glass of still water, dissolving into nothingness with a satisfying, lingering sizzle. After Coyne, McShane, Kirley, and Bane finished lathering themselves up with the sunscreen Ray had forgone, they joined him. As the waves bashed into the shoreline, the boys plunged in to meet them, diving into the water that was still chilly this early in June. The bay took its time warming up in the summer, never achieving a comfortable temperature until the hottest days of late July. But today, the chill was a welcome refreshment. The waves slapped against the rocky barriers of the cove. As their heads reappeared above the surface, hair slicked to their foreheads, the friends smiled.

Yielding to the chute created by the rock formations, they allowed themselves to be sucked out just beyond the cove before being hurled back toward the shore. With terrific effort, McShane hoisted Kirley onto his shoulders before a large swell sent them careening backward into the water in an eruption of foam and giddy laughter. Maya and Ella waded slowly in the shallows, collecting gem-toned pieces of sea glass in their hands. Only now, bobbing in the briny water, did it feel to Ray as though the summer had truly begun. With each undulating wave, he shot upward to the peak of its crest, like a spring sapling bursting purposefully through the nearly melted snow.

Nobody said anything for a while, caught up in their own thoughts or the surreal beauty of the cove. They didn't think about how lucky they were or how sad they would be to lose these days to memory, to lose these summers to jobs, to lose these bodies to time. Floating in the waves, they were, for this moment, weightless.

CHAPTER 7

Spirits of Bellevue

11:03 a.m.

A cement loading dock ran the length of the rear side of the liquor store. Its blunt edges and muted coloring provided a sharp contrast to the busy window display that invited customers into the shop on the opposite side of the building. Typically Ray would sit on an overturned milk crate back there, tossing pieces of stale bread to the birds by the dumpster until the tolling bells of St. Mary's Church signaled the start of his eleven o'clock shift. But today, he was running late. He used to arrive at his shift at least ten minutes early. Lately, though, he'd been cutting it close. He'd ended up passing out at Bane's place the previous night, an elegant, modern-style home overlooking Mount Hope Bay. Ray had slept through his alarm, and by the time he'd managed to rinse the grim taste of tequila off his breath with a rushed swig of Mr. Bane's mouthwash, he'd so reduced his margin for error that he couldn't even make a stop at Dunkin' as he raced from Tiverton back to Newport—a travesty given the vice that seemed to be tightening around his brain. By the grace of some god, he'd found a loose Advil pill rattling around in his cup holder.

Trudging past the dumpsters that reeked of rotting produce from the organic market that neighbored the liquor store, he jumped up onto the loading dock and fished the keys out of his pocket to let himself in the back door.

If Ron—the store's pugnacious owner—had ever noticed Ray's unshaven, bleary-eyed appearance, he'd never mentioned anything. And if Ron's personal store expense account (which Ray and his coworker Nate amused themselves by checking once in a while) was any indication, their boss enjoyed his weekends too.

Spirits of Bellevue consistently won the coveted title of Newport's best liquor store, the "best" distinction bestowed annually to various local businesses in myriad culinary categories—best lobster rolls, best cocktail bar, best pizza, best oysters—by the *Newport Daily News*. To be sure, Ron Giblin was a shrewd businessman. But the boutique wine shop's physical location on Bellevue Avenue certainly didn't hurt its prestige either. The store's fortunate address lent an inherent air of refinement to its luxury branding, associated as it was with the Gilded Age mansions that lined the long, historically sanctioned avenue that stretched above the city's downtown sprawl like a spine before curving into the equally stunning Ocean Drive.

Ron had built a more-than-modest living off of his connections to the Newport elite. With his vast knowledge of wine and his immoderate attention to the finicky needs of his ultrawealthy customers, he had, over the years, impressed enough of the well-to-do names who populated Bellevue Avenue to stir up local notoriety for himself. Collectors with purple-stained teeth and permanently flushed cheeks regularly meandered through the store, seeking out vintages that only Ron could procure, or requesting his counsel when stocking their home cellars.

Ray viewed his boss as a somewhat tragic figure. Ron was perpetually caught in the process of transcending to the uppermost class, striving for the same wealth and status as his customers but destined to remain forever on the fringe of their world. On paper, almost every aspect of his life could be seen as falling just short of the echelon to which he aspired: He'd lived in Middletown his whole life, but never in Newport; connections could earn him a membership at Hazard's Beach Club, but he would never manage to climb the generations-long waiting list of Periwinkle Beach Club; his only daughter attended a private school, though not the *most* private school; invitations to the summer's biggest galas and weddings requested his presence as a sommelier, but almost never as a guest. The Giblin name could reach only such heights before the elevator stopped, several tiers shy of the Vanderbilts and the Carnegies.

Though Ron had a temper as hair-trigger as it was violent, Ray had learned how to navigate his boss's tempestuous moods. The first summer he'd worked at the liquor store, Ray had watched eight other employees come and go. Each one had quit or been fired, and none had lasted more than a week or two. By now, four summers later, Ray knew when to look busy. It was a skill not unlike testing the thickness of pond ice. Another employee (since fired) had referred to this carefully choreographed maneuvering around the store—pirouetting to avoid their boss's ire—as "the Ron dance."

Closing the door behind him and remembering to clasp the heavy double lock (the forgetting of which had cost more than one employee their job), Ray heard Ron bellowing into the telephone.

"I said I need it today! You know I have this order going out . . . No . . . No! TODAY I said!"

Eternally paranoid that his distributors were conspiring against him, Ron carried out these shouting matches over the phone on a weekly basis, screaming accusations until his face turned a fitting shade of burgundy.

"You're screwing me, Marty, I know it. Yes, you are! I know it, and I have the proof!"

Careful not to make any noise, Ray stuffed his backpack behind a pallet of Veuve Clicquot and waited for the yelling to peter out before making his presence known.

"Yes, you are, Marty, and guess what? I've had enough of it! I'm going to city hall, and I'm gonna . . . Hello? Marty? Where'd . . . son of a bitch!"

Peering around the stacks of overstock wine, Ray could see Ron slamming the phone into the receiver and angrily cramming a fistful of potato chips into his mouth, chewing violently and muttering about the corruption of Rhode Island's politics. At this point, Ray knew, it was safe to leave the hallway and start moving purposefully among the store's densely packed shelves. Grabbing a few bottles of pinot noir from the nearest box, Ray made his way to the American reds section near the front of the store, glaring intently at labels and making barely perceptible adjustments to the rows of bottles.

"Morning, Ron."

"I don't believe this shit. It goes all the way to the top, I know it . . ." Ron muttered to himself, stabbing at the battered calculator on the desk between handfuls of chips. "Fucking Cianci. Vincent 'Buddy' Cianci, that mobster! Burned a guy with cigarettes! I mean Jesus Christ, these people . . . Only out for themselves! Cronies and corruption, that's all they know."

Keeping his eyes glued to the wine bottles lining the shelves, Ray suppressed a smile. The political corruption rant was a favorite of Ron's. To his credit, however, Ron was nearly as generous as he was volatile. Sometimes, on Saturdays, Ron would order a few pizzas from Nikolas Pizza down the street, urging his employees to take a break and enjoy a slice. And the hourly rate he offered his employees far exceeded the state average. At Christmas, he would routinely dole out generous bonuses. And it wasn't uncommon for Ray to leave after a particularly hectic day with a gifted bottle of wine tucked under his arm. If Ron's generosity was tacitly apologetic, it was enough to motivate the employees who had been around long enough to experience his occasional benevolence to live with his shortcomings as a boss.

Sometimes, Ray even caught himself enjoying the job. It afforded him ample opportunity to bob among Newport's upper class, and the discounted booze had been a valuable perk ever since he'd turned twenty-one. And for a college graduate with a degree in anthropology and few significant plans for the future other than a vague notion about Boston, the job was plenty suitable.

"Morning, Ron," he said again, a little louder this time.

Startled from the computer where he'd been scanning the store's terminally disorganized inventory, Ron's small eyes bounced around the room in search of the disturbance. For all his ferocity, Ron stood at about five and a half feet tall, his bandy legs holding up a semirotund torso. But in the throes of one of his shaking rages, Ron could seem to swell up and fill the whole store. The tufts of gray hair that clung to the sides of his head provided an unkempt halo for his otherwise bald crown.

"Oh! Ray, hey. Check the board for deliveries, would you?" he said in his typical harrumphing fashion. "And make sure the Campbell–Doheny order is good to go again."

Ray nodded, already making his way to the back room. The stacks of wine and liquor cases set aside for the wedding now reached his chest, and a matching tower of beer cases stood in the walk-in fridge. As the Campbell–Doheny wedding would mark the largest sale he'd ever made, Ron had become maniacal about completing the order without a single hitch. First thing every morning, he sent Ray to the back room to re-check the order. The wedding attendees would talk about who was there and who wore what, of course, but they would also be discussing what they drank and where it came from. Gossip had the potential to make or break careers in Newport, and the whole thing wound Ron into knots.

12:16 p.m.

Four summers of eight-hour shifts in the claustrophobic store had compelled Ray to devise a system for passing the time during the slack hours of the day before the postwork, predinner rush that routinely threw the store into chaos around four o'clock. First, he had determined, it was crucial to never look at the clock until absolutely necessary. Knowing the time was part of the problem. Ray typically spent the first hour easing into the shift, casually checking shelves and straightening up the beer cooler. The second objective was to turn on the stereo and choose the day's soundtrack. A spiteful former employee had nabbed the store's iPod on the day he'd quit, pocketing it on his way out the door and moving to Iceland soon after. So now the store relied exclusively on a finicky old CD player, to play an eclectic mix of albums that Ray and Nate had scavenged from their respective homes, digging up discs from storage boxes filled with miscellany from the '90s and early aughts. Beneath the puka shell necklaces, Yu-Gi-Oh! trading cards, Bop It! toys, and half-empty canisters of Axe body spray, Ray had found several CDs he'd deemed worthy of resuscitation.

With grim resolve, Ray flipped through the familiar Velcro-strapped CD case. Same options as always: Jack Johnson, Radiohead, Third Eye Blind, the Cranberries, Foo Fighters, Pearl Jam, and the Black Keys. These were the discs he'd supplied, and by now he knew all their lyrics by heart. Besides these albums, there was a stack of Nate's trippy atmospheric stuff, as well as a few Grateful Dead and Phish live recordings. It had been a few days since Ray had set Jack Johnson down for a spin, so he slipped the disc from its clear plastic pocket and placed it in the CD player. The gentle acoustic plucks complemented the faintly beachy aesthetic of the store. With "Banana Pancakes" playing softly in the background, Ray set about pretending to work.

Through a combination of osmosis and necessity, Ray had acquired a passable knowledge of wine in his time working at the store. On the rare occasion that a customer would look at him with woefully trusting eyes and ask him for a recommendation, he could usually manage to string together a few phrases he'd plagiarized from Ron's various schpiels.

"Well, if you're planning on pairing it with a red meat of some kind, I would suggest something on the heavier side. This cabernet, for example. It's bold, fruit-forward, and not too tannic. Plus, you can't beat that price point."

"Oh, well, that *does* sound good, doesn't it?"

Once, a few weeks ago, a middle-aged man with a graying man-bun had asked Ray's opinion on a pinot noir he was considering. Ray had fibbed his way through it as usual, and the man, who wore Birkenstocks and hailed from Napa Valley (he'd called it Wine Country), had ended the exchange by handing him a business card, suggesting that Ray give him a ring if he ever found himself in California in need of work. Apparently the man owned a small vineyard out there, and was planning to expand the operation over the next few years. Ray had stuck the card in his wallet without much thought, chalking it up as little more than another one of those semi-amusing interactions that broke up the monotony of his shift.

Finishing up with the Rieslings, Ray worked his way over to the rosé section. Newport was the kind of town where rosé sold like sandwich bread, especially in the summer. He took his time listing the wines that needed restocking before harvesting the necessary bottles from the back room. Using a Sharpie, he marked the boxes using a coded shorthand to denote the type and number of the remaining bottles. For Ray, there was an undeniable satisfaction in stocking the shelves, an elegant simplicity to the process. Progress could be physically visualized in real time, the stacks of wine boxes shrinking lower and lower as the shelves were gradually replenished. For a moment, Ray actually did lose track of time.

2:38 p.m.

At the store, Ray was not a guest, and this aspect of the job appealed to him. While he certainly wasn't one of the loafered Newporters who patronized Spirits of Bellevue, he at least had a well-defined role to play. Whether behind the register or stocking the shelves, he knew his function within the hierarchy: the polite and dutiful deliveryman (courteously refusing any help with the heavy cases that he carried up the steep colonial-style steps of ancient, winding staircases), or else the helpful and good-natured local (suggesting to tourists the best place for lobster rolls on a budget—the snack shack at Easton's Beach), or occasionally the nonjudgmental clerk (bagging the small pint of Popov and pretending that he did not remember that this same customer had purchased a pint of Popov not three hours prior).

The store's regular customers offered brief moments of interaction that could distract from the slow passing of the hours. Even the most mundane conversations were a welcome respite. And all kinds of characters came through the liquor store's front door, a portal into a classless human juncture in which all people, rich or poor, sought booze with which to unwind after (or before) a day of capitalistic toil. The door jingled, and in walked Old Ben, an artist who worked out of a studio across the street. He looked a bit like Kurt Vonnegut. His reedy arms swung at his sides as he meandered to the back of the store, his trench coat, which he wore no matter the weather, trailing on the floor behind him.

"Just the six-pack today, Ben?" Ray asked.

"Well, hell, I didn't see any acid hits in the back cooler there. But if you got some, I'd be happy to take 'em off your hands." The words twanged out from under his tobacco-stained mustache, and he rubbed his chin with his jerky-skin fingers.

"Not that kind of store. Sorry, Ben."

"Shit, man. I'll tell ya, there were booze stores back in the day that would sell you anything! This woulda been before my brother and I drove that van from Amsterdam to Southeast China, so it musta been '68 or '70? Shit, that was a different time, Ray-man, I'll tell ya. You know I married some chick from Kurdistan on that ride? She was a dancer . . ."

Dressed in his usual floor-length camel-hair coat, even in the summer, Larry Turbot of Turbot Esquire toe-stepped through the door to pay off the several-thousand-dollar debt he had accumulated over the past few weeks, and he left with a fresh case of wines (all of which had been recommended by a stammering and excited Ron). On shuffling, boot-clad feet, Neil Gallagher limped through the door, heading straight for the back cooler. His trembling fingers wrapped around two large bottles of Colt 45, and he left a stale cigarette smell in his wake. The cloying scent lingered even after the glass door swung shut behind him. Ray knew he'd be back within a few hours, wheezing out the same grim line with a self-deprecating smirk: "Gotta die of something, right, kid?"

Around dinnertime, Mr. Jay would arrive, charging two magnum bottles of pinot grigio to his account and tapping his foot impatiently until the bottles were bagged and deposited into the passenger seat of his car. And by the time Mrs. Baruch's Cadillac was parked askew in front of the store's wide picture windows, Ray would have her daily order of Kistler chardonnay chilled, boxed, and ready to be served.

"Oh, Ray, honey, it's a *mess* out there today. These *people*! A case of the Kistler plea— oh! My goodness, and could I get just one bottle chill— ah! So you've seen to that too! You people really are just *too* good to me. Ta-ta for now, then! Until next time!"

When the aquiline Aston Martin—one of Mr. Lipkins's two Aston Martins (one rose gold, the other jet black)—eased into view, Ray readied two bottles of Ruinart Rosé Champagne at the counter. Brandishing a black card between his tanned, manicured fingers, Mr. Lipkins paid the exorbitant price without so much as batting an eye from behind his impenetrable sunglasses.

"Cheers, kiddo," he said, sliding a twenty-dollar tip across the counter toward Ray.

That was the most he ever said, his British accent just perceptible on the first word. Ron had mentioned once that Mr. Lipkins had been a highly successful producer in the '70s and may have even had a hand in a few Rolling Stones albums.

Reginald Pike shuffled in, his pigeon toes padding in slow steps around the store. Though he couldn't have been any younger than seventy, his hair was dyed an aggressive shade of caramel-blond, and he wore tight blue jeans that accentuated his rickety legs. From an immense leather wallet, seams straining against a library of credit cards, gift cards, and IDs, he pulled a wad of bills to pay for the top-shelf cognac he'd selected.

"You've forgotten my penny," he croaked, speaking almost in a whisper.

With a forced smile, Ray placed a single penny of change in Pike's withered, outstretched hand. In Newport, these aloof, shuffling men were referred to as *trustafarians*. This, a local term, meant he'd never worked a day in his life and would live comfortably off ancestral money until the day he died, with plenty left over for the kids and grandkids and great-grandkids he would never have. Allegedly, Pike lived on a massive family estate somewhere tucked away on Ocean Drive. On more than a few occasions, he'd been seen downtown at bars where he would have been the oldest person by four decades, always alone. According to McShane, Reginald Pike was a member at Periwinkle Beach Club, and if the sun was shining, he would make his lugubrious way along the beach, a single-scoop ice-cream cone in one hand and a grimy, disintegrating tote bag in the other. Ray often wondered if perhaps Pike had been broken by the boredom of a life without struggle, walking so painfully slowly simply to fill the minutes of the day.

"What do you have for a decent bottle of vodka? And don't tell me Grey Goose—I'm completely over that one."

It was a skinny woman Ray didn't recognize, her hair dyed blond but dark at the roots. Not a dash of makeup on her face, her prim nose pointed slightly upward, exuding an indifferent confidence. She tapped a tightly rolled hundred-dollar bill against the counter, held like a cigarette between her long, pale fingers. Her blue eyes revolved about the store. Whether she was twenty-five or forty could hardly be determined, as her face contorted with such frequency that it was hard to tell where wrinkles ended and expressions began. On piston-like legs, she had jumped more than walked into the store, and she offered no greeting before charging into her request.

"Um, how about Ketel One?" Ron offered, shooting Ray a quick glance.

"That'll do," the woman said with an abrupt nod, forking the rolled bill at Ron like a relay baton. Her chipped, sky-blue nails drummed on the countertop. Moving quickly, Ray reappeared at the register with the bottle, which Ron hurried to ring up and bag.

"Thanks, tall guy," the woman said, gesturing with her pointy chin toward Ray. She then added, "See you gentleman around," as she shot back out the door, vodka tucked into the crook of her bony arm.

As soon as the door swung closed behind her, the store felt oddly still. It was as though everything had been levitating and fluttering so long as she'd been inside.

"You know who that was, right?" Ron asked.

Eccentric as he was, Ron was not immune to the island's favored pastime of gossiping.

"No," Ray said, indulging his boss's conspiratorial glance. "But she was something, huh?"

"She just moved into Moon View," Ron said, raising his eyebrows, "*alone.*"

"Wow," Ray said, unsure how one responded to such comments. "So . . . she must be rich, then."

"Like you wouldn't believe," Ron said, shaking his head. "Or, at least, her husband was."

Before he could say more, a short man with shoulder-length white hair and a bemused smile appeared at the door. Ron just about lunged across the counter to recommend a few expensive bottles that he was sure would pair nicely with the Cornish game hens Mr. and Mrs. Brooks would be enjoying for dinner.

3:21 p.m.

Succumbing to the interminable middle hour of his shift, Ray glanced at the clock before turning back to the shelves, biding his time until a delivery run allowed him a brief reprieve from Ron's watchful gaze. The several cases of wine and beer that he would load into the van were his ticket out of the store, admitting him to lavish garden parties behind towering mansions or massive weddings under tall white tents that faced the glittering blue sea. Each errand became an excursion with the possibility of discovering some new, exclusive Newport haunt. And the extravagant demonstrations of wealth that Newport or the season or both seemed to inspire in the city's upper class provided frequent opportunities for such deliveries.

After quickly loading the delivery van and double-checking the orders, Ray yanked the lever into drive, lurching the battered behemoth into the street. Though it struggled around Newport's many sharp turns and the radio could only ever pick up one or two channels, the dented old van symbolized, for Ray, freedom. It promised time to himself, out of the tense store and into the streets of Newport. He typically extended these outings as much as possible, and Newport's notorious summer traffic was usually a legitimate enough excuse for his long disappearances.

Around four or five o'clock was the ideal time to cruise along Thames Street if one didn't mind traffic. A simmering energy took over the town at that time of day, like water about to boil. The restaurants would begin cooking orders, and the savory aromas of seared tuna steaks and wine-splashed mussels with chorizo and fried calamari with fat slices of banana pepper would waft through the streets and in through the open windows of the delivery van. Ray would only ever cruise fast enough to match the flow of traffic. Couples in snappy outfits would clink drinks and laugh on bar patios. Street corner buskers would pour music into the air from dented saxophones and boxy amplifiers. Short, stocky men in stained aprons could be glimpsed hustling through the alleyways between the tightly clustered restaurants that lined the wharves, carrying tubs of dishes or long filets of swordfish in their arms. With just his big toe gently depressing the gas pedal, Ray would let the sights, smells, and sounds of Newport fill the van.

For the frequent deliveries to the mansions (or anywhere remotely near Bellevue Avenue), Ray would often take the old van for a spin around Ocean Drive. Easing slowly around the luxurious bends in the road, he would watch as the sun burned yellow across the water, making the whitecaps dance like candle flames. The van's radio could just barely pick up 96.5 FM, Martha's Vineyard's station, which issued fuzzy acoustic and bluegrass numbers that Ray would never have listened to otherwise. The van was far more trustworthy on the more open road of Ocean Drive, which featured wide lanes and generous, sloping turns. Downtown, the sneaky one-ways and cobblestoned side streets made operating the van feel like steering a king-size bed on roller wheels.

The tips could be great on these deliveries. After heaving hundreds of dollars' worth of wine up a ubiquitous grand staircase, a harried woman in slippers might press a fifty-dollar bill into his hand. Sometimes he'd be expected to leave the delivery like a great haul of Christmas presents in a wide, vaulted foyer, attended only by a member of the housekeeping staff at some lavish manor. These deliveries generally did not end in a tip. Other times, however, an animated, well-dressed man might come to the door and direct Ray down some rickety steps into a cavernous wine cellar. A ten- or twenty-dollar bill that the gentleman cracked surreptitiously from his back pocket usually found its way into Ray's hand on his way out the door.

Not only were the booze orders plentiful but the events at which they were consumed would build throughout the summer, reaching their zenith around mid-August. Come September, these cocktail sippers would have to return to whatever version of reality they inhabited for the rest of the year in Connecticut or Boston or New York. By late August, retaliating against time itself, these people would start hosting lawn parties every night, calling the liquor store just before closing time and long after sundown to see if they could get a few more bottles delivered, anything to extend the evening—and thus the summer—just a few drinks longer.

◇◇◇◇◇◇◇◇◇◇◇◇◇◇◇◇◇◇

Ray's first stop was at Mr. Derrick's. Though this was a weekly delivery, Ray had never once seen Mr. Derrick's face. The Derricks lived in an immense three-story estate, set back toward the end of Bellevue Avenue and overlooking the Cliff Walk. Even the carriage house was twice the size of Ray's home. The exhaustive delivery instructions that attended the order were always the same: Go inside to the first-floor mudroom, open the elevator door, place the wine on the lift, shut and lock the door tightly, and, finally, hit the little black button to send it upstairs. Voices could be heard from some upper floor, but the faces to which they belonged never appeared. It was rumored that Mr. Derrick was an agoraphobe, bringing the world to his dining room one dinner party at a time.

Next was the De Paul estate, where Ray endured the accusatory barking of a one-eyed schnauzer and the hostile screeching of a bright-green parrot that roosted in the kitchen. Mrs. De Paul was not present to calm the bird today, so Ray hurried to stash the hefty case of rosé in the pantry while the maid, a Chinese woman who didn't speak a word of English, distracted the parrot with a handful of Cheerios.

Quite often, Ray's deliveries would take him to the Newport Shipyard or the Goat Island Marina, restocking a massive yacht with thousands of dollars' worth of booze before the vessel pressed on for Charleston or the Bahamas. These enormous motor yachts were usually manned by tan, athletic, jocular, blond men and women from Australia or New Zealand, all of whom wore dark sunglasses and laughed loudly as they traipsed around the deck on their eternally bare feet. Though they certainly must have had to deal with their fair share of guff from the owners of these behemoths—who usually had egos to match—Ray sometimes envied these sun-soaked crews, traveling together from one stunning international port to another, chasing summer's warmth, ever on the move.

Today's delivery destinations included a motor yacht christened *Bonanza*—sixty-two feet of sleek fiberglass docked up at Casey's Marina. Carrying two cases so as to reduce the number of trips he'd have to take from the parking lot, Ray carefully picked his way along the swaying dock. Upon reaching the cool shadow cast by the boat's towering hull, he stepped lightly onto the sleek steps leading up to the deck.

"Whoa there, pal, hold on just a second. Never been on a nice boat before, have you?"

A fat, grinning man with a thick cigar clenched between his teeth stared down at Ray from the top step. The man's hair was tied back in a short, greasy ponytail, and a large pair of Oakley sunglasses covered half of his sunburned face.

"Sorry?"

"Your shoes," he said, using the cigar to gesture at Ray's feet. "No shoes on the deck."

Over the course of four trips, Ray brought the cases to the edge of the dock, kicked off his shoes, carefully set the cases aboard the deck under the man's watchful eye, reshoed his feet, and walked back up the dock for another load. Sweat stained his shirt in the late-afternoon heat. Throbbing aches ran up and down his arms from the weight of the cases, and a sharp tightness seized his calves from the multiple barefoot ascents. As Ray placed the final case of champagne down on the polished wooden deck and turned to leave, the fat man snapped a fifty-dollar bill out of a billfold and creased it at a severe angle between his chubby fingers before slapping it into Ray's palm.

Sweating and out of breath, Ray cranked the air-conditioning to full blast. The delivery list had gone flimsy in his sodden pocket. Squinting at the faded ink letters, he saw that the Ballard estate would be his final stop. Smiling, Ray eased the van back into the slow traffic of Thames Street and drove past the kitschy tourist shops, past the wharves, past the traffic, through the Fifth Ward—his own neighborhood—and down to the long, slim road that ran parallel to the water. There was a strange quiet, an almost unsettling stillness to these properties tucked away from the main roads on ancient plots of land with deeds that stretched back to the *Mayflower*'s aspirational gentry, as though noise itself were something that the most aristocratic of the aristocrats could escape.

The Ballard residence could only be described as a castle. It towered high above Ocean Drive, complete with stony spires and a winding driveway. Ray always made sure to triple-check the Ballard order before leaving the store. A delivery to the Ballard estate meant more than just a big sale; it meant that every person of notoriety at the party would be drinking cocktails supplied by Spirits of Bellevue, and word of mouth in Newport was as good as a sponsorship. If the best parties with the oldest-money crowds got their booze from Spirits of Bellevue, it had an effect not unlike placing the Nike swoosh on Michael Jordan's sneakers.

After leaving the delivery in the care of Mr. Ballard's harried personal assistant, Ray took his time coming around the curve of Brenton Point. Slowing, he peered up the hill. Moon View slouched atop a cliff facing the sea, dilapidated but stalwart. The spires that burst off the roof made the edifice look somewhat like a castle, and yet there was a faintly classical aspect to the house, too, given the massive Grecian columns that propped up the tiered roof. For the first time in all the years that Ray had passed the strange house, there appeared to be signs of human activity. A yellow backhoe emblazoned with the word BANE roved around the front yard like a giant mechanical beetle. A tall white moving truck was parked in the driveway. From his low vantage, Ray could just make out couches and chairs being ferried inside by antlike movers. One figure stood out, her blond ponytail whipping back and forth and her slender arms flailing left and right as she directed the movers.

4:32 p.m.

Having stretched the deliveries for as long as he could, Ray returned to find the store in its typical predinner state of bedlam. Ron hovered about, leaping anxiously from customer to customer as they perused the shelves. Before making his return known, Ray slipped into the refreshing chill of the walk-in refrigerator. Almost instantaneously, the sweat on his shirt congealed to his skin and a pleasant shiver thrilled down his spine.

In the cool silence of the walk-in, Ray peered over the rows of six-packs into the store. Though the sloped shelves stocked with beer hid him from view, he could see the customers through the foggy glass doors. He saw one patron laugh at the price of the bottle Ron had proffered from the top shelf before shrugging, shaking Ron's hand, and toting the bottle to the checkout counter.

The effects of the Advil Ray had downed before work had worn off, sentencing him to a dull headache. Grabbing the first loose bottle his hand landed upon in the fridge's miscellaneous back row—functionally a lost and found for beers that never sold—Ray pried off the cap with his keys and drained the heavy beer in three long gulps. It tasted bitter, maybe even skunked, but its effects were almost immediate. The beer's rich, nutty liquid burned in his nose and in his empty stomach. Just as the numbing cold of the refrigerator was becoming unbearable, a pleasant warmth spread from his chest to the tips of his extremities. The drilling pain in his skull ceased, replaced with a cool, placid serenity. The store felt warm and bright when he stepped out of the walk-in and began wandering among the shelves.

"I swear once you try that hefeweizen, you're never going to want another beer. Hell, you may not even want water anymore . . . Have a good one!" came Nate's ever-so-slightly stoner-ish voice.

The customer laughed politely at the joke, which Ray had heard Nate make more than a dozen times since they'd started working together. From behind the customer's back, Ray raised his eyebrows in greeting. The door jingled as the customer left.

"Hey, buddy," Nate said, punching the sale into the computer system.

But before Ray could respond, another customer was at the counter, with a few more forming a line behind her. Under the faded maroon beanie that Nate wore year-round was a mass of silky red hair that would fall to the center of his back were it not skillfully piled up under the cap. An equally red beard hung in long wisps from his chin, rustling and swaying with great animation whenever he launched into one of his soliloquies on the subtle brewing differences between stouts and sours.

Though he'd dropped out of the University of Vermont with one semester's worth of a theater tech degree, Nate was no burnout. On the contrary, he had an almost encyclopedic knowledge of beer and was an accomplished microbrewer in his own right. If prompted, he could talk about hops, lacing, floral notes, and citrus hints with the fervor of an apostle recounting the Second Coming. And though Ray had little interest in beer outside of its side effects, he and Nate had found common conversational ground in *Star Wars*, punk rock, the Newport bar scene, Ron's idiosyncrasies, and pretty much anything else that passed the time between employees who shared a few hours of a shift. Sometimes they'd smoke a bowl together on the loading dock behind the store or walk down to Fastnet Pub for a drink. Oddly enough, they shared a birthday—the same year, even—and thus August 23 marked something of a store holiday. Ron would buy a cake, and whatever customers happened to be in the store would usually join in the singing of "Happy Birthday" as he and Nate sheepishly blew out the candles.

"Hey, could you grab me a bottle of Meiomi pinot noir? It's for the gentleman right here." Nate gestured to an academic-looking man while he finished bagging an older woman's order and prepared to take it out to her car.

"Yeah, no problem," Ray said automatically, grateful for any task that sent him to the back room and away from the overwhelming energy of the storefront.

Ray's eyes danced along the stack of American reds in the back room, searching for the Meiomi. Finally, he saw it, demarcated by Nate's sloppy handwriting and buried under two other cases. With a heave, he managed to remove the first case and place it on the ground. But when he lifted the second case, something immediately felt wrong, like taking a nonexistent step at the top of a staircase.

A bottle dropped through the bottom of the box, tearing through the flimsy cardboard and falling to the linoleum floor with a crash. Instantly, the heady smell of wine filled the room and the scarlet liquid began oozing underneath a tall stack of cardboard wine boxes. Kicking himself for his lack of caution, Ray jumped to action. Some of these cardboard boxes had been in use since the store opened, recycled as necessary and rarely replaced for newer, sturdier boxes. Snatching the ancient mop and the grimy yellow bucket from the closet, Ray slid the teetering stacks of wine boxes to the side and started sopping up as much of the wine as he could. The wine mixed with the gray mop water to create a sickly purple haze.

"Yes, we have that vintage. Let me just grab it from the back for you."

No sooner had Ron spoken the words than his bouncing footsteps could be heard coming down the narrow hallway, right toward the site of Ray's mess. As quickly as he could, Ray grabbed the largest of the glass shards and threw them into the sink.

"What the hell happened back here?" Ron hissed, his eyes instantly ablaze. His jowls trembled as he spoke, and his stringy mustache twitched over his lip. Few things enraged Ron as much as a broken bottle.

"Sorry, Ron, the box broke. You know I'll pay for it," Ray said, mopping frantically and moving boxes out of the way as the maroon pool continued to spread.

"Just get this place cleaned up. And make sure to put down some bleach or this place will *stink*!" Ron yelled. His shoulders quaked under his overlarge polo shirt. Forgetting whatever he'd walked back for in the first place, he stomped up the rickety staircase that led to his low-ceilinged attic office.

"And for Christ's sake, make sure the Campbell–Doheny order is okay!" he hollered from the top of the stairs.

Ray managed to get the floor sufficiently cleaned up and delivered the bottle to the bespectacled man waiting patiently by the cash register. The rush had passed, and Nate gave Ray an apologetic yet mirthful look from behind the counter.

"Nothing like a good charge to the Breakage Account to get Ron's engine revving," he chortled.

"Shit, you heard that?"

"Don't worry about it, man. Can you go grab a case of Kistler chardonnay, though? Ron said he was grabbing it but—"

"Yeah, I got it," Ray said, turning toward the back room again.

"And use both hands this time!" Nate called, still laughing.

Ray flipped him off behind his back, though he was laughing too. In the back room, the smell of wine and bleach accosted his nose. He heard Ron tapping furiously away at his computer upstairs. Ray knew that Ron would never deduct a breakage from his paycheck, and he knew it had been an accident, but he still felt pretty bad. He figured there must have been a reason that wine was sold in glass bottles rather than some sturdier vessel. But still, he often wondered why something so precious would be encased in something so fragile.

7:03 p.m.

Right around seven o'clock, Ron left, grumbling a goodbye and grabbing three bottles off the shelves as he walked out. Once Ron's moped had pulled out of the parking lot and disappeared down Memorial

Boulevard, Ray slipped the Pearl Jam CD into the player and cranked the volume. Raising their eyebrows at each other, Nate and Ray silently acknowledged their new freedom. As the tension left the store, Ray felt a knot loosen in his chest, and the wine bottles seemed to relax on their shelves.

"You taking off?" Nate asked, glancing at the clock.

"Yeah, I guess so."

"Have time for a joint?" he proposed, arching his eyebrows.

"Right now?"

"Yeah, why not? We'll be quick," Nate said.

In the cool darkness of the walk-in fridge, Nate pulled an old-fashioned cigarette case from the breast pocket of his flannel shirt. The hand-rolled cigarettes shrouded Nate in an ever-present cologne of the earthy tobacco leaves and toasted paper. Using only the tips of his calloused fingers, he selected a thin yellow joint nestled among the white cigarettes and lit it at one end before passing it to Ray.

"So how much longer do you think you can stand working here?" Nate asked, exhaling a thick cloud of smoke.

Releasing his own cloud, Ray shrugged.

"Definitely till the end of the summer. Beyond that, who knows? How 'bout you?"

"Man, you know I'm staying here," Nate said.

"You don't want to go back to school?"

Nate's turn to shrug.

"Maybe someday. But school's so expensive. I have a job now where I make decent money, and I get to buy craft beers at a majorly discounted price. So it doesn't really make sense for me to go back just yet, you know?"

The pot turned Ray's thoughts inward, and he imagined the ten grand in student loans that he would soon have to start paying off. The image morphed from a theoretical number on his computer screen to its physical representation in neat stacks of cash. He pushed the thought away.

The bell on the front door dinged, and Nate rushed off to man the register, saluting Ray on his way out. Ray lingered in the refrigerator.

Until Nate had said it out loud, Ray had never considered the liquor store as a legitimate career possibility. Keep working at the liquor store even when the summer crowds departed in September? It seemed preposterous to Ray, at first. He knew his friends would have been flabbergasted at the notion. But, he thought, his gig at the liquor store was no less "real" than a nine-to-five sales job, was it? Were his paychecks any less "real" than those he would receive at the end of a forty-hour week spent in a cubicle?

Standing beside the chilled racks of beer, he allowed his imagination to tolerate the idea. It was a good job that he knew how to do and for which he was relatively well paid. He made nearly as much as his mother did working the reception desk at the Hotel Viking, after all. It would allow him to remain in Newport, a city he loved, and close to his family. His brother still worked in Newport too. Tony had never considered moving to Boston—had never even gone to college besides the few credits he'd earned at CCRI. Lots of people worked retail jobs or restaurant jobs in Newport—most people, in fact. However, something about earning a salary felt crucial to Ray, as much a part of life as graduating from high school, getting married, and raising a family. Why was that, he wondered? If the liquor store gig satisfied Nate, why shouldn't it satisfy him? The barrier between "summer job" and "real job" suddenly took on a porous quality in his imagination. At first, it felt like clarity. But the more he thought about it, the more confused he became.

CHAPTER 8

A Newport Night

To avoid his mother's adamant insistence that McShane come inside and eat a bowl of black beans reheated from the pillow-size Ziploc bags eternally stocking their freezer, Ray walked down to the end of the road to await his friend's car. The neighborhood was quiet this evening. Most of the houses lining the street were shabbily appointed cottages like his own, though construction had begun on a six-story parking garage that would, within the next year or so, subsume the majority of the block. The hope was that it might ease the parking shortage that bottlenecked traffic at the far end of Thames Street during the peak tourism months. Bane Concepts construction vehicles rested like massive archaeological skeletons in the lifeless dirt pit that would eventually be the foundation of the parking garage. By a stroke of luck, Ray's parents' home had been spared the fluorescent pink eminent domain notices that had one day appeared on their neighbors' doors.

Waiting for McShane, Ray counted fourteen Irish flags hanging out of windows or attached to doorside flagpoles along his street. Others sported Italian or Portuguese flags, a few American Stars and Stripes, Red Sox flags, or the Rhode Island flag with its golden anchor emblazoned over the word

HOPE, rippling slightly in the intermittent warm gusts. Headlights turned the corner onto the street, and Ray recognized McShane's father's Cadillac. A Gucci Mane track was blaring from the speakers.

McShane had to shout to be heard over the sound of the music, calling to Ray through the window as he pulled to a stop.

"My bad. Meant to get here earlier but I can never find this place back here."

"No worries, man," Ray said, sliding into the passenger seat.

As soon as Ray had clipped his seat belt, McShane handed him a slim metal flask. The liquid seared Ray's throat, and he suppressed a cough.

"Damn. Whiskey?" Ray yelled.

"Scotch! Good stuff, too," McShane said, lowering the volume on the stereo. "One of my dad's colleagues brought it to dinner tonight. Fucking epic."

Ray noticed the McShane family crest etched on one side of the flask; a lion that looked like it was doing the "Thriller" dance while moonwalking under a banner of Latin words. At one time, Ray might've been able to translate the phrase, though all of the vocabulary and declensions he'd committed to memory seemed to have left his head as soon as he'd completed the required introductory Latin course as a St. Bede's freshman.

The street noises disappeared along with the traffic as the car nosed into the Kay Street neighborhood. Tall hedges hid massive porches and broad colonial-style homes. McShane parked in front of a large, emerald house on Ayrault Street. The late-afternoon sunlight limned the neighborhood in a mango-flesh glow. A blue tarp covered one side of the Finches' home, now in its fourth year of renovations. It was a three-story Newport historical house, and as such, they'd had to wage a bitter war against the notoriously persnickety Newport Historical Society to undertake their ambitious renovations. The house's location was ideal, within walking distance of the bars and biking distance from everything else, yet far enough from the downtown strip to enjoy quiet evenings on their back patio. Not that the Finches were a quiet family. Even from the street, Ray could hear loud voices emanating from their backyard.

Without bothering to knock, they walked through the front door, fixing themselves drinks at the kitchen bar before proceeding outside to join the festivities. The small crowd assembled on the patio, presumably a coalition of Finch's extended family, wore brightly colored pastel clothing, and each hand held a strong drink that sloshed within its thin-stemmed flute or sturdy glass tumbler with each emphatic gesture of its holder. Long strings of pearls clattered against the women's necks, and needlepoint belts with cartoonish images of sailboats, martini glasses, and lobsters encircled the men's waists.

"Mr. Finch, how are you?" Ray asked, hand outstretched and ready to meet Mr. Finch's enthusiastic shake.

"You watch the Sox tonight?" Mr. Finch asked without a second's hesitation.

Ray always felt that Mr. Finch's unblinking blue eyes were staring through him more than at him. The Sierra Nevada Pale Ale in his hand looked as much like an accessory as the sleek watch on his wrist, though the beer would likely make its way to the crown of his bald head later in the evening—a favorite party trick of his.

"No, who'd they play?"

"Blue Jays," he said, shaking his head ruefully.

"Going downtown tonight?"

"Yeah," Mr. Finch replied, nodding. "We're meeting some friends at Norey's for dinner. Then maybe Speakeasy. We'll see."

Ray nodded approvingly, as though he too was mulling these options. In truth, they both knew where the other would be going for the night or could've made decent guesses. With some significant exceptions, Newport could be a somewhat predictable place.

"Hey, Mr. Finch, by the way," Ray began, making a conscious effort to look his interlocutor in the eye, "I wanted to thank you again for setting up that interview for me. The one in Boston."

"Don't mention it," Mr. Finch said, slapping Ray on the shoulder. "Phil's an old friend. Bit of a prick, but a good friend. I've got a few more calls I could make if you're still considering law school too."

"Aren't you always telling me not to become a lawyer?" Ray joked.

Mr. Finch shrugged, chortling. "It depends what you're looking for out of life. I want this, for example," he said, making a broad sweep of his arms that seemed to encompass the house and the party and the tasteful cutlery all at once. "So I had to find a career that lets me have this, right? My father was a lobsterman. He loved it. We lived in a shoebox apartment in Pawtucket. All we ate was lobster. The place stank like shellfish all year long. To this day I can't stand the taste of lobster. I know, I know, it's ironic, right? Living in New England and hating lobster. But my father, he loved chugging off on his own in the boat at dawn every morning and hauling in his traps. He lived for it. Do you see what I'm saying here? I like practicing law fine. I wouldn't say I have a passion for it, but it's a trade-off, right? Either you work a job that gives you the life you want when you come home at night, or you work a job that gives you life while you're on the clock. Those are basically your two options. Do you see what I'm saying? You're following this, aren't you?"

"I think so, yeah," Ray replied.

"If you take that second option—nothing wrong with the second option! Nothing at all—however, making a career out of something you're deeply passionate about, it's very rare that that career is as lucrative as the job you don't want to do, right? Maybe I'm not being clear . . . Okay, here's an example. Say you have an economics degree, right? Say it's from Harvard or Princeton or something. You could walk onto Wall Street tomorrow and, boom, you're hired, you're making six figures, you're living in a doorman building in Murray Hill, you've got a membership at Equinox, etcetera, etcetera. Right? But here's the catch—and there's always a catch if you go this route—you're going to work eighty hours a week for two or three years before things cool down for you. A miserable few years, Ray. Miserable! I know people who've done it! Okay, so now let's consider the other side of this. You have your fancy economics degree, and you decide that your real passion is gardening. You can't get enough of it, and you refuse to work any job that doesn't allow you to garden all day every day. Maybe you get a job at a greenhouse or a nursery or something. I'm not a gardener myself, mind you, but I imagine they'd work in such places. You make far less money, sure, but you have no qualms about waking up and going into work in the morning. See what I mean? Do you see what I'm saying here, Ray?"

"What, so there's no third way? No, like, in-between?" Ray asked. "Like, what if that person with the econ degree or whatever who loves gardening started a gardening business? Couldn't they make a boatload of money *and* enjoy their work?"

"I'll say two things about that," Mr. Finch said, pausing to sip his beer. "One, that rarely happens. Most people on this planet work whatever job allows them to make enough money to pay rent and put dinner on the table. Let's remember, too, that this notion of matching your passion to your work would be ludicrous to most people in this world of ours, Ray. While most third worlders are selling—I don't know, oranges—on the side of some street for the equivalent of American nickels, we're over here in America deciding whether or not to make an obscene amount of money simply because it makes our soul feel yucky. What privilege! What a country, right? But let's pretend for a second that it does happen, just for conversation's sake. This is point number two, by the way. So this hypothetical economics whiz and gardening enthusiast starts a business. Well, guess what? Now they're running a business instead of gardening all day. That poor fool is sweating over Excel spreadsheets instead of troweling dirt, or whatever those guys are into. They're probably working eighty hours a week for the first few years just to get this business off the ground. At that point, why not just work on Wall Street? At least there you'd get paid for your work. You'd have some assurance that your hard work will not, ultimately, be for naught. Starting a business, you're probably not clearing a check until year two or three! My point is this: Doing what you love rarely makes you rich, but being rich almost always allows you to do what you love. See?"

"Well," Ray said, raising his glass to Mr. Finch, "you've given me a lot to think about."

"Do you have any kind of head for math?"

Ray recalled the long afternoons spent in office hours with turtle-necked math professors in college and the dread that would grip his stomach when the calculus exams at St. Bede's were placed before him on his desk.

"No, not really. Why do you think I was an anthropology major?"

"Well, that means Wall Street is probably out for you. Maybe you get lucky and score a position at some burgeoning tech startup or something, but that's rare. And it's too late for you to become a doctor—which I can't recommend either, by the way. But that doesn't matter. If it's money you're after—*real* money, I mean—then law school is probably your best bet," Mr. Finch replied, clinking Ray's glass. "You read books and wrote papers for your archaeology classes, right? Anthropology, right, that's what I meant. Law school is no different. Reading, studying, memorizing, and typing it up into a paper. Law school. Think about it. I could get you another interview for a paralegal gig to work while you're studying for the LSAT, too, if you want. Couldn't hurt come application time. Just let me know."

"Ray, honey! How are you? I hope he's not talking your ear off, is he?"

Mrs. Finch's voice had to be loud to carry over the noise of the party. She finished pouring herself a fresh glass of chardonnay before reaching up onto her tiptoes to give Ray a hug. A man that Ray vaguely recognized as one of Finch's uncles winked conspiratorially and slipped a drink into his hand as he ambled toward the kitchen. Now equipped with two drinks—a flute of prosecco in his right hand and a Moscow Mule in his left—Ray began to circulate, smiling politely and talking with animation to the guests he'd met at Finch parties past.

"I heard she's a divorcée," said a short blond woman in a bright Lilly Pulitzer dress.

"I heard she divorced a Ridgemont," asserted a tall sandy-haired man with wire-rimmed glasses and a light tan.

Swirling a perspiring beverage in his hand, the man basked in the gasps his comment inspired.

"No! A Ridgemont?" yelped an older woman, holding a hand to her mouth.

"Just what I heard," the man said, nodding sagely.

Ray lingered by the bar as they spoke, pretending to fix himself a drink. The name Ridgemont didn't sound familiar to him. But he'd spent enough time around this niche demographic to know that any multisyllabic surname that could be pictured on the spine of an old leather-bound book usually meant old money. Rockefeller. Vanderbilt. Carnegie. He made a mental note to ask Coyne about it later.

After several more speculations about Moon View's newest resident and a few more cocktails, the topic changed. The crowd, which had grown to more than two dozen people, was becoming anxious to leave the house, bemoaning Newport's strict and, they agreed, puritanical laws that required bars to close at one o'clock. And as food was only ever served in the form of decorative little hors d'oeuvres at these semicasual functions (tonight's dish was a gravlox canapé the size of a matchbook), they had grown hungry. For a party of this size, Ray's mother would have bustled relentlessly from the kitchen to the dining room with platters of empanadas and croquettes, trays of brimming mojitos, and plates stacked high with rice and black beans that she would have prepared weeks in advance. Each guest's eating habits would have been documented and evaluated like a test, which could be passed only if second helpings were requested.

Ray tripped on his way up the narrow staircase as he stole away from the party to an upstairs bathroom. Mr. Finch's words were still ricocheting around in his head. Boisterous conversations from the backyard came in indistinct bursts through the bathroom window. Maybe law school wouldn't be such a bad idea, Ray thought. He wouldn't mind being able to host parties like this rather than attending them as a guest. He racked his brain, but he couldn't think of anything he was particularly passionate about. He liked going to the movies, and hanging out at the beach, and driving his old Volvo around the island at sunset, but those things sounded to him more like the makings of a very lame Tinder bio than potential careers. So why shouldn't he go to law school? Still, for reasons he couldn't fathom, the notion of becoming a lawyer seemed almost as absurd as continuing to work at the liquor store.

Buzzed and curious, Ray opened the medicine cabinet affixed over an ornate sink. Between a small box of dental floss and a travel-size bottle of mouthwash, he noticed a translucent orange pill bottle with a peeling label. Flattening down the label with his thumb, he could make out the word *Clonazepam*. He didn't recognize the name. On an impulse, he clumsily pried open the bottle and popped two of the round white capsules into his mouth, chasing them with a sip of his Moscow Mule. He returned the bottle to its place between the floss and the mouthwash and closed the medicine cabinet. His reflection in the mirror was stained with crusty flecks of toothpaste. Ray stared himself in the eye for a long moment, yielding himself to the hyperawareness that *this* was what he looked like. They were the same dark eyes, thick eyebrows, arrow-straight nose, broad mouth, shaggy hair, and goofy ears that he'd known all his life. But he looked older, he thought. Older than whenever he'd last undertaken this unsettling exercise. The skin that clung just under his eyes had a faint lavender hue, and his cheekbones seemed to be pushing their way through his somewhat sunken cheeks. Shadows caught in brief pits and shallow caverns around his nose and above his chin. He considered the possibility that he was simply tired, that a few decent nights of sleep, a few days off the booze, and a long jog or two might erase these subtle changes from his visage. Grabbing his drink from its perch on the edge of the bathtub, he tore himself away from the mirror and went back downstairs to the party.

◇◇◇◇◇◇◇◇◇◇◇◇◇◇◇◇◇◇◇◇◇◇

"There you are! Where the hell have you guys been?" Attempting to yank a fresh polo shirt over his head while holding a beer in his hand, Finch called down to them from the balcony that overlooked the patio. "I've been looking all over this place for you guys!"

"We've been right here! Your dad's trying to get us drunk," McShane yelled.

"Enjoy, fellas," Mr. Finch said, returning from the bar and pressing espresso martinis into Ray's and McShane's hands.

"Stay away from him. He's a bad influence," Finch shouted. "You guys ready to go?"

"What about Kirley and Coyne?" Ray cupped his hands around his mouth to be heard.

"Meeting us down there." Finch's voice was muffled by the shirt caught over his head.

"Where?" McShane hollered.

"West Deck! Hold on." Setting the beer down on the railing, Finch finally managed to pull his arm through the sleeve. "I'm coming down."

Keeping his attention on the Dark and Stormy that one of Finch's blond aunts had poured for him on his way out the door, Ray kept stride with McShane and Finch as they worked their way through the Kay Street neighborhood toward downtown. Cold beer bottles sweated in their back pockets, and they snuck sips from their drinks so as to avoid the prying eyes of Finch's scrupulous neighbors. Finch kept hushing them until they reached the clamor of Thames Street. Newport was too small for anonymity, and infamy spread as quickly as notoriety, if not faster.

"What should I do with this?" Ray asked, holding up the empty tin mug that had so recently been brimming with rum and ginger beer.

"Just toss it in those bushes. My parents have dozens," Finch replied, waving a hand casually toward a row of bushes surrounding an expansive lawn.

Ray deposited the exquisitely wrought cup into an empty recycling bin across the street. He jogged to catch up with McShane and Finch. His footfalls felt peculiar, as though one leg was longer than the other.

"Want one?" Finch asked, proffering an open pack of cigarettes.

McShane was already lighting up, taking a grateful drag as the tip of the cigarette burned orange in the darkness.

"Sure, why not?" Ray replied, accepting the cigarette and catching the lighter when McShane tossed it in his direction.

"Since when do you smoke?" McShane asked.

"I don't," Ray said, smirking.

By the time they arrived, the bar was raucous, and they had to shoulder their way through the crowd to order drinks.

"Well, look who it is!"

Sweaty and grinning, Bane left his ensemble of Tiverton friends by the bar to greet McShane, Finch, and Ray with backslaps and hugs. It was not long before he disappeared again, though, off to make good on his offer to buy a round. Twelve tequila shots materialized on the bar, and Bane coolly handed several bills to the bartender like a father sneaking cash to his college-bound son.

Crammed together like rush hour subway passengers, with space only to raise drinks to their lips, they shouted conversation into each other's ears over the din. Stretching to his full height and focusing his blurred vision, Ray scanned the teeming waterfront deck for familiar faces. At one end of the dock, he saw McShane and Kirley chatting with two slim brunette girls who appeared to be twins. Nearby, Coyne's wild gestures and emphatic facial expressions could only mean that he was lecturing a cornered Giants fan on the dominance of Tom Brady's career with the Patriots. At the opposite end of the bar, Ray spied Maya and Ella sipping gin and tonics and dancing to the pop music that blared from the mounted speakers. Finch had barely made it past the bouncer before he'd bumped into one of his innumerable cousins, and now they were laughing in the corner over some recent family gossip. Ray recognized a few bartenders and waiters from the restaurants downtown; a few people he'd worked with at the liquor store; people he'd met once or twice out at the bars; some guys with whom he'd attended high school or college; and some friends of his brother. There were hordes of people he'd never seen before.

Thoroughly drunk and having evidently lost track of the brunette duo, McShane and Kirley joined Maya and Ella on the dance floor, pumping their arms and kicking their legs with abandon. Feeling a small glass being nudged into his palm, Ray looked up to see Bane, winking with a shot glass poised at his chin.

"For you, bud," he said. "Grey Goose."

After a hollered discussion of changing bars, the crew was gathered, and Ray felt himself being swept along like a jellyfish in a wave. Crossing the street, they filed clumsily into the line at the entrance to O'Brien's Pub. The bouncer—a thick, grizzled man with a pirate's beard and a few missing teeth—had busted plenty of their fake IDs over the years. Drunken conversation made the time pass quickly, and soon enough they were inside. While his friends pressed their way to the bar, Ray walked out to the patio. He'd noticed some old friends, Newport guys he'd known since his family had first moved to Rhode Island. Somehow Rossi, Souza, and Jonny had managed to secure one of the highly coveted patio tables. More likely than not, they had ordered a few Mudslides around noon and hadn't moved since. After his dad had been stationed in Newport, Ray had cemented a friendship with these guys through church league basketball teams and middle school classroom antics. Though they'd fallen out of touch somewhat when Ray had been accepted to St. Bede's, they'd remained friendly whenever they bumped into each other on these booze-clouded evenings.

"Jonny, dude, you're looking yolked! What got into you?" Ray asked.

"Ray, man, how've you been?" Jonny responded, friendly as ever. "Basic training. Just got back from Missouri."

"I guess that explains that god-awful haircut too."

"Yeah, man, I know it," Jonny said, laughing and running a hand over the bristles of his military standard haircut. "I better pay your brother a visit, huh?"

Within minutes they were laughing and rehearsing anecdotes from their middle school years. They caught Ray up on the gossip he'd missed too. Apparently, another girl from the neighborhood had gotten pregnant, and another guy—a kid they'd all played little league baseball with—had overdosed on opioids. A few acquaintances had moved to Providence, and a few more were planning on living with their parents for another year or two to save money. Someone had an art exhibition opening at RISD this fall, and someone else had just been offered a tryout with the Providence Bruins. Seeing McShane gesturing to him from the bar, Ray exchanged bro-hugs with each of them one more time and told a parting joke before heading back inside. The joke hadn't been funny, but they were all too kind or too drunk not to laugh. Or maybe they were laughing because he'd stumbled into an empty chair when he turned to leave.

Staring into the warm haze of the bar, Ray sipped the rum and Coke that McShane had bought for him. Faces blended in the dim light, and the smell of stale beer, cigarette ash, and billiards chalk perfumed the air. In one corner, he saw a few of the younger faculty members from St. Bede's. Over by the defunct jukebox was a guy he recognized as an intermittent patron of the liquor store. The young mailman who delivered his paychecks sat on a stool at the other end of the bar, whispering into the ear of a waitress. She was still wearing the apron from wherever her shift had ended. People he'd met once or twice mingled with people he'd never seen before, and the room blurred into a runny watercolor of faces.

"Whatcha lookin' at?"

The kinked smile and darting eyes could only be Kirley's.

"I think I have to get out, man," Ray said.

"Not feeling this bar?"

"This island."

The Killers' "Mr. Brightside" pumped from the overhead speakers, and the bar patrons sang along with drunken gusto. The sweating bartenders' hands never stopped, flying from one glass to another, filling a beer at the draught, placing a lemon over the rim of a cocktail glass, swiping a card, and wiping down the bar with a rag in a ceaseless fervor of motion.

"What do you mean?" Kirley asked, slurring slightly.

"I feel like I know everyone in this bar."

Sticking a cigarette between his lips, Kirley scanned the bar with restless eyes, ping-ponging from face to face. He wore the same pinstriped suit he'd worn at Maya's get-together, and again, he'd exchanged his loafers for a pair of unlaced Converse.

"I guess so," he said with a shrug.

"Did you end up passing that exam?" Ray asked.

"The CPA exam? I passed the first one, but not the second one yet. I think there are four of them."

"How's that internship going?"

"It's boring. Really fucking boring. Good experience, though, you know?"

"Still excited about being an accountant?"

Kirley laughed and took another drag from his cigarette.

"*Excited* isn't the word I'd use. I'm fine with it, though. The money's good."

Ray clinked his glass to Kirley's and took a purposeful swig. The cold bubbles rumbled in his chest. Another slurred consensus was reached, and they stumbled down to Dockside in time for last call, despite their earlier proclamations that they'd finish the night at O'Brien's. The crowd was tightly packed, and the mass of heads undulated and bobbed like buoys on a rough sea. At the bar, McShane encouraged Bane to buy a final round, making long-winded appeals of the carpe diem variety.

The bartenders flickered the lights, signaling last call.

"Fuck Newport, man! Last call at twelve forty-five? Such bullshit, dude," Finch garbled, propped against the back wall and fumbling a lighter between his uncooperative fingers.

A mass exodus filtered into the streets, Ray's gang among the throng. The river of people coursed up the wharf toward Thames Street, from there breaking into rivulets that trickled toward apartments and late-night pizza slices.

Semiconsciously, Ray slowed his pace and fell back a few strides from his friends. When they turned up Narragansett Avenue, Ray kept walking up Thames Street in the direction of Broadway. He had a vague notion of paying his brother a visit. Gradually, the crowded street petered out into emptiness. An almost total silence replaced the din of the bar, and he was enveloped by the tense stillness of a city street at night. He could hardly see his own hands when he raised them before his eyes, and he stumbled when the road switched abruptly from smooth asphalt to a long stretch of cobblestones. After a while—he wasn't sure how long—he made it to Broadway. But for a young couple arguing in front of the 7-Eleven down the street and a supine man crooning from a bus stop bench, the streets were empty. The towering arches of city hall and the pointed spire of St. Mary's Church were bathed in a cold shade of blue.

The window of Tony's apartment was dark. Ray thought about ringing the bell anyway, but decided against it. He wasn't even sure what he'd say if Tony answered the door. Plus, he figured Tony had an early shift at the barber shop tomorrow morning. Or maybe he was out finishing a drink at one of the intimate little bars nestled along Broadway that let regulars linger on for a while after last call. Ray turned and walked back in the direction he'd come from.

It didn't take him long to get back to the Finch household, despite an unplanned detour. He had walked so briskly that he'd overshot Kay Street by several blocks before the sight of one of Salve

Regina University's campus statues signaled to him that he'd gone too far. By the time he arrived at the Finches' place, the fine hairs at his temples and behind his ears were damp with sweat. Knowing the front door would be locked, he tiptoed around to the back porch and walked in through the French doors that separated the patio from the kitchen. The Finches' ancient brown Labrador grumbled at Ray, hobbling dutifully toward the potential burglar. A brief sniff of his hand cleared him for entrance, and he crept through the cavernous hallway and up the narrow staircase to the third floor. Placing his ear to Finch's door, he heard nothing but a few labored snores. Again descending the stairs and passing back through the kitchen, he circled around the outside of the house to the backyard, doing his best to limit the creaks that groaned from the old floorboards with each footfall. Looking up to the roof, he saw the orange glow of a lit joint being passed back and forth.

Back upstairs, Ray crawled cautiously over Finch's slumbering body to clamber through the bedside window and onto the roof. There he whistled softly to McShane and Kirley, who were giggling in a cloud of blue smoke.

"There he is," McShane said, somehow still full of energy.

"Where'd you go?" Kirley asked between drags.

"Bumped into some guys I know."

A fresh joint was lit and passed into Ray's outstretched fingers, and he took it gratefully.

"Is Finch okay?" he asked.

"Yeah, he'll make it," McShane said, chuckling softly. "You know how hard he goes at these family parties. Fuckin' maniac."

"His parents came in after us," Kirley said, smirking.

To the amusement of Finch's friends, Mr. and Mrs. Finch consistently managed to push their carousing so late into the night that by the time they'd eventually return home, their son and his companions were usually already sleeping soundly.

"Damn," Ray said, shaking his head and exhaling a gray plume through his nose. "Respect. Good for them."

Already the hit was making his head feel too heavy for his neck.

They stared out from their rooftop perch at the houses that lined the blocks in every direction. From atop the tall house, they could just make out masts and sails swaying in the harbor like decorative umbrellas in a cocktail.

CHAPTER 9

Rum Floater

Saturdays follow Fridays like a smooth, generous chaser. At a certain age, drinking away an entire weekend is time well spent. Somewhat ironically, alcohol catalyzed the memories—funny stories made funnier, dramatic stories made more so. The sleepless nights and stomach-churning mornings were endured in the name of experience.

McShane held a lit cigar out the window of his father's Cadillac with one hand while steering with the other. The briny smell of the salt marshes mixed with the pungent aroma of the cigar smoke as the car sailed down Ocean Drive. An osprey stood sentry atop a telephone pole where it had built a formidable nest. In an attempt to inhale a few gulps of fresh air into his lungs, Ray rolled down the passenger window as far as it would go. Kirley had refused to leave his bed this morning, citing a hellish headache.

"You want a cigar?" McShane asked, peering over his Ray-Bans.

"Dear god, no," Ray groaned. His head was killing him too, but the thought of skipping out on a trip to Periwinkle had never occurred to him.

"Now, what kind of self-respecting Cuban turns down a cigar, huh?" McShane joked.

"A hungover one. You have to smoke that thing?"

"My dad will kill me if I stink up the interior," McShane mused, ignoring Ray's question and taking another puff.

The sun muscled through the dull gray clouds that hung low over the island. A lone fisherman ambled slowly along the shoreline, his fishing rod poised at an angle over his hunched back. A party of cyclists whipped around a turn, and their skintight jerseys flew past Ray's window in a panting neon blur.

Rae Sremmurd's *SremmLife2* had just been released, and "Black Beatles" throbbed through the Cadillac's high-quality speakers. The thumping beat and Swae Lee's smooth, gentle hooks were medicine to Ray's pounding headache. McShane had always had an insatiable taste for rap music. Even back at St. Bede's Prep he'd regularly pulled up obscure music videos on the dorm computers in order to enlighten—or, more often, to shock—his classmates with YouTube clips replete with guns, drugs, piles of cash, and scantily clad women jiggling their derrieres on the decks of sleek yachts or the hoods of luxury cars. He'd twice seen Riff Raff in concert. He even went so far as to wade through hours of unlistenable SoundCloud tracks in an effort to feed his appetite for the newest movements in the genre. Lately, he'd been closely following the Chicago rap beefs and the revelation of Atlanta trap music. He'd been listening to Lil Durk long before most people had even heard the name.

The sky cleared abruptly as they veered around Brenton Point, the sun beaming across the bay like a spotlight. Ray dug through the glove box and shielded his eyes with the first pair of sunglasses he could find.

"I think those are my mom's," McShane scoffed.

"I can't stand this sun right now," Ray mumbled. Glancing into the rearview mirror, he saw his bloodshot eyes staring back at him through a pair of large, purple-tinted orbs with transparent frames.

"Oh, cheer up. Lookin' like a beauty out here today!" McShane said. He flicked away the cigar butt, and the small brown stump erupted in a plume of sparks as it bounced against the pavement.

McShane's arms threatened to burst through the tight sleeves of his Lacoste polo shirt. He appeared to have recently gotten a haircut. Ray ran a hand through his own hair, which was starting to splay out in little wings over his ears. It had been almost a month since he'd gotten his haircut, just before his interview. He realized, with a small twinge of guilt, that this meant he hadn't seen Tony in almost a month, either.

"Oh," McShane said, looking down at the rubber flip-flops on Ray's feet.

"No good?" Ray asked.

"Do you have anything leather? Or canvas, even? Wait, I probably have an extra pair of Sperrys back here . . ."

One hand on the steering wheel, McShane grasped at his backpack in the rear seat. Within seconds he procured a battered pair of leather Top-Siders and placed them in Ray's lap.

"They might be a little tight," he said.

"Thanks," Ray said.

It wasn't the first time Ray had failed inspection. Periwinkle Beach Club had a stringent dress code. It was the kind of established, conservative institution so exclusive it had come under fire for racism and anti-Semitism on more than a few occasions in its long history. Usually, those local tabloid stories were dismissed with a few passing references to tradition, member limits, and a half-hearted explanation that nothing could be done about memberships passing from one generation to the next. Periwinkle Beach Club—to which McShane's family belonged as ancestral members—had been founded by the original rumrunners and railroad tycoons who had commissioned Bellevue Avenue's most spectacular mansions. Ray had looked up the history of the storied beach club on Wikipedia after the first time he'd been invited along by McShane. The brief entry revealed that the beach club had been established in the 1890s by Newport's well-to-do class as a means of avoiding rubbing elbows with the influx of mill workers from Fall River who'd been granted access to Newport's beaches via the creation of a new trolley line. Though much smaller in size than Newport's more noteworthy beaches such as Easton's or Sachuest, Periwinkle Beach Club was situated on the far reaches of Ocean Drive, deliberately distant from the nearest trolley stop. The waiting list to become a member was generations long, and even then membership was not guaranteed. The family names mounted on the cabana doors accrued a proud tarnish with each passing summer.

The shoes were tight, and the old leather felt clammy against Ray's skin. He recognized the Sperrys as McShane's go-to pair from back at St. Bede's. He didn't mind, though. In his experience, the potent snobbery of the beach club was well worth the trouble. The sand at Periwinkle was really no different from the sand at the adjoining beach (aptly named Reject's Beach and separated by a thick, closely guarded rope). However, twice a day, at sunrise and sunset, a tractor combed up the seaweed that low tide had left on Periwinkle's shoreline and deposited it on Reject's side of the rope. This tedious process was performed so that the members' picturesque beachfront views wouldn't be obstructed by the dark, slimy salad of the deep. Furthermore, the main clubhouse boasted an exquisite buffet, an in-ground pool, and a superb bar. The clam chowder was among the best in New England. And nobody left the beach sober when drinking on the McShane tab. Hungover as he was, Ray was looking forward to spending an afternoon in the shade of an umbrella watching waves crash against the distant rocks.

"Good afternoon, Mr. McShane. May I take those for you?"

There was an irony in McShane's handing over of his father's car keys to the valet. In addition to intermittent caddying gigs at Newport National Golf Club, McShane himself worked as a valet at Gurney's Newport Resort & Marina during the summers.

"I'll come home every summer just for this," McShane said, leaning against the bar and gazing fondly at his surroundings.

The yellow-trimmed clubhouse doorway framed the glimmering ocean and the immaculate khaki sand that stretched beyond the patio like a portrait. Cell phones weren't allowed on the premises, so the people seated on the white wicker chairs that surrounded elegant glass tables conversed in hushed tones under sun hats and over iced teas.

Each time Ray crossed the threshold into the club, he would be seized by a strong compulsion to mentally record every detail of the experience. The members were particularly fascinating to him. They wore designer clothing that had acquired a time-faded look so perfect it might have been planned, as though to give the impression that, despite their extravagant wealth, they had never been corrupted by the bourgeois materialism of the nouveau riche. It seemed, to Ray, to be a display of some kind, a nonverbal assertion that they'd achieved—or, more likely, had always had—an economic stratum that did not require the proof of new shoes. They might as well have been nude, for they wore their self-assuredness in their skin, which was lightly tanned from sailing excursions and idle afternoons spent sipping drinks on Periwinkle's patio. They were peacocks who never felt the need to reveal their ostentatious plumage, confident that the reputation of their species preceded them.

In a side room adjacent to the bar, a handful of ancient men in navy blazers drank Heineken draughts and watched a PGA tournament on a flat-screen television. They smiled politely at Ray as he walked by. Reginald Pike shuffled slowly along the water's edge, a vanilla ice-cream cone dripping down his hand. At one extreme of the beach, a middle-aged man in a derby hat practiced with his pitching wedge in the sand. Blond children in tennis whites—whites were mandatory if one wished to so much as look at the tennis courts—scurried around the cabanas, their rackets swinging at their sides. Women in elegant one-piece bathing suits and flowy beach coverups dipped their pedicured toes in the club pool.

"Could we get two Beachcombers?" McShane asked the bartender. "And we'll do a rum floater on those, please."

One of the many young Eastern Europeans who staffed the clubhouse in the summer hurried to fulfill the order, snatching two cups and filling them with ice.

"Myers's or Goslings?" she asked. Her English was accented, and she held up two bottles for McShane's appraisal.

The Beachcomber was Periwinkle's signature drink—a blended concoction of white rum, sour mix, chopped mint, and lime juice that tasted as refreshing as it smelled.

"Myers's is fine, thanks," McShane said, invoking the tab and deploying his member voice.

"Thanks, man," Ray said, clinking his glass.

They left the bar without tipping because, by design, there was no tipping at Periwinkle. Rather, the members contributed a generous donation of sorts to the staff at the end of the summer, a pot that certainly came to a substantial sum, especially when converted to Hungarian forints or Ukrainian hryvnia. Actual money never changed hands at the club. Instead, surnames were swiped like credit cards, and no card was declined.

"We're just getting started," McShane said after a long sip.

"Are we gonna get kicked out again?" Ray asked, chuckling.

Two summers prior, they'd been quietly excused from the beach after smuggling in their own beers and carousing a bit too loudly. The prickly club manager had given McShane a stern warning, though there wasn't much he could do beyond a curmudgeonly recitation of the club's policies. Of course, the story always brought McShane and Ray enough pleasure in retrospect to make the sallow manager's finger-wagging remonstrations feel almost worth the trouble.

"We'll see," McShane laughed, placing a few crab cakes next to the heirloom tomato panzanella on his platter.

The staff stood behind the buffet, wordless and eager. They clasped their hands behind their backs, waiting to be sent on an errand or to jump into action when a child inevitably dropped one of the pristine china plates. They wore crisp white polo shirts and starchy khaki shorts. Firm smiles were affixed to their faces.

But Ray recognized the look in their eyes. Their pupils held the same glint that his wore when he was hauling crates of exquisite wine up to sprawling homes or fetching bottles at the liquor store. Tongs laden with a mound of smoked salmon hovering just above his plate, Ray had a sudden urge to speak with these staff members, to learn what might be behind that subtle glint. What had they overheard when the members thought no one was listening? Did they relish opportunities to commiserate about rude members and demanding bosses from behind storage closet doors or from the safe distance of the employee parking lot? Were they homesick for some dish that they hadn't yet procured here on this odd little island in the Atlantic?

But, Ray wondered, if they were to respond at all, would they answer his questions honestly? He was on the other side of the buffet, after all.

"You coming?" McShane called.

The smoked salmon fell with a damp thud to Ray's plate, and he joined McShane at the table.

The light lunch settling in their stomachs, they stepped down off the slightly raised stone patio and onto the beach. As soon as their bare feet touched the sand, a skinny boy with a dark tan appeared at their side, clutching two folding chairs in his gangly arms. With spry, eager movements, he arranged the chairs and scampered back up the beach to the clubhouse. Moments later, he returned, planting a wide umbrella in the sand and laying thick white towels across the chairs, his movements punctuated by a series of deferential nods. Sipping the cool drinks, McShane and Ray drifted into a light sleep as the mild June sun settled on their skin, rousing only to refresh their beverages.

◇◇◇◇◇◇◇◇◇◇◇◇◇◇◇◇◇◇◇◇◇◇

"Another round?" McShane suggested, stirring.

The empty glasses lay on their sides in the sand.

"Sure, I'll grab it," Ray offered, hoisting his reposed limbs back to life.

One awkward, sleepy step after another, he lumbered up the beach to the clubhouse.

"Two more, please," he said to the bartender, who was by now familiar with his face and the drink order that attended it.

A bony, older woman with dyed-blond hair looked back over her shoulder as she passed Ray on her way to the tennis courts. Halting and turning to face him, she looked at Ray as though she recognized him.

"Sorry, I know you're not really supposed to ask this anymore, but, what *are* you?" she asked, her plucked brows knitted and her rouged lips drawn into a smile.

This late in June, his tanned pigmentation had attained an ambiguous shade of copper that occasionally prompted such questions. Ray knew it would have been easy to feign misunderstanding here, to force her to ask the question again to see if she could hear herself. But resisting the urge, he fell back on his impulses as a gracious guest.

"Cuban," he said, adding a disarming smile. "Half."

"Oh!" she said.

Though her face was creased with soft wrinkles, her taut limbs were disturbingly toned for her age, as though she had willed her body into fitness. But rigorous Pilates and tennis lessons six days a week could turn the clock back only so far.

"You're a member here?" she asked. "I'm sorry, it's just that I don't recognize you, and I thought I knew everyone around here!" she added with a terse laugh.

"No, I'm not," he said, more defensively than he'd intended. "I'm a guest."

Her head nodded quickly, as though he'd given a correct answer. Smiling once more, she continued on toward the tennis courts.

The bartender snickered as he handed Ray the drinks. Ray ignored him, but he felt his ears turning red as he took the brimming glasses in his hands and walked back toward the beach. But he paused at the edge of the patio. He suddenly felt very old. It was almost July. When he was much younger, he'd often imagined what he might look like, feel like, and be like in his twenties. For some reason, he'd always imagined a tall version of himself wearing blue jeans and laughing with his friends, who were also wearing blue jeans. It had seemed like such a distant, important age back then, as though crossing the threshold of one's second decade on earth might confer a certainty about things like a finishing glaze on a piece of glass. But Ray didn't feel solid. Rather, he felt as though his certainties were streaming off of him in steady rivulets, pouring out of him faster than he could gather them up again. If only they could be channeled in some—any—direction.

A few members seated on the patio began to eye him with mild curiosity. He set the drinks down on the nearest table and marched to the club's front desk.

"I would like to put my name on the waiting list," he said to the desk attendant. "For membership."

The fastidiously appointed clerk eyed Ray over his wire-rimmed glasses, a subtle smirk playing across lips.

"Is that so?"

"Yes, please," Ray said. He fought to keep the tremor out of his voice. Though he'd been asleep just minutes ago, his heart was pounding and he felt a rush of energy thrill through his veins.

"Well," the clerk said, fidgeting with his bow tie, "you should know that, at present, our waiting list is over thirty years long. And even then..."

The clerk stared coyly at Ray, awaiting his response. Ray fought the urge to pluck the man's conspicuous toupee from his scalp.

"The waiting list," Ray said. "Please."

"Very well," the clerk said, arching his eyebrows and snickering slightly. "But you should know that adding your name to the waiting list does not guarantee membership. There are significant fees, an application process, recommendations considered, etcetera, etcetera. You understand, yes?"

Ray nodded. Blood pulsed like a drumbeat in his ears. Sighing, the clerk uncapped an elegant fountain pen and opened a large leather-bound notebook.

"Your name?" he asked. The pen was poised over a blank slot on the page, just under a slew of scrawled names and their dates of entry.

"Raymond Wilson."

Ray watched until the clerk had finished printing his name in the slot, blotting the wet ink before closing the notebook and replacing it in a drawer under the desk.

"Well, Mr. Wilson," the clerk said with a strained smile, "we'll let you know when membership becomes available for you."

Before turning to leave, Ray pulled a wrinkled five-dollar bill from his pocket and stuffed it behind the neatly folded kerchief in the pocket of the clerk's blazer.

"Thanks," Ray said, though the clerk was too baffled to respond. His mouth opened and closed in mute protestation as he tried to remove the bill from his pocket.

Ray grabbed the two cocktails from the table on the patio and rejoined McShane under the umbrella.

PART II

JULY

A man accepts his failures more easily—or perhaps summer's insanity is gone? A man notices ordinary earth, scorned in July, with affection, as he settles down to his daily work, to use stamps.

—ROBERT BLY

CHAPTER 10

Home

On the rare nights he spent at home, Ray would sleep deeply, recovering the slumber he'd lost to late nights boozing with friends and morning shifts at the liquor store. He'd spent the past three days in Bristol, jumping off the McShanes' private dock until dark and partaking in the carousing that accompanied the annual Bristol Fourth of July parade (the oldest of its kind in the country, a fact of which the township was so proud that the median lines on the street were painted red, white, and blue rather than yellow). Ray had hardly slept in seventy-two hours, and he was exhausted by the time he got back home to Newport.

The Wilson-Domingos' squat house sat among the multitude of nondescript cottages that lined the blocks of the Fifth Ward. It was a sleepy neighborhood on the periphery of Newport's more picturesque sections, functioning as the elbow that connected the boisterous action of Thames Street to the reverential calm of Ocean Drive. The old Volvo sedan that Ray's parents occasionally allowed him to borrow sat in their narrow driveway. For all its quirks—a rear windshield that took hours to defog, a tendency to refuse ignition on cold winter mornings, a sunroof permanently jammed halfway closed—Ray loved the jalopy. It was the only consistent image he had of a home, standing sentry in front of every house he'd ever lived in.

The house next door had been abandoned ever since Hurricane Sandy had felled a massive tree that cleaved a gaping chasm through its roof. And the house that had been their neighbors' on the other side had been demolished, replaced by wire fencing and the expansive dirt lot that would eventually become a parking garage.

"You look hungover, *niño*."

It was his mother's typical greeting when he emerged from his bedroom at an hour she deemed unreasonable.

"Is there any coffee?" Ray grumbled, ignoring her accusation.

Wordlessly, she poured a small cup of espresso for Ray and another for herself before sitting back down at the kitchen table. It was probably her third or fourth of the morning. If battery acid could give her more of a kick, she probably would have imbibed that instead.

"Jesus, this stuff is wicked strong," he said, recoiling from the bitter flavor.

"Please," she said, waving a dismissive hand. "You don't even know. Back home we have coffee that would melt your teeth if you tried it. Your father could never handle it either."

Nearly three decades had passed since she'd left Cuba, and still she talked about it as though it were a house across the street, gesturing out the window whenever she invoked her homeland.

"Think they drink coffee in Japan?" Ray asked.

Ray's father was four months into a six-month deployment on Okinawa.

"Who knows?" she said. "That man is probably too busy buying cocktails for local girls to worry about coffee."

"That doesn't sound like him."

"You don't understand, *mijo*. When those Navy boys dock up, the women come flocking. Foreigners are like golden tickets. It's the only time in the world a white man gets to feel exotic."

"Yeah, well, he's not really a boy anymore, *mamá*," Ray said, smiling at the thought of his pentagenerian father wooing admiring Japanese girls.

"He hasn't changed one bit since I met him in Santiago, you know that?" his mother said. "Even then he was always talking about running away, traveling the world. His mind was always on to the next place. Can't sit still, that man . . ."

A wistful smile spread across her face as she tucked a strand of gray hair behind her ear. She'd spent almost two decades moving around the world from one Navy base to the next, joining her husband each time the command came down the chain that he was being relocated to San Diego, Charleston, Corpus Christi, Singapore, and Whidbey Island. But after he'd been stationed in Newport, she'd refused to leave. She was tired of uprooting her life every few years and pulling their two nearly high school–aged sons out of one school after another. Ray's father had joined the Navy right out of high school and hadn't ascended high enough in rank to have much agency over where he and his family lived. So while he was shuttled around the world, taking extended leaves to return home every few months, Ray's mother had built a home for her family and a life for herself in a small cottage (partially subsidized by the U.S. Navy) in Newport's Fifth Ward.

"I thought he was stationed at Guantanamo when you met him?"

"Yes, but nobody would hang around that awful place. All the sailors would go to Santiago to find the most beautiful women," she said, speaking with the conviction of a war historian.

This part of the story Ray had heard. He forced down the rest of the acidic coffee and placed the small cup in the sink.

"And where is *el príncipe* off to today, a royal ball?" she asked. Her voice was thick with sarcasm, though she smiled as she spoke. "You know, when I was pregnant with Tony, I worried my children would feel out of place in this country with an American father and a Cuban mother. Seems silly now, right? You and your *hermano* have taken to this place like a goose to water."

Knowing better than to correct her (she claimed the mistranslated idioms made perfect sense in Spanish), Ray stepped inside the pantry. He'd stashed a pint of bourbon behind the neat rows of Goya products that lined the shelves. He slipped the slim bottle into his back pocket, covered it with his t-shirt, and slung his backpack over one shoulder before returning to the kitchen.

"Gotta go," he said, "I'm meeting up with Josh."

"You boys stay out of trouble. Be good, *mijo*. You know I don't like that house."

This was a recurrent admonishment of hers, and she capped it off with a reproachful shake of her head. Ray pecked her on the cheek on his way out the door.

"I know. He's older now, *mamá*. He's a graduate student. Can I take the car?"

"Fine, but I need it back in the morning—I have the early shift. The hotel is fully booked this week. I hope you and Josh behave." Then she called after Ray's departing back, "Wait, *esperate*, Raymond."

The screen door had just clattered shut. Sighing, Ray walked back into the kitchen.

"I don't see you for three days, and now you're back out the door?"

"*Lo siento*. I've been working a lot lately."

"Ha!" she laughed. "So getting drunk on the beach is work now? Your brother cuts hair sixty hours a week, and he still comes home for dinner some nights. Have you talked to him recently? He has *una novia* now, did you know? Have you met her yet? A waitress at Clarke Cooke House. Red hair. He hasn't brought her to dinner here yet."

Ray shrugged. He felt a little bad that he hadn't known Tony was dating someone. "I don't know, *mamá*. I haven't talked to him in a few days. I'll go see him soon, though."

"Have you seen his new apartment?"

"*Claro*. I helped him move in, remember?"

"I told him it was too expensive, but he doesn't listen. Both of you in such a rush to leave my house. If it weren't for Christopher, I'd have nobody to cook for."

Christopher was a man in his late thirties who rented a room on the second floor of the Wilson-Domingo house. He was a gregarious, self-effacing, and appreciative dinner guest and had become a fixture at their table over the years, sometimes accompanied by a new boyfriend and always bursting with stories to share. A hairstylist at a tony salon on Thames Street, he and Señora Wilson-Domingo had become fast friends ever since he'd offered to cut her hair for free in exchange for a plate of her picadillo, its savory aroma wafting up from her stove and taunting him in his upstairs quarters.

"Anyway," his mother continued, "Tony told me to tell you that if he refers you to the barber school, you can get a discount, and he'll get a hundred dollars, too, if you complete the course."

"I don't want to be a barber."

"*Por qué no?* Tony makes good money. You want to work at the liquor store forever? It's not enough money, *mijo*."

"I'm thinking about going to law school, actually."

The words felt odd leaving Ray's mouth. His mother dropped her pen onto the table and set down her crossword puzzle.

"*En serio?* You want to be a lawyer now?" she asked, almost whispering. "Since when?"

"Mr. Finch said he could set up some more interviews for this year. Paralegal jobs. And then I could apply to law schools next fall."

"I've never heard you talk about wanting to be a lawyer before. This is what you want?"

"Sure," he said, shrugging.

His mother stood up from the table and embraced him in a tight hug.

"*Estoy tan orgulloso de ti*," she said, kissing him on the cheek.

Ray laughed and pulled back.

"I haven't even done anything yet. It's just an idea, that's all."

"If it's what you want, then it's what I want," she said, beaming. "You are so lucky to have such friends."

The brunt of Ray's good fortune had stemmed from the intrepid *Providence Journal* columnist who had lambasted St. Bede's in a scathing article published nearly a decade ago. In the fiery verbiage of the front-page story, she'd condemned the school for being institutionally racist and also asserted that St. Bede's Prep was dismissive of students who did not come from moneyed areas like New Canaan or Bergen County, ignoring the many qualified students in their own zip code. Within a month of the article's publication, U.S. representative David Cicilline of Rhode Island's First Congressional District had taken up the cause, condemning the school for its throwback elitism on every local network (no doubt to the benefit of his political career, considering the public's lukewarm, at best, perception of the posh school) and demanding institutional change. Even Senator Sheldon Whitehouse (a member, it should be noted, of Periwinkle Beach Club) called on St. Bede's—his alma mater!—to address the issues raised by the article. Soon enough, St. Bede's introduced the "401 Scholars Program" (a nod to the single area code that covered the entire state of Rhode Island), which would provide one deserving local student per year with a full scholarship.

On the day the envelope arrived, marked with the red crest of St. Bede's, Ray had torn it open with bated breath. His mother's tears had stained the acceptance letter as she read it over and over again, babbling excitedly in a flurry of Spanish and English about how her son would go from St. Bede's right on to Harvard and then on to a distinguished career in the Senate, perhaps even the presidency. At the time, his dad had been stationed on an aircraft carrier off of Hawaii but had called home to express his pride. Tony, who had just finished barber school, had locked Ray in a bear hug so tight he thought his ribs might break.

After he'd been accepted to St. Bede's, the world of preppy affluence had entered Ray's consciousness in trickles at first—classmates talking about vacations to the Bahamas at Christmastime or discussing the best ski lodges in Switzerland, girls removing their pearl necklaces before mounting their dressage horses, and guys debating the merits of this or that country club. Once he'd made friends, the trickle grew to a torrent, accepting invitations to their pool parties and regattas, joining them for dinner at restaurants he'd never been to, and watching Celtics games from box seats.

One spring day, late in his freshman year, Ray had been invited to hang out by some of the guys in his class for the first time. He'd spent most of that first year in the library, memorizing Latin declensions and skimming the Bible stories that his classmates seemed to know by heart. The weather had just started to turn warm after a brutal winter.

"Hey, Ray, my dad said I could take the boat out this weekend. You in?"

That weekend his mom had chauffeured him to the address in Tiverton that Bane had provided. They thought they'd taken a wrong turn when the map directed them to follow the narrow, twisting path off the main road. After nearly two miles of winding, tree-lined road, the massive Bane estate had risen up in front of them. The immense, multilevel, modernist house perched on a neat acre of land overlooking the Sakonnet River.

"My god, it's like a castle!" Ray's mother had whispered.

Back then, instinct, and not the experience he had accrued since that day, had told Ray not to mention anything out loud about how big the house was or how reclining on the yacht and sipping Mr. Bane's whiskey had been the single most luxurious moment of his life. To that point, he'd only ever seen such things in music videos and Bond movies.

He'd superseded his circumstances then, he told himself, so why not again? If he'd belonged with this crowd in high school and college, why not now, as they progressed at warp speed toward adulthood? With the right job, the right suit, the right car, and the right tastes, he believed he could be enmeshed completely, joining their world so seamlessly that when he appeared at the same garden parties and weddings that they attended in future summers, they wouldn't give the unlikeliness of his presence any more thought than they did this summer. The difference would be that he was no longer tagging along as a guest on their summer escapades but rather that his own social schedule had happened, by chance, to bring him to the same summer functions, independent of their plans.

It was not that Ray feared he would lose his friends—not at all. The history that bound them was stronger than titanium, forged in study halls, grim church services, bonfires, long drives, athletic events, and innumerable drunken nights. No, he did not fear that he would lose them. What he feared was that it would eventually become inconvenient to be his friend. They would want to eat at restaurants he couldn't afford and spend their leisure time at pastimes—golf, tennis, sailing, skiing—that he had neither the upbringing nor the time nor the funds to pursue. Their kids would go to different schools, and their bachelor parties would be held at locales that priced out his company. They'd make sincere offers to cover his costs, but it would be too embarrassing to accept. Their conversations would revolve around stocks, promotions, car purchases, and destination vacations to which he would have nothing to contribute. Their houses would be large enough to host massive parties—even parties in his honor, perhaps—but he would never be able to return the favor. These were the fears Ray admitted to himself only occasionally. And he knew them to be, at least in part, irrational. But at twenty-two, newly graduated from college and staring down the looming decades that would eventually make up his life, no longer anchored by the academic institutions and schedules that had planted Ray and his friends—at least superficially—on an even plane, the boundary between rationality and irrationality was fraught with fissures.

Ray turned to leave again but his mother stopped him, pulling him back into a hug.

"*Darle mi amor a* Josh. Be safe."

"I will," Ray said, his hand on the doorknob.

"And you don't need this," she added, pulling the pint bottle from his back pocket and glaring reprovingly at him as he rolled his eyes and stepped out the door.

"*Te quiero, mijo.*"

"*Te quiero, mamá.*"

CHAPTER 11

The Cactus

There was nothing particularly offensive about the Anwars' summer house, in and of itself. And yet, over the course of the several summers in which Josh had taken up residence there, the mere mention of the house had come to elicit sharp intakes of breath and remonstrative headshakes from the dozen or so island parents who knew—or presumed they knew—what occurred within its shabby walls.

The summer house's infamy had arisen through somewhat peculiar circumstances. Emigrating from Egypt in the late nineties, the Anwars had sought to build for their children a distinctly American life. The lifestyle afforded by Dr. Anwar's thriving anesthesiology career allowed for a generous amount of experimentation on this front. However, in each of their efforts to achieve the suburban picket-fenced normalcy they'd envisioned, they had missed the mark by just a little. These occasional missteps in presentation fascinated and delighted Ray almost as much as they frustrated Josh. For instance, one summer, the Anwars had dug an in-ground pool into their yard, despite the fact that Rhode Island received about two months of pool weather per year and beaches were never more than ten minutes away.

"Dad, you can't even swim!" Josh had bellowed at his father, screaming to be heard over the sound of the backhoe digging great bucketfuls of dirt from their backyard.

Another time, Dr. Anwar had purchased a massive Ford truck, though he'd had to buy a footstool so that he could clamber up into the driver's seat on his squat legs.

"Dad, you're a doctor! What the hell do you need this truck for?"

On Super Bowl Sunday, they decorated their house with the emblems and flags of whatever two teams were playing.

"Look at this. Who does this?" Josh had scoffed, gesturing at the Baltimore Ravens and San Francisco 49ers banners strung neatly over the garage door and shaking his head.

The summer house had been another such misfire. While many Americans of a certain financial class might purchase a vacation home at some point, few would think to buy a second house in the same town as their first. It occupied a little square patch of scrubby lawn and sat atop a crumbling seawall overlooking Narragansett Bay. Like most of the houses in Island Park, it fell just short of charming in its asceticism. Grimy white doors were decorated half-heartedly with bits of sea glass or clamshells collected from the rocky shoreline, succumbing to the public's nautical expectations only begrudgingly. Some of the houses in the area had been ravaged by nor'easters and hurricanes so many times that they looked as though they might collapse into a heap of whitewashed clapboards and dingy shutters at the slightest breeze. If it weren't for the ocean view, an ungracious looker might dismiss the whole neighborhood as an eyesore.

Not long after the get-together at Maya's house, Ray's mother had sent him out for a fresh canister of bay leaves and he had bumped into Josh's mother at the grocery store. Mrs. Anwar had asked the expected questions about his graduation, his family, and his plans for the summer, each query inflected with her musical, accented English.

"Ray! Hello! How are you, *habibi*?" she'd asked, her dark eyes impossibly sincere for the cereal aisle.

She'd embraced him in her short arms, her mass of coarse, curly black hair pressing against his face.

"I'm good, I'm good, thanks. How are you? How's Josh?" Ray had asked.

"Oh," she started, sighing. "He's not talking to us right now."

The feuds between Josh and his parents came and went like monsoons, building to destructive proportions before petering out into a drizzle. He would berate their parochial conservatism and the limits of their foreigners' grasp of American teenage life. Back in high school, whenever Ray would go over to Josh's house to study or eat dinner and the inevitable fight would break out—a harsh mix of shouted colloquial English followed by a slurry of equally impassioned Arabic—he would stare intently into Dr. Anwar's elaborate saltwater fish tank, feigning interest while waiting for Josh's vitriol to wane. Though he'd mellowed since high school, Josh's temper remained somewhat easily triggered. Once he'd decided to side with liberalism, the conservative leanings of his parents had riled him up. When he'd become an atheist, his parents' Christianity had rubbed him the wrong way. They had locked horns repeatedly over the subject of marijuana, Josh's partaking of the drug, and whether or not it was indeed safer than alcohol (as he would often assert at the top of his lungs). Ray supposed the cigarettes had been the cause of some more recent row in the Anwar household.

"Oh. Well, how are his studies going?" Ray asked, changing the subject.

"Good, good, you know. He's already planning his . . . how do you say it? Not dissection, but . . ."

"His dissertation?" Ray offered.

"Yes! Yes, he's over at the summer house working on it. Won't talk to anyone. Oh, but you should go say hi! He'd love that," she said.

By his senior year at St. Bede's, Josh's relationship with his parents had become so combustible that he'd moved into the summer house permanently. And it was to the summer house that he returned on school breaks. In many ways, the move had salved his relationship with his parents. The interactions he'd had with them thereafter were, by comparison, pleasant. While they disapproved of the raucous bashes he would occasionally host, the patience and politeness he would exude whenever he returned home to do laundry had made the semi-estrangement palatable for both parties.

"I'll try to make it over there," Ray said.

The truth was that none of them—Ray, Kirley, Maya, McShane, Ella, Finch, Bane, or Coyne—had had much contact with Josh since the last summer after high school. Though he would join them out of a sense of nostalgic duty at a few gatherings every year, he would usually disappear by sunrise, as he had at Maya's get-together. A few summers back, he'd gotten to feeling like people were using him for his summer house. Kids flirting with adulthood but still stuck at home in the summers were always looking for a place away from their parents to drink and smoke and have sex and throw up (though not always in that order). Just before they'd all gone off to college, an encounter with an Island Park neighbor—an older dude with gauges stretching his earlobes—had turned Josh on to psychedelics.

"I wonder if you'd do something for me," Mrs. Anwar said, grabbing Ray's hand and locking him in her obsidian eyes. "Would you ask Josh to stop smoking cigarettes?"

The sincere request bore the weight of a final hope, a last-ditch effort. Tony the Tiger grinned stupidly from the Frosted Flakes box on the shelf.

"Back in Egypt, so many people die of the smoking," she continued. "He won't listen to us. And he's always admired you, *habibi*. He'll listen to you."

Ray shifted uncomfortably in the aisle before answering.

"Okay, sure. I'll try," Ray managed to say, knowing that he would've confessed to murder to free himself from that baleful stare.

"You promise?" she asked, still clasping his hand.

"I promise."

"Thank you, *habibi*," she said, hugging him again. "And say hello to your mother for me!" she called over her shoulder, pushing her cart toward checkout.

◇◇◇◇◇◇◇◇◇◇◇◇◇◇◇◇◇◇◇◇◇◇

By the time Ray was steering the old Volvo around the bend toward Island Park, he wasn't sure whether he would, indeed, suggest that

Josh quit smoking. He wasn't even positive that he'd actually go inside. He thought about driving right past the house and back to Newport. Who was he to tell Josh how to live? Why shouldn't he smoke cigarettes? Ray was no paragon of human health. None of them were. At twenty-two, they felt indestructible. Drinking past midnight, eating buffalo chicken pizza at dawn, and sleeping in snatches, they had yet to encounter a pain that a Dunkin' Donuts iced coffee and Advil couldn't relieve. And yet, the encounter with Mrs. Anwar in the supermarket lingered in his mind. He'd made a promise, after all, and Ray liked to think of himself as the kind of person who kept the promises he made.

The summer house was exactly as Ray remembered it, though he couldn't recall ever having been to the place sober. And even if he'd ever arrived that way, it certainly wasn't how he'd left. The riotous, unmowed grass of the patchy lawn speared his ankles as he walked through the gate. A messy patch of overturned soil by the mailbox had at one time been the site where Josh planned to grow all his own produce. He'd been dating a vegan girl at the time. No zucchinis or tomatoes had ever grown there, but at least now, nearly four years later, tufts of young green grass poked up through the soil.

Ray tapped gently at the door and called Josh's name. This, too, was a first. In summers past, he'd barely broken stride, walking straight through the front door. To him and everyone else that debaucherous summer after high school, the house had been like a second home. But for Josh it had actually been his second home, and then his primary one. A brief pang of guilt twisted in Ray's gut. Again, he thought about jumping back into his car and driving away.

"Ray? Holy shit, man, how are you? Come on in."

Josh went for a knuckle bump while Ray, who panicked as soon as Josh opened the door, extended his hand for an inappropriately formal handshake. Ray cringed internally as Josh's closed fist met his open palm, but they quickly remedied the cumbersome greeting with a brief, mildly awkward, back-slapping hug.

The house was still shabbily decorated, but at least now the smell of cheap fruit-flavored vodka didn't accost the nose upon stepping through the door. The empty liquor bottles that used to be displayed in rows above the kitchen cabinets—the sad trophies of adolescent males—were gone, replaced by funky clay pots and nonstick pans. A few family pictures and a smattering of rather tacky landscape paintings depicting local vistas hung from the same walls where flattened thirty-pack cardboard beer boxes had once been pridefully duct-taped.

The thin floorboards squeaked as Ray followed Josh to the backmost room of the one-story, railroad-style house. The cramped room overlooked the bay. Unlike the front quarters of the house, this room looked and smelled familiar to Ray. It was the aroma of the dingy furniture that had trapped innumerable clouds of cigarette and pot smoke in its fibers. The only discernible change to the room was that several bumpy, cratered rocks, a few notebooks, and a laptop had replaced the ever-present glass bong on the coffee table. A single potted cactus had been placed in one corner too, Ray noticed. It was nearly Josh's height and bore only a slightly different hue than the faded green wallpaper.

"Sorry about the mess. Trying to get a jump on my dissertation," Josh said, gesturing to the rocks strewn across the table.

"Actually, I was gonna say this place looks cleaner than ever," Ray joked.

"Right, ha, yeah," Josh intoned, rubbing the wiry black hairs that sprouted from his chin.

"So, what's the dissertation gonna be about?" Ray asked.

"Rocks," Josh replied flatly.

After a moment, Ray realized it was a joke and laughed. It would have felt strange to sit directly across from each other, as though they were at an interview or a lunch date, so they sat adjacent to each other on the teal wraparound couch.

"No, I'm actually planning on writing about igneous rocks and their possible correlation to crude oil deposits."

"Sounds fascinating," Ray said sarcastically.

Gently picking one of the rocks up off the table and weighing it in his hand, Josh laughed again and shook his head.

"It's not, actually. It's wicked boring. It's pretty much the same thing all geologists dissertate—is that a word?"

"Beats me."

"Okay, well, anyways, it's the same kind of dissertation that all geologists do. So we can get jobs afterward."

"Like a university position?"

"No, no. Ha! No. With an oil company."

The way he said it made it sound like a confession more than an explanation, and from under his thick brows a somewhat apologetic glint shot through his dark eyes.

"Isn't that, like, joining the enemy?" Ray asked.

More chin rubbing and laughter.

"Yeah, well, money makes the world go round, right?"

"Tell me about it."

"Finch told me you were thinking about law school. That true?"

"Yeah, thinking about it."

"You never thought about going to grad school for anthropology?"

Ray shrugged.

"Not really. I want to make some money—real money, you know? At least with a law degree, I know I'll get a job, right?"

"Sure," Josh said. "I guess I never really pictured you as a lawyer, though."

"No? So what did you picture me as, then?"

Josh laughed and ran a hand through his thick hair.

"I'm not sure. Something different, I guess."

Staring through the window at the undulating sea as he'd done on innumerable occasions in the past, Ray felt like he was seeing the vista for the first time. Every other time he'd looked through the grimy square window out onto the bay, he'd been drunk or high or both, expending his (admittedly, in those moments, limited) focus on an evaluation of his buzz more than the coolly lapping waves that crashed against the rocks below.

"You mind?" Josh asked, pulling a beaten pack of Marlboros out of his shirt pocket.

Though he'd paused to ask politely, a cigarette was already perched on his bottom lip, his thumb triggered on a Zippo.

"Your house," Ray said, waving him on with a loose flail of his hand.

No sooner had Ray spoken than the flame jumped from the lighter and began crisping the tip of the cigarette. The fire toasted it a light shade of brown like a marshmallow before it smoldered into a morbid gray-black.

"My bad, you want one?" Josh asked, offering the pack.

"I'll just take a few hits of yours, if that's cool. Better not waste a whole one on me," Ray replied.

Nodding, Josh took another deep drag. As a personal rule, Ray tried not to smoke tobacco. Occasionally, he would succumb to a proffered cigarette, though only when alcohol had undermined his defenses. He prided himself on never having purchased a pack of cigarettes. But maybe, he thought, Josh would be more comfortable if he accepted the offered smoke, clearing any suspicion of judgment by way of self-incrimination. Nobody could tell a crass joke in front of a nun, after all. Besides, he rationalized to himself, each hit he took from the cigarette would be one less puff going into Josh's lungs.

The cigarette tasted like old raisins and ash.

"What's up with the cactus?" Ray asked, exhaling.

"It was here when I moved back in at the beginning of the summer. My parents must've stuck it there at some point."

"Do you ever have to water it?"

"Nah, I don't think so. It stores water inside itself or something, so it never dies," he explained, gladly accepting the cigarette back from Ray's outstretched hand.

"Yeah, I guess that's, like, cactuses' whole thing, right?" Ray said.

"I guess so. Hey, you want some tea? I was just about to make some when you came," Josh said, standing up.

"Sure, yeah. Sorry to barge in, by the way. I know you're studying and stuff."

"Don't mention it," Josh said. The comment sounded sincere enough to Ray, and he allowed himself to relax a little.

Stepping awkwardly over Ray's legs, Josh moved in jerky steps to the kitchen. Ray heard the faucet release a torrent of water and then the meek beeps of microwave buttons being pressed. There was a flicking and popping sound, too, followed by the metallic clunk of the Zippo being shut.

Ray pawed at one of the larger rocks resting atop the glass table. It felt rough against his fingertips and satisfyingly earthen and solid when he picked it up, weighing its pleasant heft in his hand. Worried about disrupting anything Josh might have been working on, however, he quickly placed the rock back down on the table and shuffled along the couch until he was next to the cactus. Its green skin was faded and creased, but it looked as sturdy and dignified as an old war veteran. The smooth grooves of the plant felt almost fake, faultless as a fiberglass surfboard. With the tip of his index finger, he gently touched one of the tiny, sharp spines that poked out at even intervals along the cactus's ridges. It was pliable but wickedly sharp.

"Doesn't that hurt?" Josh asked, setting two mugs of jasmine tea down on the table next to a pile of bluish stones.

Ray yanked his hand back into his lap. He hadn't heard Josh return to the room. Josh's feet were sporting a tired pair of Nike mid-calf socks—the kind that had replaced ankle socks in popularity in the late aughts after the YouTube video, entitled "The Ultimate Lax Bro" and featuring an exemplary character in Brantford Winstonworth, went viral, giving a name and an identity to a subculture (that is, lax bros) that had existed at New England prep schools for several years by then.

Was it possible that Josh now maintained a shoeless household, Ray wondered? After all the Steve Madden stilettos and Adidas Sambas and Hunter boots and Converse low-tops and UGG slippers and Vans and Jack Rogers sandals and Rainbow flip-flops and Sperry topsiders and sand-coated bare feet that had tromped through this place over the years? It was difficult for Ray to fathom, but then he recalled seeing a Swiffer WetJet propped up against the refrigerator in the kitchen.

Somewhat sheepishly, Ray removed his sneakers and placed them tidily in the corner before replying to Josh's question.

"No, not really. If I pressed harder, it probably would, though. You've never touched it?"

Cocking his head to one side, Josh reached for the cactus. He pushed his finger slowly against one of the thumbtack-size spines.

"Cartoons always made it look worse," he said.

Maintaining space between them, he slouched into the seat Ray had vacated. The rich aroma of the jasmine tea swirled in Ray's nose.

"You think those spikes work, man? Like, in the wild, I mean," Ray asked, again testing the sharp bristles with his fingertips.

"What do you mean?"

Josh took a small sip of the tea before recoiling back from the brim and setting the mug down on the table. Still too hot; he'd have to find something else to do with his hands. His fingers tapped a rhythm against the cigarette pack in his pocket, and he eyed the yellow guitar that rested in the corner opposite the cactus. His knee bounced up and down as his heel tattooed a beat onto the carpeted floor.

"Like, do you think those needles keep animals from busting them open and drinking all the water out in the desert or whatever?" Ray asked.

"I've never really thought about it," Josh replied, a hollow laugh escaping from his throat as he shook his head.

With a motion so quick that Ray nearly missed it, another cigarette appeared between Josh's fingers, and he torched it to life. As the smoke swirled up to the ceiling, everything about him slowed down. His leg stopped bouncing, his fingers stopped drumming, and he sank deeper into the plush couch cushions.

"They must be pretty pissed, though, once they get all bloody opening it up, and it's just water," Josh said, chortling.

"Yeah," Ray agreed.

"Like, for that effort I want a steak."

"Or at least beer. Even shitty beer would be cool. Like PBR or something."

"Yeah, what if cactuses had beer in them?"

"All these wasted animals walking around, all scratched up. You imagine that?"

A wave of nostalgia washed over Ray just then. Sitting on the decrepit couches that furnished the St. Bede's dormitory common rooms, Ray and Josh had spat these nonsense hypotheticals back and forth for hours. The riff played itself out, and the laughter left a dull ache in their stomachs.

The cigarette smoke and the steam issuing off the mugs of jasmine tea melded into one another in the close air of the room. Combined, the vapors smelled something like the clouds of incense that would burst from the thurible with each emphatic swing of a monk's arm during the excruciatingly long church services they'd been subjected to at St. Bede's. Ray took a sip of the tea. The hot, caffeinated liquid mixed with the tobacco in his bloodstream, uniting to create a comfortable weightlessness in his hands and feet.

After a long while that felt like a short time, the tea had gone tepid and they'd smoked all but the last three cigarettes in the pack. A twelve-pack of Corona had been discovered in the refrigerator, and Ray gave up borrowing hits off Josh's cigarettes after the second beer. It was easier for him to smoke his own rather than passing one back and forth.

"One more each, then we split the last one on the way down?" Josh suggested, proffering the nearly empty carton in Ray's direction.

"On the way down where?" Ray asked, reaching for one of the three remaining cigarettes.

"Oh shit, dude, I thought I already mentioned it. There's this live band that plays at Scugg's down the road."

"Can we walk, or do we have to drive?" Ray asked, glancing at the several empty Corona bottles that stood among the rocks on the table.

The room was starting to feel more like he'd remembered it.

"Yeah, man, we can definitely walk. It's just down the boardwalk."

A foghorn sounded from across the bay, and a long red barge passed by the window, mounds of coal piled on its deck. Nearly sunset, violet streaks shot across the rippling water. A seagull beat its wings furiously, a large quahog clasped in its beak. Once it had ascended several stories into the air, it released its quarry. The quahog careened down to the shore, shattering into pieces as it made contact with the rocky beach. Orange clam meat splattered against the salt stained stones of the shoreline. The seagull squawked and dove to its dinner.

"And this band . . ." Ray began, tilting the warm beer up to his lips.

"You know, they suck, but they're good," Josh said.

A pleasant warmth spread from Ray's fingers and toes up through his limbs and into his chest, rubberizing his bones and wrapping his torso in a thick blanket.

"I think I know what you mean."

Scugg's made no attempt to hide that it was a dive bar. The Coors sign flickered only its two Os, which stared from the window like a pair of neon bat eyes. Like nearly every other structure in Island Park, the building was flat and boxy, built like the clusters of barnacles that clung to the sides of rocks, ever prepared to weather a rogue tide. Hurricanes ravaged Aquidneck Island every few years. Inconveniently built right up against the sea, Island Park was particularly vulnerable to flooding. The clapboards that held Scugg's together looked as though they had been beachcombed from the rocky shore across the street. Inside it smelled like cigarettes and flat beer, and Ray's sneakers squelched against the sticky cement floor.

"This place is an institution," Josh said, buzzed and reverent.

The majority of the people in the mostly male crowd wore oversize Patriots jerseys or Bruins hats pulled low over their eyes. From a shelf over the bar, a boxy TV displayed a football game. A series of uproarious hollers broke out as Tom Brady converted on a third down, and Ray jumped at the abrupt noise. Recovering, he high-fived a large, bearded man to his left, and the apprehensive stares with which Ray and Josh had been greeted dissipated from many of the drinkers' faces, replaced by a glassy-eyed contentedness as they returned to their draughts.

"Wait, it's July—how is there a Patriots game on?" Ray asked.

"Oh, yeah, they're always playing a Pats game on the TV here. I think this is Super Bowl fifty-one, where they came back on the Falcons," Josh said, squinting at the screen.

A few younger guys milled around a pool table in the back room. Every few minutes the clack of two pool balls connecting rang out from the table, followed by approving grunts or dramatic guffaws.

"What can I get yah, hon?"

The bartender was a short, thin woman, and her long hair was dyed a ravenous shade of black. Though she looked to be about forty, her tight clothes, heavy makeup, and the dim lighting of the bar made it difficult to discern her age with any certainty.

"Two whiskey Cokes," Josh said, yelling to be heard over the din that ensued after Danny Amendola celebrated a touchdown with a showstopping spike.

"You got it, hon," she said.

Winking, she spun in balletic fashion to the liquor shelf behind her. Procuring two plastic cups from some unseen lower shelf, she tossed a handful of ice cubes haphazardly into each one. Whiskey splashed onto the bar as she poured, and the soda foamed up over the rim.

"You get the next round," Josh said as Ray pulled open his wallet.

"Sure."

"It's cash only, by the way."

The bartender released Josh's change from her long, shellacked fingernails with another wink, which was made more dramatic by her long, fake eyelashes.

Shimmying sideways to squeeze through the Patriots' loyalist crowd amassed by the bar, Ray and Josh emerged into the back room. A few people were setting up instruments atop a busted plywood stage.

"The band will probably go on after the game ends. The bar puts on these old Sox and Pats games once or twice a week. It's pretty much the only time they get a crowd in here. The band's actually not half bad."

They planted themselves in a grimy booth, and Ray's pants squeaked against the stained rubber material. The cocktails were strong, and they drank them fast. Slithering through the wall of bodies again, Ray bought a second round. The Coca-Cola left a sweet, sticky rind on his lips. A few more jersey wearers from the bar began to seep into the back room as the Patriots sealed the overtime win.

A balding man with a droopy mustache and an immense gut bobbed drunkenly over to their table.

"Man! Wha' a win, am I right? Damn can Tom Brady throw a football," he slurred.

"Pretty great," they agreed, nodding.

The man staggered away as Ray raised his eyebrows slightly at the back of the man's retreating head.

"Welcome to Island Park, right?" Ray joked.

"What do you mean?"

Josh's eyebrows assumed sharp angles over his eyes, and he looked directly into Ray's face as he spoke. His fingers, which had been drumming against the table, froze.

"Oh, just, you know, like, super local right?" Ray stammered.

After a long pause, Josh's fingers started drumming again and he looked away.

"Man, I love this place," Josh said, gazing fondly into the milling, drunken crowd. "You've been hanging around with those other guys too much, dude. In Newport. Drinking cocktails on yachts or whatever. This is what bars are like, man. Real bars, I mean."

"It's definitely got character," Ray offered, in a weak attempt at diplomacy.

A guitar chord split the air, and the celebratory crowd by the bar shuffled into the back room, drawn by the successive entertainment. The reddish-purple light that hung over the stage intensified, and the ruby hue descended over the faces of the crowd, casting their bodies in a demonic pallor.

"Hell yeah, man, here we go," Josh said excitedly, all traces of malice gone from his voice.

As the band finished tuning up, Ray managed to slip through the crowd again, only to find the bar without its tender. After about a minute, the front door opened, and the bartender appeared, stubbing out the last nub of her cigarette on the cement outside. Cool air licked at Ray's face until the flimsy door swung shut with a weak slap.

"Shit, I'm sorry, hon. I thought everybody'd be watching the show," she apologized.

"Me too," Ray said, gesturing at the empty bar.

"Right, good thinking," she laughed. "Same?"

"Please. Hey, think I could bum a cig?"

It was a request he'd only ever seen executed in movies, but the words felt natural as they sprung from his tongue.

"Oh sure, hon, don't worry about it," she said.

While fishing a cigarette out of the bejeweled back pocket of her dark jeans, she simultaneously tossed a few ice cubes into two plastic cups with her other hand. Balancing the cigarette across one of the cups, she pushed the order across the bar.

"Thanks," Ray said, passing her the cash.

"Don't mention it. But don't tell your mama I gave it to you—'cause those things'll kill you!"

Dark-purple lipstick stained her teeth when she smiled.

"Right, yeah," he replied, forcing a laugh.

Back in the booth, Josh thrilled at the cigarette Ray had managed to scrounge, holding it up like a trophy.

"Great fucking work, dude! You're just in time—they're about to start."

The pounding drums and charging guitar chords filled the cramped room, pinning Ray to the booth. The rhythm crashed like waves over the crowd. Ray had been expecting some older guys in faded Led Zeppelin tour T-shirts blasting away passionately at a dream they'd never quite given up. But the singer was a woman, and she didn't appear to be much older than he was.

A beautiful, haunting wail soared from her throat, throbbing through the microphone and suffusing the room. It was a sound unlike any Ray had heard before. Usually at bar gigs like this, the instruments were too loud and the vocals couldn't be heard, and the performers generally faded into loud background noise. But this group was different. The singer's light-pink hair swung wildly about her face as she sang, her eyes closed.

"What are these guys called?" Ray shouted to Josh as he drained the last sip from his drink.

The flimsy plastic cup crushed easily, and Josh dropped it to the ground, where it joined dozens of its fallen brethren.

"The Aardvarks."

The zonked crowd nodded along to the rhythm. It was impossible to tell if she was singing covers or originals, but Ray didn't especially care. A desire to know her name, her life story, why she was singing at Scugg's in Island Park, and why she had pink hair gripped him suddenly, and he could think of nothing else.

The Aardvarks finished their set around one in the morning. Scugg's wasn't the kind of bar that respected Rhode Island's last-call law, or at least not strictly. The crowd in Patriots jerseys and faded black hoodies ambled soporifically toward the door. A few fluttered around the bar before leaving, like moths deciding whether or not to land on a lamp.

Following a few smokers outside, Josh managed to bum another cigarette. Still in the back room, Ray's feet carried him up to the sagging plywood stage. The room was empty but for a bearded man wearing a ratty red Portsmouth High School Football sweatshirt passed out in a booth and the Aardvarks packing up their instruments.

"Hey, great set," Ray said.

It was another line he'd only ever heard in movies, and it sounded phony as it left his mouth. The singer whirled around as though she'd felt a fly buzzing next to her ear.

"Huh? Oh thanks, yeah, we appreciate it."

The depth of her voice somehow complemented her tall stature and the thick, rubber-soled boots she wore, giving her something of a Viking aura. Standing below the stage, Ray had to arch his neck to speak up to her.

"So why are you guys called the Aardvarks?" Ray asked. He wondered if he sounded as drunk as he felt.

"It's really just so we're at the top of any alphabetical list when people look online for local bands to book," she replied.

Flicking her wrists in small, practiced circles, she wound an aux cord over her arm.

"Can I ask you another question?"

"That is another question," she said, her lips forming a bemused smile.

Though the skin on her face was smooth, the pads of her fingers were calloused and rough from years of pinning guitar chords to their frets. Her right thumbnail was grown to an impressive length, longer than her other nails and finished in a daggerlike tip.

"Why is your hair pink?"

The drummer, who had tattoos covering every inch of his left shin and a beanie pulled low over his ears, lifted his head up from his disassembled drum kit and looked from the singer to Ray with quick, flitting glances. The singer cocked her head to one side before answering, narrowing her eyes at Ray. Her lips were still formed in a thin smile.

"It's just how I like it," she said finally, shrugging.

Turning her back to him, she resumed winding up the cord and zipping her wickedly angular electric guitar into its case.

Back outside, Ray found Josh tired but buzzed. The whiskey lightness had left their feet, and they trudged back to the summer house. The cool evening air felt clammy on their skin, and the briny smell of the ocean stuck in the back of their throats. The moon sent a butter-colored path across the dark bay, and swollen waves lapped rhythmically against the seawall.

"You can crash on the couch, if you want. It's actually pretty comfortable," Josh said as they stumbled through the front door.

The screen door thwacked shut behind them.

"Yeah, I remember."

"Ha, right, of course."

"You gotta come out with us in Newport sometime, man. The guys would love to get fucked up with you again," Ray blurted.

Twisting the locks on the door, Josh said nothing for a moment. Ray's heart pumped a steady pulse into his fingertips and throbbed in his ears.

"I don't know. You've always gotten on better with those guys than I did."

Josh wasn't wrong, Ray knew.

"That was a good time," Ray said, collapsing onto the couch in the back room. "I talked to that singer."

"Oh, yeah? Was she cool?"

"Yeah, man, I think so. You ever think about, like, if we did just exactly what we wanted?"

"What do you mean?"

"That singer. Like, she just woke up one day and decided to start a band. Another day, she woke up and decided to dye her hair pink. She's doing exactly what she wants."

"Maybe. You're probably romanticizing it a bit, though, don't you think?" Josh's voice sounded weary, and he leaned against the doorframe.

"Yeah, you're probably right. Maybe I'm drunk. Night, Josh. Thanks for letting me crash, homie."

"Yeah, don't mention it. Night, man," Josh said.

A faucet turned on, and Ray heard a toothbrush rasping against teeth. A few minutes later, a door closed and mattress springs groaned.

Still wearing his shoes, Ray let his feet dangle off one end of the couch, his neck twisted against the cushions. When he closed his eyes, he felt like he'd just spent all day on a boat, so he tried to keep them open for a while. Long, slow waves swept across the dark ocean, and he stared at the moonlit whitecaps until, finally, he was overtaken by sleep.

◇◇◇◇◇◇◇◇◇◇◇◇◇◇◇◇◇◇◇◇◇◇

It wasn't the sun's light that woke Ray in the morning, but rather its heat. Beaming through the window, the rays seemed to shoot directly into his eyelids. The faux leather material of the couch cushions clung to his face as he peeled away his cheek. Sweat coated his sideburns and palms, and his feet felt clunky and numb. At some point in the night, he'd managed to kick off one of his shoes, and his shirt dangled from one shoulder like a sling. A goldfish seemed to be turning circles in his stomach, and his tongue felt swollen and dry. Terribly thirsty but unable to move, he fought a trickle of saliva down his arid throat.

By craning his neck, he could see the cactus. It stared down at him—judgmentally, he thought—from the corner. Reaching out a clammy hand, Ray stroked the smooth, flat part of its rind. His finger left a thin trail of moisture.

With his index finger, he clawed at the smooth green cactus skin, gently at first and then more purposefully. The motions were awkward and imprecise, but he couldn't bring himself to sit up into a more comfortable position; the effort would signify that the day was truly beginning, and he preferred to remain in limbo, caught between sleeping and waking. Picking at the cactus skin was the most constructive thing he could think to do. Beyond his control at this point, his finger moved independent from his thoughts.

One of the tiny cactus spines nicked him, and a dot of blood appeared at the tip of his index finger. Still, he did not stop, continuing to scratch until a wet groove appeared. Moving mechanically, he ran his nail along the groove, stripping away one filmy layer at a time.

At last, he burst through the translucent greenish membrane, and his finger poked into the cool water within. The soft cactus flesh felt pleasant and refreshing against his rigid finger. Drawing away, he licked at the water that coated his fingertip. It tasted like celery, with a hint of iron where the cactus had drawn blood. Drying his finger against his pants and taking a deep breath, he sat up. With effort, he managed to wrestle his shirt over his sore shoulders. Stretching his aching neck, he didn't notice when Josh walked into the room, toting two mugs of steaming coffee. A cigarette dangled from the corner of his mouth.

"Where'd you get that guy?" Ray asked, gesturing to the cigarette.

The smell was nauseating, and Ray took a mug and breathed in the coffee steam to block it out.

"Went out earlier to pick 'em up," Josh grunted.

The black coffee burned Ray's tongue, but within a few minutes sensation began returning to his extremities.

"Sorry, no milk or sugar here," Josh apologized.

"No worries. It's good like this."

Lighting up, Josh held the pack out to Ray as he took a long drag. Three cigarettes were already missing. Holding up his hand, Ray shook his head. His throat felt as though it were covered in sun-chipped paint, and his brain throbbed against his skull. Cocking his eyebrow briefly, Josh nodded and returned the pack to his pocket.

"You do that?" he asked, gesturing to the pulpy hole in the cactus.

"Oh, yeah. Sorry. I don't know why . . ."

"It's okay," Josh said with a shrug, taking another drag.

Droplets from the leaking faucet in the kitchen smacked at intervals against the empty sink. A few seagulls squawked from their perches along the seawall. The faint smoldering sound of the cigarette as Josh inhaled and the large wet gulps of coffee that Ray couldn't manage to drink smoothly resounded in the shabby room.

"Why'd you do that, though?" Josh asked after a while. "Why'd you claw up my cactus? Kinda weird, dude."

"I thought you said it was your parents'?"

"Same thing," he said.

"Sorry, man," Ray said.

Another gulp of coffee. An ancient man with a metal detector and big, clunky headphones ambled slowly along the shoreline, pausing now and then to lift a rock with his toe before moving on. The smoke danced in the bright rays of sunlight that seeped into the room.

"Listen, I have a ton of stuff to get done today," Josh said.

"Right, your dissertation. My mom needs the car back, anyway."

Pulling himself to his feet, Ray felt the blood rush to his head, and for a moment, his vision was blotted out by a dark-red screen. Patting his pockets for his keys and his wallet, he stumbled toward the front door.

"Good times, Josh. I'll see you around," he said.

Waving casually in Ray's direction, Josh nodded and picked up one of the rocks, holding it close to his face.

Ray lingered in the doorway.

"Hey, Josh," he began.

"Yeah?" Josh droned, still eyeing the rock.

"Maybe cut back on those cigs. They're no good, dude."

His eyes flashed up as though Ray had clapped or shouted. But then they returned to the rock in his hands.

"Yeah," he said, shrugging. "I know."

CHAPTER 12

The Prudence Island Ferry

A combative rooster pecked at Ray's ankles as he stepped out of the car. Having long ago overcome his trepidation around the bird's aggressive squawks and bandy orange legs tipped with razor-sharp talons, he feinted a kick, and the rooster squabbled off under the porch. A few cats licking themselves on the steps lunged away from his feet as he ascended up to Kirley's room. Two more skittered across the roof, and one shot in through the door ahead of him. According to Kirley's most recent estimate, thirteen cats lived on the premises in total, in addition to ten hens, one ornery rooster, a family of ducks, and a handful of rabbits.

Like most of Ray's friends, Kirley had been spending the summer at his parents' house. However, Kirley's arrangement was slightly different. His parents allowed him to occupy the attic apartment on the top floor of their house. Turning to the side to squeeze past several grandfather clocks (of which Mr. Kirley had an impressive collection), Ray stepped into Kirley's room.

Until it had been hit by a car on West Main Road, a large German shepherd named Doozey had patrolled in circles around the house. It was on Doozey's former bed, a thick circular mattress pad, that Kirley now snoozed in the corner, having evidently been too drunk last night to summon the energy to climb up onto the king-size bed in his bedroom. The jacket of his pinstriped suit lay over his torso like a rumpled blanket. The ceilings were low, and every wall was covered with yellowing old maps of Rhode Island. A brimming ashtray rested among rolling papers, poker chips, novels, and a coin collection on a low wooden table in the corner. Like the rest of the house, the space was cluttered and dusty, and nearly everything looked antique, as though a nineteenth-century shipping vessel had crashed and all the burst wood and maps and artifacts had solidified with ramshackle abandon into the Kirley estate.

"Wake up, Kirley."

Propping himself up on one elbow, Kirley rubbed his eyes and began to pluck cat hairs from his clothes absentmindedly.

"You didn't happen to see Mr. Bittles on your way in, did you?" he croaked.

"Is that the yellow one?"

"Orangish, yeah."

"Yeah, I think he was on the stairs."

Yawning and nodding, Kirley pulled himself to his feet. An ancient compass resting on the desk caught Ray's eye, and he picked it up, feeling its weight in his palm. The room could have been a pirate trading post. A stack of oil portraits sat on a wooden bench in one corner, awaiting the deductions of the RISD museum's team of forensic art historians to determine whether they were indeed the Gilbert Stuart originals that Mr. Kirley claimed them to be. Beside these was a paint bucket filled with wax-colored pieces of scrimshaw, intricate images carved into their smooth sides with jet-black ink. Next to the bucket was a large wooden crate, brimming with bundles of fireworks left over from the Fourth of July. Kirley, a rather industrious pyrotechnic, crossed state lines to purchase these items in New Hampshire each year, deploying them during his annual extralegal backyard event. The maps, pinned at angles onto the sloping section of the ceiling where the roof began, perfumed the cramped space with the sweet, musty smell of old paper.

"Is this new?" Ray asked, holding up a retractable spyglass.

"New to me, yeah," Kirley replied. "My dad got it at some auction last weekend. He says he got it for a steal."

Despite Ray's best efforts to place it down gently, it thudded heavily against the rickety card table.

"You ready to go?"

"Yeah, gimme a minute," Kirley said.

It was nearly five in the afternoon, but Kirley preferred to sleep during the day, keeping mostly nocturnal hours when he wasn't interning at BankNewport. From the small bathroom, the sound of water splashing against his face echoed through the attic. A busted wicker chair creaked against Ray's weight when he sat down. He found an old lute under the chair, and he picked at the tinny strings while he waited. With his other hand, he thumbed through a milk crate filled with vinyl records in faded, dissolving album sleeves. A kitten napped in a hatbox under the table. Several guitars were mounted on the wall over the dog bed. They were the only items in the room that weren't coated in a thin layer of dust.

"Hey, Kirley, you ever heard of a band called the Aardvarks? They're local."

Kirley yanked his tie over his head and slipped his arms through the sleeves of his suit jacket.

"Don't think so. They any good?" he asked, sitting down on an overturned bass drum to pull on his Converse. He didn't bother tying the laces.

"Yeah, I saw them play at Scugg's recently. This girl can really sing. They play the kind of stuff you'd hear on 95.5 WBRU. You know, alternative, punk rock kinda sound."

"You were in Island Park?" Kirley asked, raising an eyebrow.

"Yeah, hanging with Josh, actually."

"How's he doing?" he asked.

"He's good. The same."

As they stepped down the narrow staircase to the driveway, several cats skittered under the house ahead of their feet. Kirley's dad was bent over a workbench, a pair of thick goggles covering his eyes. He hunched over an enormous grandfather clock with a long set of tweezers poised in his hand.

"Mr. Kirley, how are you?" Ray asked, extending a hand.

The face of the clock had been removed, exposing a network of cogs and mechanical joints. The pendulum lay heavily against the wood backing. There was a clicking sound followed by the metallic whir of the cogs as the clock hands went round in a full rotation. A red hen waddled under the workbench, its striated feet clipping against the asphalt.

"Just fine, son, just fine," he said, peeling off a rubber glove and meeting Ray's hand with a quick, firm shake. "Are you two still planning on taking the ferry to Prudence tomorrow?"

They both nodded.

"Good, good. That's good. Say hello to her for me. And do me a favor—make sure that hack captain isn't gunning the engine when he docks up, would you?"

After four decades of running the Prudence Island Ferry, Mr. Kirley had sold it to the highest bidder at the beginning of the summer. Now Mr. Kirley used his retirement to make a second career of what had previously been a lifelong hobby: snooping around flea markets and yard sales throughout New England, buying whatever artifacts caught the attention of his keen eye, fixing them up, and then selling them for a tremendous profit to museums and collectors. Nineteenth-century American grandfather clocks were a particular specialty of his.

A cat slunk around Ray's calves, arching its spine. Kirley paused in the driveway to shake his father's hand.

"So long, Pop," he said.

"You boys stay out of trouble," he called as they left, chuckling to himself and adjusting the goggles over his eyes.

This gentle admonition was an inside joke of sorts. Not one harsh word had ever passed from Mr. Kirley's lips to his son's ears. Not even when Kirley had been arrested for marijuana possession the previous summer. It seemed that his parents had taken the same parenting approach to Kirley as they had to the legion of stray cats that padded about the property, feeding them when hungry but otherwise letting them do as they pleased.

Ray buckled himself into Kirley's Saab. Forgoing the seat belt (he found them too constricting), Kirley plopped into the driver's seat and rolled down the window. Fiddling with the radio, he landed on Cool

102, and the bopping rhythm of a Sublime song streamed through the car's old speakers. Expertly maneuvering the stick shift, Kirley merged into the traffic on West Main Road. Ray settled back into his seat as Kirley turned down a shortcut, cruising in the direction of Newport.

"Are we going to be late? You said we wanted to catch it at sunset."

"We've got plenty of time," Kirley said.

Gradually, the expansive dairy farms overlooked by Portsmouth's Middle Road—and the pungent scent of manure that drifted up from the sprawling pastures—were replaced by the suburban neighborhoods and strip malls of Middletown. The sun had only just begun its long descent when they crossed into Newport. Each curve of Ocean Drive revealed a new picturesque vista more jaw-dropping than the last, made all the more resplendent by the historical mansions erected by the tycoons of yesteryear that appeared at intervals along the scenic road. But today, Kirley's Saab swerved around the puttering tourists and impatiently bypassed the magnificent estates. The car careened around the bend toward Brenton Point.

"Hey, slow down. Look."

Following Ray's finger with his eyes, Kirley slowed the car and peered through the open window. The moving trucks had left, though a few of the Bane construction vehicles remained parked in Moon View's sloping driveway. But the yellow excavators and churning cement trucks were not what had caught Ray's attention.

"Am I high, or . . . is that a *giraffe*?"

Kirley brought the car to a complete stop, right in the middle of the road. Sure enough, behind the tall stone wall that encircled Moon View was the long, spotted neck of a giraffe. Even from the bottom of the hill, they could see that its height was tremendous. Their eyes traveled up the giraffe's neck to the animal's tapered head, which arched skyward to munch on the tree limbs that bordered the immense property.

"That's wild. I guess she's got the space for it," Kirley chuckled, slowly accelerating again.

The smooth road bent around the coast, and Moon View faded from the rearview mirror. A dirt path that cut through an overgrowth of bushes and trees appeared on the right, and Kirley brought the car to a halt on the shoulder, lurching the stick into park.

"We'll have to walk from here."

"Where are we going again?" Ray asked, unbuckling his seat belt.

The image of the giraffe galloping around the estate grounds wouldn't leave his mind. A long joint stuck out between Kirley's lips, and his small thumb flicked at a cheap lighter he'd pulled from the pocket of his pinstriped jacket. Turning his back to the wind and using his suit jacket as a shield, he finally managed to light the joint. After a couple of drags, he passed it to Ray. The thick, sour smell whipped away in the breeze as they dodged vines and crouched under branches to get through the overgrowth, working their way slowly down the wooded path.

"It's called the Bells Mansion Estate. It's been abandoned since the late 1800s."

"Where the hell do you find these places?"

Shimmying over a rusted fence with an ancient sign that read "NO TRESPASSING" hanging at an angle on its links, they paused to catch their breath. The crumbling stone ruins of the old manor rose up before them. Decades of time, looters, and storms had stripped it of everything but its thick stone skeleton. In its heyday, it must have been as massive and as grand as the Breakers or Miramar or any of the other mansions on Bellevue Avenue. One wing of the once-sprawling building still stood nearly intact.

"My dad has all these wicked old maps of Rhode Island. Some of them go all the way back to the colonists—you know, Roger Williams and Oliver Hazard Perry and all that. It's how my dad piloted the ferry around before GPS. But then he just got really into collecting them. Anyway, a few of the old ones mark ancient stuff like this, and sometimes the sites are worth checking out."

Using an old rope that some previous expedition had left hanging from a rusty beam that jutted out of a second-floor window, they squirmed up through the crumbling cement frame. Old shards of glass and rusty nails scraped their palms as they hoisted themselves onto the landing.

The Atlantic Ocean could just barely be seen through the dense leafage of the surrounding forest, immense trees that had probably been saplings when the Bells Mansion was built. A riotous, wild garden had grown through the cracked cement of the second-floor ruins. Grass and weeds and colorful wildflowers burst from beneath tumbled stones and ashy dirt. Through the crumbled arch of a window, cars that from their vantage looked like Hot Wheels toys careened around the soft bends of Ocean Drive, passing from view in fleeting blips. Vibrant graffiti covered the walls. Despite the collapsed chimney stacks and dull gray cement of the walls, the graffiti, wildflowers, and verdant overgrowth revitalized the abandoned wing, filling the decaying space with color and life. Somebody had painted a smiling, neon-yellow banana over the fireplace. Closing his eyes and listening to the wind whooshing through the trees and into the cavernous space, Ray wanted to share this place with the world and hide it in his pocket all at once.

◇◇◇◇◇◇◇◇◇◇◇◇◇◇◇◇◇◇◇◇◇◇◇

The Prudence Island Ferry had never made much sense to Ray. For one thing, Prudence Island was very nearly deserted. Sitting squarely in the middle of Narragansett Bay, the small island housed fewer than two hundred residents who lived there year-round. Lighthouses outnumbered cops two to one (as in, two lighthouses and exactly one cop, who, by all accounts, spent the majority of his shift drinking red wine from a cask with the Portuguese men who fished for scup on the island's eastern shore). The ratio of deer to humans was even more disparate, and, as a result, Prudence had a severe deer tick problem. Nearly every resident had contracted Lyme disease at one point or another. There used to be a one-room schoolhouse, but it had recently been closed down by the state when attendance shrank to just three students (ages nine, twelve, and seventeen).

And yet, tourists loved to visit this strange little New England haunt, a demand for which Mr. Kirley's former livelihood, the Prudence Island Ferry, had answered the call. Twice a day, every day of the year save Christmas, the massive, flat hunk of steel would chug back and forth across the bay from Bristol to Prudence Island. Eager tourists with their bicycles and picnic baskets would join the occasional local on board, the latter party making their weekly pilgrimage to the mainland for groceries or supplies.

Though his father no longer ran the ferry (which meant he now had to pay the modest five-dollar fare), Kirley still enjoyed chaperoning his friends across the bay every once in a while. He would treat them to a tour of the island's more remote locales and scenic views that he'd discovered over the years. Standing in the bow, Ray tasted salt on his lips from the sea-foam blasting off the hull.

"How's that internship going?" Ray asked. "Think it will lead to anything?"

As much as Ray hated questions like this when they were asked of him, he couldn't help asking it of his friends. The heavy stern of the ferry plowed through the choppy water, and they gripped the rubberized rails to keep from being thrown off-balance.

"Well," Kirley started, "I kind of always thought I'd be running this thing. I never really wanted to before, but now that I can't . . . But the internship is good. Boring, you know, but good. If I get offered a job, I'll probably take it. They say you can make a lot of money if you stick with the company for a few years."

Composed of a hunk of thick stainless steel and an immense, churning engine, the ferry mowed through the water, a foamy wake the width of a highway trailing behind. Growing up near the ocean had done little to diminish its divinity for Ray and his friends. Noses pointed into the whipping breeze, they spent the rest of the ride staring silently into the rolling green waves.

It wasn't long before Prudence Island's ancient wooden dock came into view. The tourists stepped unsteadily onto the weather-eaten boards, clutching their bikes and smelling of bug spray and sunscreen. The dock groaned and squeaked when Ray and Kirley jumped down from the bow, bobbing with the steady roll of the tide.

"Stop by the store?"

The island's economy revolved around a single convenience store, a small, square hut situated just beyond the dock. Despite its monopoly on Prudence Island's commerce, it was a small wonder that the little shop could stay open at all. The store had no name—why would it need one when there was nobody against whom to be distinguished?—and was run by an ancient woman who had been working the register every day save Christmas since it had opened in 1953.

Pushing through the foggy glass door into the shabby store, they nodded a hello to the nonagenarian proprietor, and she creaked a nearly imperceptible nod back at them in welcome. The shelves were orderly and neatly arranged, though most of the items were coated in a thin layer of dust. It appeared that selling out of a particular item was a rarity. There were a few souvenir snow globes and tree ornaments perched on the top shelves, but these they bypassed. Instead, they grabbed a few packs of peanut M&M's that were sure to be a little stale. Everything was priced in whole numbers, no ninety-nine cents or tax, and only bills of twenty dollars or less were accepted.

Back outside, they faced the conundrum that the handful of kids who'd grown up on Prudence Island must have dealt with on a daily basis: Now what? Kirley had an inkling about an old Navy warehouse on the south end of the island.

"It'll be a little tricky to get there," he said, his lips sneaking into a smile. "But it'll be worth it. And keep your eyes peeled for arrowheads. The Narragansetts used to come out here sometimes to hunt deer. Way before all this." Swinging one arm across his body, he gestured toward the spattering of houses that dotted the shoreline.

A rogue wave kicked briny water up over their shoes. Their feet squelched with each step as they picked their way over the craggy rocks.

"What happens when that lady dies?" Ray asked, gesturing back to the shop over his shoulder.

"They'll probably close it down or something. Maybe she's willed it to someone. My dad says it makes less than three hundred dollars a year in profit, but that lady works forty hours a week anyways."

The July sun beat down on the backs of their necks. A burn the shade of Tabasco sauce was already staining Kirley's cheeks and nose.

"It wouldn't be so bad a job, would it? Nobody tells her what to do. Free snacks. An ocean view," Kirley mused. "Know what's crazy, man? I could be the richest motherfucker in Rhode Island, but I bet I'd still get jazzed about free snacks and an ocean view."

Pausing on a slab of pudding stone, Ray skipped a flat rock into the bay. It smacked against the water three times before sinking under the surface with a satisfying plop.

CHAPTER 13

Folk Fest

For locals, the appeal of the annual Newport Folk Festival was not, generally speaking, the music. Rather, the three-day outdoor concert series provided a welcome excuse for aquatic enthusiasts from all across the state to congregate and flaunt their vessels and admire others' boats. The music could hardly be heard over the thrum of boat engines or the slap of kayak paddles. The bands playing from the arena stages on the shores of Fort Adams were an afterthought, background noise. The sleek yachts that anchored in the harbor en masse were compelled to set sail not by the world-class entertainment of the festival, but by the urge to be seen.

And then there were those who sought to glimpse this nautical peacocking display. As was their custom, Ray and Finch biked the length of Ocean Drive, pausing at Hazard's Beach Club (exclusive, though not nearly as exclusive as Periwinkle) to catch their breath. Today, however, there was no time to enjoy a refreshing IPA on the beach, as they normally would at this point in the ride. Stowing their bikes in the bushes, they rushed to grab the kayaks from Finch's family's cabana and launched the vessels into the sea, paddling furiously until they were clear of the incessant tide.

Curiously, despite the luxurious offerings of a Hazard's Beach Club membership—privacy, weekend barbecues, a fully stocked bar, fresh towels—Finch hardly ever went, claiming to prefer Reject's Beach because there were no lifeguards or family friends supervising the quantity of Modelo beers he imbibed in a given afternoon. In similar fashion, he kept his distance from Speakeasy (a historically relevant, if overpriced, downtown bar) despite the fact that the mere mention of his surname to the bartender would be met with a dry martini. He preferred Dockside and West Deck, the proletarian bars that his extensive network of cousins, aunts, and uncles were less likely to frequent. Just so, his parents had recently bought a boat, and yet still he insisted on paddling out to the Folk Fest boat assembly via kayak. It was a strange, prideful strain in Finch, a rebelliousness of sorts, some kind of masochistic impulse to deny himself the fruits of his parents' labors, if only slightly.

Finch took his intoxication very seriously, especially during Folk Fest. Today he had zipped a collection of imported beers and a baggie heavy with weed into a waterproof sailing bag pilfered from his younger brother (a world-class sailor with a legitimate shot at making the Olympic team). With the same exquisite taste as his mother, Finch had also packed an assortment of the kinds of snacks that one could purchase only at a purveyor like Whole Foods or Trader Joe's—artisanal granola, Parmesan crackers, chocolate-covered espresso beans, and jalapeño-flavored sweet potato chips. Mrs. Finch would probably harangue him later for raiding the pantry, though her remonstrations would no doubt be good-natured in tone.

"So you're all set up with Pinnacle, then?" Ray asked.

By way of response, Finch gave one sharp nod of his head. Though he was a witty companion once he loosened up a little, getting Finch to talk had always been a bit like singing a periwinkle out of its shell. A few drinks never hurt either, when trying to inspire loquaciousness in Finch.

Not only had he graduated summa cum laude with a degree in economics, but he had also taught himself, in his spare time, the software company's preferred coding languages. He'd even negotiated for a higher salary upon being offered the job, having had multiple job offers to leverage in his favor.

"How about you? Are you gonna go and be the next Jane Goodall or something?" Finch asked, freezing his paddle above the water so the joke could land.

Laughing, Ray sent a splash of water at him with a smack of his paddle.

"She was a primatologist, dick," Ray said. "And no. Actually, your dad is setting up some interviews for me. Paralegal jobs, that sort of thing. I'm thinking of applying to law school in the fall."

Finch snorted a laugh.

"What's so funny about that? Can't see me in law school?"

"No! No, it's just funny," Finch chuckled. "My whole life, my dad told me that if I could be anything else, I shouldn't become a lawyer."

"He doesn't like it?"

Finch shrugged.

"I think he likes it fine. The money can be good, if you do it right."

Just as their shoulders began cramping and their grips slackened, they heard guitar chords blaring across the water. Mustering a final reserve of energy, they dug the paddles into the blue-green swells and propelled themselves toward the sound. More and more boats began drifting into Newport Harbor, schooners, catamarans, and Grady-Whites amassing like a flock of seagulls floating atop the lulling waves. There must have been at least a hundred boats bobbing around the harbor, all clustered near one another. A few dads had taken their families out on their forty-two-foot powerboats, though these were made to look modest by the sweeping yachts that cruised through the crowd. Stout men who wore their shirts unbuttoned, their chest hairs rustling in the wind, captained these vessels, their eyes fixed straight ahead, determined not to notice the stares that followed them as they glided across the water.

Everyone but the congregation's most Celtic participants was tanned and smiling. It wasn't even noon yet, but the sun was already hot. A few people tossed beers from their decks, and Ray and Finch caught them gratefully. The foaming light beers mixed with the froth of the sea in their mouths as they fought to maintain their balance and drink the beverages at the same time in the churning wake. The harbormaster motored sternly through the assembled watercraft in his black pontoon boat. Ray figured it must be the poor bastard's least favorite day of the year, charged with the impossible task of allowing people to have fun without letting them get out of control. His usual power had been neutered by official orders from the city council not to disrupt the carousing celebrations of the wealthy concert donors who were watching from their yachts, as the annual festival generated millions in tax revenue for the state.

A long, elegant white sailing yacht cruised past Ray and Finch. A girl waved to passing friends from the bow. Bracelets jingled like wind chimes on her wrist, and retro purple sunglasses obscured her face. The light breeze fluttered her short-cropped blond hair as she floated on endless legs across the polished deck. On the bow of the elegant sloop, the wind catching her hair, she could have been on the cover of a magazine. She wore a simple white one-piece suit, its modesty belied by her Botticellian figure.

"Who's that?" Ray asked.

Polishing off his beer and following Ray's eyes, Finch nodded exuberantly, acknowledging the awestruck look on his friend's face.

"Jessie Biddle," he said, eyebrows raising and lowering. "You don't know her?"

The name sounded familiar to Ray, but Finch filled in the details as they bobbed in the wake. She was an enigmatic blond girl from an old-money family with deeper Newport roots than the Redwood Library. At its highest tiers, Newport gossip had its central cast of characters. These much remarked upon individuals, hidden in ultraexclusive East Coast haunts for most of the year, would resurface in the summer, popping up at restaurant openings, making appearances at galas and at Periwinkle Beach Club, or showing up in the glossy photos of *Newport Life Magazine*. Jessie Biddle was one such character, though Ray had never before crossed paths with her at Periwinkle or any of the other rarefied spaces to which he was occasionally granted access. In the photos, she'd be seated next to a party of equally photogenic men and women sipping rosé, smiling genially from some rooftop with the bay glimmering in the background. It was rumored that she spent most of her time modeling in New York, but evidently even she was helpless to the pull of Newport in the summer.

"Didn't you work with her at the Pearl?" Ray asked Finch, already paddling toward the yacht.

It was a safe bet. It seemed as though working at the Black Pearl, one of Newport's most famed restaurants, was an integral part of every rich, blond local girl's education, a requirement to graduate into the real world (or, at least, whatever version of the real world these entrancing women would come to inhabit). None of them had any particular need for the job, their fathers' credit cards firmly holstered in their purses. And eager suitors would have gladly paid for their dinners—including drinks, appetizers, and dessert—all seven days of the week. But working a part-time shift waiting tables or hostessing at the Pearl had become, to the restaurant owner's surprise and benefit, a mark of local cachet—a rite of passage, of sorts. Working at the Pearl, for these young women, was a sort of finishing school, the final stop of their adolescent trajectory toward high-societal relevance. This seemingly menial part-time gig was, for them, equivalent to being featured on the cover of the Vineyard Vines catalog (which many of them had)—that is, many people saw them and, in seeing them in that setting (whether smiling in the pages of the catalog or hobnobbing among the tables at the Pearl) knew them to be local women of the highest class, according to the shallowest of metrics. It was more of a social affair or a hobby than a job, with the result being that orders were often wrong and drinks delivered late, but so charming were these blond summer hires that complaints were never made.

"I think she was a hostess there with me, like, five years ago. But I don't think I ever talked to her," Finch said.

The sound of the paddle churning through the water diminished Finch's voice in Ray's wake. Like Odysseus and the Sirens, it would have taken several feet of rope and a sturdy mast to keep Ray from paddling in pursuit of the fluttering canvas sails ahead. He was propelled by a slight buzz and a rush of adrenaline. When would he have another opportunity to meet such a girl, he wondered? People like her mixed with the hordes that formed the population atop which her high station was mounted so rarely that to let this fleeting moment pass by unpursued would, in Ray's estimation, be equivalent to missing Halley's Comet. Maybe her stunning looks hid a cruel, arbitrary, and downright horrible personality (which he couldn't seriously believe), but he wanted, at the very least, an opportunity to find that out for himself. July was almost over. Out of breath but smiling, he drew up beside the stunning hull of the sailboat, marring its painterly image with his dingy green plastic kayak.

"It's gorgeous," Ray called up to Jessie.

Evidently caught off guard, she turned toward the sound of his voice and peered over the top of her sunglasses. Looking down off the bobbing deck, her sharp blue eyes landed on Ray. The seawater had dried in his hair, curling it into ringlets over his ears, and his smile revealed a set of large white teeth that sharply contrasted the russet tone of his skin.

Heart beating in his palms, he felt the pregnant pause that followed stretching into its third trimester. It was rare that he took a chance like this, always so concerned about offending someone that he ended up deferring to everyone, amiability disguising his fear of controversy. Maybe it was something about being on the water, mixing in this great soup with the aristocrats, that had compelled him to paddle up to her boat. Or maybe it was the beams of gold light that seemed to emanate from Jessie Biddle, even from a distance. Perhaps it was just the booze.

"You work for Ron, at that liquor store, right?" she asked.

It was not the first time that he'd been recognized in relation to his job. Even so, plenty of times he'd bumped into regular customers downtown who hadn't recognized him without their wine delivery weighing in his arms.

"That's what I'm best known for, sure," he replied, before rushing to add, "but I'm actually thinking about—well, I'm going to go to law school."

"I see. And we worked together at the Pearl, once, didn't we?" she said, turning her attention to Finch.

Choking down a sip of Smirnoff and panting as he brought his kayak parallel to Ray's, Finch nodded emphatically. A tribute to her noble upbringing, her manners were effortless, as much a part of her as her poreless skin. Elite politeness of this kind could not be learned or purchased at any price but only engendered by a childhood spent under the judgmental gazes of the ancestral portraits that no doubt hung from the walls in her home.

"This spot's no good, Jess. We'll have to take her to the other side, where the water's deeper. These idiots are crowding me," a man's voice called from the cockpit.

A stubby, unlit cigar was jammed between his teeth, and he was talking mostly to himself. His head whipped back and forth, glaring at the morass of boats charging about the harbor, unaware of the guests dripping onto his deck. A dark vein throbbed in his neck. Stubble peppered his chin and jawline in that handsome way that certain rich guys could get away with, looking as though they wore European cologne even from a distance.

"That's my father. He's paranoid. Last year we nearly got wrecked by a drunk speedboater. But I'm afraid I have to go—captain's orders and all that," she said, rolling her eyes and adjusting her sunglasses.

A motorboat sped by, sending a large swell up under the kayaks. Grabbing the bow of the Biddles' yacht, Ray managed to stay balanced. However, having downed upward of four beers and half a dozen vodka nips, Finch was knocked clear of his vessel, his limbs flailing. The smack of his chest hitting the water was followed by a large splash. Moments later, he reappeared at the surface, a sheepish grin poking out from under the soaking hair plastered to his forehead.

"However, I would love to hear more about the things you *aren't* best known for," Jessie said, her prim lips forming a wry smile.

Reaching past her agitated father into the cockpit, she snatched a business card from a console on the dashboard.

"It's the house number, but I'm almost always there," she said, leaning gracefully over the bow to hand the card to Ray.

From the design on the card, it appeared that her father's business was nautical in nature. On one side, the headquarters' address was listed in figures of latitude and longitude. BIDDLE SEA CONCEPTS was printed in neat black ink across the opposite side, with his name—Rick Biddle—printed just underneath. It was probably more of a hobby than an actual business, for so it went with the idle rich. However, the Biddles' relationship to the sea was as lucrative as it was historical. Throughout the eighteenth and nineteenth centuries, the Biddle family had been renowned shipbuilders. The ships that left their Newport workshop would immediately be filled with rum, molasses, or the enslaved (though the family would appreciate it if everyone could just go ahead and forget about that last part) and would then proceed directly into the routes of the infamous triangular trade.

"Thanks," Ray said, clutching the card between his salt-encrusted fingers.

The yacht disappeared beyond the pier. Still holding the card up to his face as though studying it for clues, the sea rising and falling beneath him, Ray felt as light and directionless as a piece of driftwood bobbing in the tide.

"You bastard," Finch said, grinning and tossing a beer at him.

Lunging to catch the bottle, Ray forked the business card high above his head to keep it from getting wet. He secured the card in a pocket of the dry bag, and they relaxed into the rhythmic hum of music from the shore and the pleasant ebb of the sea beneath their kayaks. The massive amps on the stage sent reverberations through their bones, mixing with the effects of the joint that they passed back and forth. A feeling of dopey bliss settled in their chests. The light breeze dried the salt on their skin, and they drifted carelessly with the tide.

CHAPTER 14

High Tide

As his mother had claimed the Volvo to visit a cousin in Worcester, Ray had had to get creative. He hoped Jessie wouldn't mind the bright-yellow moped he'd spent a day's earnings to rent for the afternoon.

The house came into view, and Ray's pulse quickened. It was an old château walled off by beech trees on the side facing the road while the opposite facade boasted a broad deck and large picture windows that overlooked the water—a metaphor of sorts, wealth hidden publicly but flaunted in private. At the door, he tucked his hair behind his ears before self-consciously flopping it back over them and knocking. He wished he'd visited Tony for a haircut beforehand. The ancient iron knocker swung heavily against the door in three evenly timed knocks.

After a moment, the thick oak door swung wide, revealing Jessie standing at the threshold. The house was big enough that they must have had maids, but the Biddles would die before being seen to allow the help to answer their door.

"Please tell me that's yours," she said, pointing to the yellow moped.

It looked comically small in the massive driveway. She wore a navy-blue summer dress and another pair of retro sunglasses with white frames perched atop her head. Her short blond hair was pulled back in an abrupt ponytail. Only after a few tries was Ray able to operate his mouth.

"It's ours, actually. For the day," he said.

"Divine," she said, smiling.

Together, they walked up the driveway to the moped. Though he hadn't noticed it on the yacht, she was nearly as tall as he was.

"Do you know how to drive this thing?" she asked, seating herself primly behind him.

The seat offered little choice but for her to lean into him, though she somehow managed to position herself gracefully on the narrow cushion. Any and all awkwardness was vanquished by her unflappability. As Jessie linked her hands firmly around his waist, Ray buzzed the engine to life.

"Oh yeah, I'm an excellent driver," he said, grinning as he pulled out onto Bellevue Avenue. "I've taken one lesson."

The rushing wind frolicked with Jessie's hair as the moped maneuvered around the sweeping curves of Ocean Drive. Looking down at the hands clutched across his stomach, Ray noticed a small black key tattooed on the inside of her left pinky finger. He wondered if Jessie's parents disapproved of the small tattoo. Maybe she'd done it to feel a small rush of rebellion—a reminder that, while her surname engendered certain generations-old expectations, she herself still had some little agency to become a Biddle of her own definition.

Perhaps it was by this same impulse toward decaffeinated rebellion that Ray had caught her eye: a boy with a curious, hyphenated last name who lived at an address neither she nor her parents had heard of, whose parents were not members at a yacht club and who had, in all likelihood, no clue as to the significance of the Biddle name. He was somebody her parents could never possibly have set her up with—nothing like the lanky, ex-lacrosse players with square jaws and perennially windswept blond hair on the fast track to a finance career in New York. At the same time, however, perhaps Ray had been seen at enough of the right places with enough of the right people to be deemed, by her calculated standards, a suitable date. Ray didn't delude himself into thinking that this Ocean Drive excursion would eventuate in a Campbell–Doheny wedding of their own. Like all things this summer, it would be thrilling, if temporary.

Mansions built to fairy-tale proportions erupted out of the earth to their right, dramatic spectacles of architecture and wealth that hearkened back to a time when fortunes were defined by things so grand and singular as trains or oil. To the left, the Atlantic sparkled pure blue in the afternoon sun. Ray had been checking the forecast on his weather app every day, and he was thrilled to see that his planning had paid off. Was Jessie equally awed by this vista, he wondered? Or had its majesty dimmed for her, having spent her entire life looking out of mansion windows rather than into them? Ocean Drive was the prettiest place Ray knew, and Jessie's motionless rapture behind him suggested, he hoped, that she concurred.

Not that anything could have been heard over the low whine of the little engine beneath them anyway, they rode on in silence, letting the sublime speak for itself. But they did communicate, with little, almost imperceptible gestures: squeezes of their hands, pressing their bodies close together to negotiate particularly sloping turns. Slowing, Ray pulled off onto the grassy field by Brenton Point. A group of children laughed and flew brightly colored kites on the wide lawn, their parents watching from picnic blankets or waiting in line for a frozen lemonade from the Del's truck parked by the shore. Wordlessly, Ray took Jessie's hand and led her toward a break in the trees that lined the knoll.

"Ah, so this is the part where you kill me," she said with a smirk.

Ray laughed, and not just out of politeness (though he would have even if it hadn't been funny).

"I want to show you something," he said.

Ray took the lead, holding back the branches and vines for Jessie as they walked. A short distance down the path, they came to the sagging chain-link fence. Bittersweet vines grappled and tugged at the fence like seaweed in a trolling net, and the rusting, almost illegible sign threatening trespassers dangled from a single nail. It was all exactly as Ray remembered it from when he'd come here with Kirley a couple of weeks earlier. Stepping up onto one of the many rambling old stone walls that coursed through New England like veins, he held out his hand to Jessie, pulling her up after him.

Almost casually, she looked over her shoulder toward the path. Indecision flickered through her eyes, whether to follow Ray over the fence that had at one point forbidden trespass or else be exposed as an insulated rich girl, morally opposed to rule breaking. Clutching the sides of her dress, she hopped down off the wall and stepped through a fault in the beleaguered fence, joining him on the other side.

"I've never been back here," she said.

"You'll love it, I think."

Truthfully, he was starting to worry that she'd hate it, that she might find it strange that he'd brought her out to this ruinous old mansion. It was entirely possible that his impression last time had been clouded by the joint he and Kirley had smoked. Maybe she was already thinking of some guy named Trevor who picked her up in a convertible BMW and took her to Castle Hill for lemon drop martinis at sunset—a nice, clean date where she didn't have to walk around so much.

Through another twist of brush, the cavernous stone building appeared, planted firmly in the rutted earth. Trees twisted and skewered through the foundation, poking through windows and breaking through the roof.

"It's an old mansion. The Bells Estate, it's called."

Gazing at the grim beauty of the ruins, Jessie said nothing. Ray had timed it correctly, the sun beginning to set and permeating the trees with a dappling of greenish-gold light. The building looked ancient and wrecked, tossed here by a tornado from another era. But the lighting gave the ruins an ethereal filter, reinvigorating it with life. Ivy scrawled its walls, choking the stone and yanking the edifice back into the earth like a squid with its hapless victim.

"The best part is upstairs," Ray said, setting his foot on a tree that hugged the closest wall of the building.

Still entranced, she followed him from branch to branch as they monkeyed their way into the second floor. Here, the evidence of humanity was more recent, though the spellbinding nature of the interior remained intact. Glass bottles lay shattered in corners, and piles of ash demarcated former fires and secretive rendezvous. Joint roaches littered the ground like fallen acorns, and wildflowers sprouted up out of every loose crack.

The graffiti was just as vibrant as Ray remembered, and the overgrowth seemed taller and more verdant than it had been at his last visit.

"You could have told me we'd be scaling buildings," Jessie said, brushing her hands together and redoing her ponytail. "I might not have worn a dress," she added, laughing.

"Sorry. I wanted to surprise you. Look at this garden—it's all wild. And how about the graffiti?"

The marvelous colors exploded off the craggy walls and fell in surreal drips to the floor. Shapes and letters twisted through one another to create three-dimensional visuals bordered by the ivy that would soon be the images' demise. The walls were devoid of the curse words and slurs that one might have expected to find in such a place, given the dubious muse of the typical graffiti vandal. By some unspoken agreement, the artists had decided to keep this place sacred, a small bastion of artisanship hidden within the ruins. While abstract, neon images and words constituted the majority of the exhibition, it was clear that the artists had, over the years, experimented with both medium and form. Some walls bore splendid frescoes depicting landscapes, while others displayed immense, intricately detailed murals of ships or portraits of figures.

From his backpack, Ray pulled a bottle of prosecco and two champagne flutes. He unwrapped the foil that had managed to keep the bottle passably chilled and poured the fizzing liquid into the glasses. He handed one to Jessie and gently clinked his glass to hers.

"I thought I'd seen everything on this island," Jessie said, after taking a small sip of the prosecco.

As though viewing an exhibit at the Metropolitan, she walked slowly from one image to the next, pausing here and there to sip from her flute or lean close to make out a small detail. Ray followed just behind, watching for reactions in her unyielding eyes. They paused beside the defunct fireplace. Just as the orange sun punched through the gaping chasm in the ceiling, she turned to Ray, and, stepping closer, kissed him. Her lips were the shade and texture of raspberries.

CHAPTER 15

Polo

Kirley had worked at the Newport International Polo Grounds every summer since he was fourteen years old, starting out as a young grunt raising flags, replacing divots, and setting up chairs. So when he'd finally been offered the coveted bartending job, responsible for quenching the irrepressible thirst of the sprawling crowds that the Saturday polo matches attracted, he had accepted enthusiastically. His internship at the bank was boring and unpaid, and the weekly bartending gig was neither. And thanks to Kirley's recommendation, Ray had joined him behind the bar that summer, frantically scooping ice and slicing limes side by side every Saturday evening after his shift at the liquor store.

There is a reason that the quintessentially preppy Polo brand features a horseman raising his club. The distinct flavor of New England's upper-class aesthetic reached its zenith in these polo matches. Balancing champagne glasses and finger sandwiches on their laps, the snappily dressed crowd cheered and clapped as the horses charged onto the pitch. Polo, as a sport, has no *Hoop Dreams* analog. On their own dime, players flew whole fleets of horses from Spain or Monaco or Jamaica or wherever else they might come from to various locations around the world on a weekly basis throughout the season. Newport Polo played just one match a week, on Saturdays, though the postmatch saturnalia was always liable to bleed into Sunday morning. The horses beat the earth raw running up and down the field, muscles and tendons straining after the ball. The players, for reasons Ray did not lead the lifestyle to understand, would sweat as much as the horses, soaking through their collared shirts and streaking their riding boots with dark mud.

Earlier in the summer, Ray had witnessed a horse die after taking a bad fall. The usually boisterous crowd had fallen to a hush. The head bartenders had snapped at Kirley and Ray to bow their heads and look away. But the display of grief had felt performative and disingenuous to Ray, the crowd's rosy-cheeked faces taking on an ashen severity when the large creature lay crumpled in the grass before them while they turned a blind eye to the fact that these same horses were routinely crammed into crates and flown great distances according to the fickle whims of their owners. A horse had died to entertain a couple of hundred spectators with rich tastes for a single summer afternoon. They'd still finished the game that day too.

At the polo matches, the bright pastel costumes favored by the island's affluent class were worn with a tongue-in-cheek nod to exaggeration. They wore audacious Lilly Pulitzer plaid pants and oversize bow ties, sun hats the circumference of kiddie pools, and powder-blue blazers. As with nearly everything that occurred among Aquidneck Island's elite circles in the summer, they were here not out of any driving passion for the sport of polo but rather to be seen watching polo. Laughing gaily, they mooned about in conscientious bewilderment of themselves. From the trunks of their expensive cars, they pulled lavish tailgates—tables complete with silverware, coal-fired grills, and delicate china sets. Wads of cash swelled their seersucker pockets, and the urge to spend increased as the night progressed.

This they did at the bar, ordering bottle upon bottle of Veuve Clicquot Champagne (priced reasonably at two hundred dollars per). The hours disappeared in one frantically poured cocktail after another: two Dark and Stormies here, three Pimm's Cups there, a margarita for the young lady, a scotch for the gentleman. Ray's fingertips went numb between the subzero ice chests and the sweltering afternoon heat. His fingernails stung at the edges with each lime garnish he chopped and placed delicately on the rim, and the sickly sweet smell of grenadine lingered on his hands for days afterward. Behind the bar, toiling to beat a rush, was one of the rare times that summer that Kirley removed his pinstriped jacket and rolled up his sleeves, a rag draped over one shoulder.

There was much to love about the job too. The tips were incredible, each of the bartenders pulling in close to three hundred dollars a night. But watching the sauntering men with their young wives have to wait in a line and ask for something nicely was, for Ray at least, priceless. An air of resentful bashfulness accompanied their orders, their sallow faces sporting the incredulous look of people unaccustomed to standing up to order their drinks.

Finally, there was a lull, the last of the rush gamboling off to their folding chairs. It was nearly six, and the blushing sun wobbled unhurriedly towards the horizon.

"Think it's time yet?" Kirley asked, his voice sly as ever.

Grinning, Ray snagged two ice-cold cans of ginger ale from the drawer under the bar. Pouring half of the sodas down the drain, they filled the rest back up to the brim with vodka or gin or scotch or whatever else was close enough at hand to sneak into the concoction in quick, surreptitious draughts. They were careful that their clandestine motions were not seen by the head bartenders—a pair of bitter, middle-aged twin sisters with harsh Cockney accents who already distrusted the constant laughter and obstreperous joking of their wily young employees. The especially pushy customers were easier to deal with after that first doctored soda, and the time slipped by faster too. However cumbersome it might have looked in actuality, their hands felt fluid and dexterous as they roved about the bar pouring drinks and accepting cash.

"Here's what I want," said one older, spray-tanned man wearing a crisp white shirt with a neckline deeper than the Mariana Trench. "Ice, vodka, and a splash of cranberry juice—just a splash! And no garnish—I know everyone's hands have been in there all night."

"You got it," Ray said, his voice thickened by the spiked Sprite he had hidden behind the icebox.

Out of the corner of his eye, he saw Kirley tilt a generous pour of whiskey into a Coke can, inconspicuously swishing the sinister concoction before taking a swig.

Jerome Fitz, their boss and the founder of Newport Polo, was a lithe man in his middle fifties. He stood at average height with bright, wild eyes. Starting with just a few horses and a fly-bitten patch of land, he had built up these polo matches from next to nothing, netting a fortune for himself along the way. Of course, it had helped that both his second and fourth wife not only believed in his aspirations but had been the independently wealthy descendants of old-money families. Though she had not been fiscally involved in the creation of Newport Polo, his current wife (the sixth) was equally invested—both emotionally and financially—in the curation of her husband's passion project.

Supposedly he had once been a professional ice luge competitor before a shattered spinal vertebra had prematurely ended his career. Whether inspired by his remarkable full recovery or propelled by his indomitable ego, Fitz played polo with a vengeance, lunging to the very edge of his saddle and straining after every loose ball. His daughter, Molly, also played. She had attended St. Bede's for a few years before being expelled for repeated plagiarism infractions. Perhaps out of resentment for their having graduated from St. Bede's while she'd been forced to attend a second-rate all-girls school in Middletown, Molly had always maintained an icy attitude in her dealings with Ray and Kirley.

"Are you guys drunk?" she asked flatly.

In these moments—which were more frequent than they would have liked—Ray and Kirley were never sure how to respond. On the one hand, she was their age and, like most people their age on the island, enjoyed drinking to excess. On the other hand, she was the boss's daughter, the princess of the polo grounds—a tutu-pink riding helmet taking the place of her tiara. Then again, they were fairly drunk by this point in the evening, and deciding how to reply to her point-blank inquiry had become something of a challenge.

"Nope," Kirley said. His eyes crinkled, and he took a long sip from his can. "Wasted. Totally. Completely insane."

Rolling her eyes, Molly stomped off in her riding boots in the direction of the stables. The assembled crowd had reached the grounds' max capacity, a mass of pastel colors and floppy hats. In this impressionistic blur of color and movement, something caught Ray's eye. It was a woman sitting cross-legged on top of a car, an old Subaru wagon. Counterintuitive as it may seem, her nondescript attire announced her presence in the sea of loud colors as clearly as if she had strutted onto the premises on stilts. She wore ripped jeans and a long-sleeve white T-shirt, her dyed-blond hair yanked back in a sloppy bun that revealed long, dark roots near her forehead and temples. Smoke trailed off the end of her cigarette, and her eyes never left the game. While cigars and pipes were more than welcome at these events, cigarettes would have been considered far too proletarian for such a setting. A can of Budweiser warmed between her bare feet.

"That's that loony who moved into Moon View," crowed one of the sisters (Ray had never been able to tell them apart).

"Is it? That's not at all how I pictured her," said Jeff, using a fistful of bills to shield his eyes from the sun and peering into the crowd. Though technically employed as a bartender, Jeff treated the job like a hobby, as his trust fund certainly didn't require him to work in this lifetime. He was one of Fitz's numerous step-nephews. Though he could mix a cocktail as well as the next guy, he was more interested in schmoozing with the crowd, constantly popping out from behind the bar to kiss a friend on the cheek or to offer free shots to women in tight dresses.

"She's crazy?" Kirley asked. His words were a bit slurred, and his eyes were red and puffy from the joint he'd just hit behind the Porta-Potties.

"Oh yeah. Married some hotel tycoon and divorced him a month later. I heard she might be a lesbian too," Jeff remarked casually.

As the crowd died down and the sun threatened to set, Ray and Kirley steadied their eyes and began mopping up the bar top. That's when Jessie appeared. She wore a simple lavender top and white pants, forgoing the gaudy outfits that most of the attendees had donned for the evening. To Ray's somewhat inebriated perception, she was cast in the same alluring glow that had shrouded her edges that day on her father's yacht—a golden energy that seemed to pulsate just below her skin. And just like that first time, or when she'd opened the door for him at her house two days ago, she seemed to materialize out of nothingness.

"Tell me, Mr. Bartender, what have you by way of gin?"

"Gordon's," Ray said, holding the bottle up for her inspection, "or Bombay."

"The Bombay, please. With tonic and lime," she said, adding another "please."

With drunken fluidity, Ray poured and mixed the drink and handed her the perspiring glass. Taking a small sip, she glanced up at him over the rim of the cup.

"Very refreshing."

Ray let out a breath he didn't realize he'd been holding.

"Don't work too hard," she said, turning to leave.

Winking once, she waltzed away, back to whatever perfectly modest yet tasteful tailgate encampment had brought her here, taking the last rays of sunset with her.

CHAPTER 16

The Causeway

For Ray and his pals, no Aquidneck summer was complete without a jump off the causeway. It stood about forty feet above the inky harbor below, though it always felt much higher at the pivotal moment before the jump. The causeway connected Newport to Goat Island, a speck of land home to little more than the harbor, a few houses, and a luxury hotel. Beneath the causeway, impressive yachts and long schooners swayed in their moorings, bobbing like ice cubes in the oil-slicked harbor water.

It was crucial to time the jump right around sunset. From that height and next to the infinite horizon of the bay, the sunset bathed the vista in a warm orange glow. Standing there on the bridge, waves lapping at the buoys and boat hulls below, towels draped over bare shoulders, one felt that they were precisely where they ought to be on an Aquidneck summer evening.

At the bridge's highest point, right in the middle of the arch, a few guys from the Navy base shotgunned beers before leaping and flipping wildly off the edge and plummeting downward into the blue expanse. The old fishermen sitting on overturned paint buckets waved, smiling and reeling in their lines so that the boys could jump. They couldn't have been catching much anyway. The harbor water below was black with the oil discharged by the boats bobbing on either side of the bridge.

Technically, it was illegal to jump off the causeway. But if one acted quickly and kept their eyes peeled for cops, the illegality of the act could be rendered moot. Perching on the cement railing, Ray worked up the nerve to jump.

"All clear over here," Coyne said from the other side of the bridge, making sure no boats were passing underneath.

"Jump, pussy!" Kirley called.

Heart hammering in his throat, Ray leaped off the ledge. He hung in the air for several long seconds, his muscles clenched and his face screwed in anticipation of the watery impact. With a crash, he hit the water and then—silence. Deeper and deeper, he sank into the black. Everything slowed down but his pulse, which bongo riffed through his rib cage. The water became colder the deeper he sank. Kicking his feet, he resurfaced, tasting the acrid gasoline flavor of the harbor water. It was a bizarre feeling of accomplishment, jumping off great heights like this. Adrenaline pumped through his veins as he let out a triumphant holler.

After clambering onto the dock, he scaled the wooden slats back up to the crest of the bridge. Wrapping a towel over his shoulders, he waited for Kirley and Coyne to return from their respective jumps.

"Damn. Why do we always wait so long to do this?" Coyne asked, toweling off his head. His short hair stuck up at odd angles.

Kirley and Ray shuffled to stand on the side of Coyne's good ear. They stood in contented silence for a while, leaning against the railing and basking in the warm light of sunset and watching the Navy guys hurl themselves, one after another, into the water.

"Hey, Coyne, how was that interview today?" Kirley asked.

Coyne shrugged and draped his towel over his shoulder.

"It was okay. I didn't love the feel of the company, really. It pretty much seemed like I would just be cold-calling people all day, which is kind of exactly what I want to avoid. The money is pretty good, though."

They nodded in agreement. The idea of spending forty hours a week in a cubicle, especially after romping about the island all summer, was completely repulsive.

"You can always go work for your uncle, though, right?" Ray asked.

"Who, the guy in Quincy? Isn't he in plastics or something?" Kirley asked.

Again Coyne shrugged.

"Yeah, plastics. And Quincy would be okay, I guess. It's close enough to Boston. But I'd actually kind of like to avoid that too. I mean, I'm sure he would take care of me. And I'd make good money, obviously. And from what he tells me, the job isn't terrible. But working for my uncle, I don't know . . ." he said, trailing off.

"What about the internship? Think they'll offer you?" Coyne asked, repositioning the microscope on Kirley.

"Nah, they didn't end up offering me a job. They wouldn't even write me a recommendation, actually," Kirley said, smirking and shaking his head. "Actually, they fired me. Last Friday."

"Damn, that's bullshit," Coyne said.

"Not really. I showed up high a few times, and I kept fucking up little things. The last straw was when I forgot to lock up the registers. And I screwed up the count once or twice, which they take pretty seriously since that's, like, the whole point of a bank, you know? And I might have made some inappropriate comments at the company retreat back in June. I thought they were all drunk, too, at the time . . . It's all right, though. I'll find something else. The world's always gonna need accountants. And I've still got the bartending gig to float me through the summer in the meantime," Kirley said, grinning ruefully.

"You still gonna wear that suit everywhere?" Coyne asked.

Kirley shrugged. "Yeah, I think so. Dress for the job you want, not the job you have. Isn't that a phrase?"

"Yeah, but I think it applies to people who already have a job," Ray said.

Kirley laughed and whipped at him with his towel.

"Listen, if there's one thing I've learned from all those goddamn cats at my parents' place, it's—"

"How to lick yourself clean?" Coyne interrupted, chuckling even before he could get the joke out.

"No, dick," Kirley snorted. "It's how to land on my feet. I'm not worried about it. I'll get a job. A good one too. I already have the suit."

It was almost eight o'clock, and the sun was still pinned to the horizon, washing the sky in a stunning copper-pink hue.

"What about you, Ray? You gonna keep working for crazy Ron?" Coyne asked.

With July dwindling all too quickly to an end, they couldn't help but gauge each other on the topic. The notion of employment and the looming "real world" had, in early June, been little more than a tickle at the back of their minds. But it was now galloping at breakneck speed to the forefront of their consciousness.

"Yeah, right," he said, laughing and looking down. "Actually, I got an offer to do some paralegal work at this firm in Cranston. I'm still thinking about law school. But I'm looking for something up in Boston."

It was a lie, but they nodded approvingly. Though none had yet panned out, he had been driving up to Boston every few weeks for interviews—a few of which Mr. Finch had arranged. But he was getting disheartened, not by the fruitless interviews themselves but by the prospect of these summer days coming to an end. At this point, getting the job felt just about as bad as not getting it. All the salaried jobs just felt like exercises in abstruse company policy and imaginary goals and shallow, intangible achievements. Other jobs could be pictured, had definite weight and objectives. Waiters brought food to hungry people. Barbers cut long hair into shorter, better hair. Taxi drivers took people from one place to another. There was a dignified simplicity to the nature of these livelihoods that appealed to Ray. He'd always imagined himself as the kind of person who could explain what he did for a living in one word.

Standing on the causeway, however, he could not bring himself—refused to allow himself—to believe that he could be satisfied with these professions. The thrill he'd felt seeing his name inscribed on Periwinkle's registers still charged through his bones. If the actual work of a law career remained a dubious, abstract entity in his mind, the image of himself in a three-piece suit smoking postdinner cigars felt real enough to be touched, a phantasmal figuration of himself that disappeared as soon as his mind's eye blinked.

Boston had become a troubling specter in the recesses of his psyche. The traffic, the city's unimaginative fixation on sports, the coterie of pudgy white guys getting beer-drunk three times a week and cosplaying adulthood. But it was clear to Ray that these associations were symbolic. The wall popped up right out of the earth in front of him, just as soon as the season ended. If Newport was summer, then surely Boston was autumn. The quaint, academic streets littered with ocher leaves, young professional couples smiling as they huddled together in their knit caps and shoulder bags and sipped thermoses of coffee, breathing in that pleasant burnt smell in the air. Autumn was when things began to die.

PART III

AUGUST

One day you discover you are alive. Explosion! Concussion! Illumination! Delight! You laugh, you dance around, you shout. But, not long after, the sun goes out. Snow falls, but no one sees it, on an August noon.

—RAY BRADBURY

CHAPTER 17

Silver Linings and Green Animals

The train trundled slowly along the tracks. Tree branches struck the windows as it rounded turns, and narrow stone passages gave way to rickety bridges overlooking the sea. Jessie stared out the window at the placid bay. Ray adjusted his blazer so it wasn't bunched up around his shoulders. Jessie turned and smiled from the seat across from him, tucking a strand of hair behind her ear.

"Is that new?" she asked.

Ray ceased fiddling with the blazer and smiled sheepishly.

"Is it that obvious?"

"It's nice," she said, smiling and turning back to the window.

He had bought the blazer the day before at a boutique menswear shop on Thames Street, in addition to an Oxford button-down, cuff links, a dark leather belt, a pair of loafers, and slacks that actually fit his lanky legs. The clearance-rack khakis from Marshalls he'd worn all through high school had exposed his ankles to the slushy snow he'd often had to wade through to get from the dormitory to the classroom building in the winter. Though he'd spent more than he'd planned to at the shop—more than a week's pay—all thought of the expense had left his mind when the shopkeeper had encouraged him to admire himself in the large mirror. He'd hardly recognized the dapper figure staring back at him.

"Celebrating something, may I ask?" the old shopkeeper had asked, in his kind, wavering voice. "An engagement, perhaps?"

"A job offer," Ray had replied, the mustachioed tailor fluttering at his side, clasping the cuff links into place at his wrists. "And a date."

Neither response had been a lie, and he'd watched himself stand up straighter in the mirror as he'd spoken. Earlier that day, he'd made a delivery to a small cottage in the Point neighborhood. There had been nothing particularly remarkable about the delivery, at first—a few bottles of pinot noir to accompany a dinner party of some kind. A man Ray recognized had answered the door, directing him to the wine cellar in the basement. Ray had seen him often at the liquor store, perusing the shelves with his wife before inevitably settling on the same few bottles of pinot noir that they always bought. The man had followed Ray down the narrow staircase and helped him slip the wine bottles into the snug, climate-controlled shelves.

He was not a terribly old man, though he had gray hair and carried himself with a professorial air, wearing a cardigan despite the summer heat. It was after they'd finished stocking the shelves in the cellar that the delivery had become memorable for Ray. When they'd ascended back upstairs to the foyer, a young woman was standing on the staircase that led to the second-floor bedrooms.

"Baby, was that the wine guy? I thought I saw the van," she'd called from the staircase.

She wore only a plush bathrobe, which she had fixed haphazardly about her waist. Ray was sure he did not recognize her, though he was certain that she was not the frumpy woman who wore neck scarves and accompanied her husband on his indecisive perambulations around the liquor store.

As soon as Ray had emerged from the basement staircase behind the man, however, she had inhaled sharply, quickly pulled the robe closed, and scurried up the stairs on her bare feet. Ray had pretended not to notice when the man's face turned the shade of watermelon flesh, averting his gaze and stepping quickly to the door.

"You've worked for Ron for some time, haven't you? I've seen you around the store," the man had said. They were standing in the doorway of the cottage. Ray had been walking quickly toward the delivery van to leave, silently cursing the man for not tipping, when the man's voice brought him back to the stoop.

"Yes, a few years. Mostly just in the summers," he'd replied.

"That makes sense, then. I'm only down here in the summers. I spend the rest of the year in Newton," the man said. "Not an easy man to work for, is he? No, no, you don't have to answer that," he'd chuckled. "Ron is a good friend of mine. We grew up together. You must be doing something right if he's kept you around this long. He goes through employees like secret cigarette smokers go through breath mints—which is a lot, speaking as one such—but don't mention that tidbit to my wife. Tell me . . . Raymond, is it?"

"Ray."

"Tell me, Ray. Have you given any thought to what you might do for a career? I assume you've gone to college, as you mentioned you worked only in the summers. You seem sharp, well-mannered, hardworking . . . discreet. You must be all these things if you've put up with Ron for this long—no easy feat, I'll repeat."

"I've been giving some thought to law school."

"Law school! An excellent pursuit. I'm afraid I can't be of much help myself—I'm in finance, you see. Ah! But I do know . . . here . . ." the man pulled a thick wallet from the back pocket of his trousers and began rifling through its folds. He procured a bent business card, which he handed to Ray.

"Give this man a call if you'd like. Feel free to drop my name—Henry Blanchet."

Ray turned the card over in his hands. "Douglas P. Ironbolt: United States Federal Judge of the District of Massachusetts" it read in neat black print, bordered on one side by the Massachusetts state flag and the scales of justice on the other.

"Doug is another old friend of mine. I manage his money, see. I'm sure he'll be able to find something for you . . . with my recommendation, of course."

As he spoke these last few words, the man had extended his hand to Ray and fixed him with a grave stare. Ray had nodded, meeting the stern gaze and silently acceding to its implication. When he'd pulled his hand away, he'd discovered two crisp fifty-dollar bills in his palm.

"Thank you."

"Nonsense, Ray," Blanchet replied, waving him goodbye. "Thank *you*."

A few hours later, just as his shift was ending, Ray had received a call at the liquor store from a Massachusetts number. It was, of course, Judge Ironbolt. He'd told Ray about how highly recommended he'd come and how, because he couldn't wait to speak to him, he'd called the liquor store personally, asking for Ray. The call had lasted less than fifteen minutes, but by the end of it, Ray had been offered a paid internship in the judge's Cambridge office. He would begin in September.

"Buy yourself a suit," the judge had said. "I reckon you'll be needing one from here on out."

As soon as his shift ended, Ray had walked on air the whole way to the boutique clothing shop, unable to suppress the grin on his face. He'd gone from the tailor to a bookstore, where he'd purchased several tomes of LSAT prep materials.

A waiter pushed a cart up the narrow aisle of the train, pausing to place an ice bucket and two glasses on the table between Jessie and Ray. A perspiring bottle of Chablis was nestled among the ice cubes, and the waiter, with several robotic, professional movements, uncorked the bottle and poured out two glasses of the pale-gold liquid. He nodded obsequiously before pushing the cart up to the next table.

"Cheers," Ray said, holding his glass up to Jessie and taking a sip. He savored the citric, lightly floral flavor of the Chablis.

"Yes, cheers," she said, raising her glass. "To your first time on the Newport Dinner Train. I can't believe you've never done this before!"

Ray had seen the old maroon train go by many times, lurching along the old railroad tracks that skirted the edge of the island, elegantly dressed men and women sipping drinks in the windows. His parents had spent an evening on the dinner train one year on their anniversary and had enjoyed themselves, though they'd been so flabbergasted by the expense of the prix fixe menu that they'd never done it again.

"My mother and I used to ride the train for afternoon tea every Sunday in the summers, until I grew out of that. It was very exciting, though, when I was a girl," Jessie said. "Isn't it wonderful?"

"It is," Ray replied.

They sat in silence for a while, contentedly watching the picturesque vista pass by through the windows.

"What does your tattoo mean?" Ray asked after a while.

Jessie looked at him in confusion for a moment before laughing and peering down at the small key on her pinky finger, as though just noticing its presence.

"I forget I have it sometimes. It's so unlike me, don't you think? But I suppose that's why I got it. I was nineteen. It's supposed to be a skeleton key. You know, those keys that can open any door? It seemed deep at the time. I do like it. But to answer your question, I guess it has something to do with a sense of possibility. Like I can open any door in life, or something like that. That sounds silly, doesn't it?"

Though Ray couldn't imagine what closed doors Jessie had encountered in her life, he said, "Not at all."

Prudence Island came into view across the bay as the train chugged into Portsmouth. Ray drank the first glass quickly and poured himself another. He topped off Jessie's glass before returning the bottle to the bucket.

"Where does it stop?" he asked.

"Oh no, you're not bored, are you?" Jessie asked. "I so wanted you to enjoy this."

"No, no! I'm not bored. Really," Ray stammered. "Just curious."

"It's okay if you are," Jessie said, laughing. "I suppose it is a little stuffy. Maybe a little touristy too."

Ray wiped his hand on his pant leg and reached across the table, placing his palm in Jessie's. Her hands were cool and dry, and she smiled as she laced her fingers in his.

"It's great," he said.

"It's a while longer, I think. Oh! But I've just had an idea. Something else I'm sure you haven't seen."

Before Ray could protest, she caught a passing waiter by the arm.

"Excuse me, I'm so sorry, but could you please ask Roger to stop at Green Animals? If he gives you any fuss, please tell him that Jessie Biddle would be thrilled for the favor."

"Certainly, Ms. Biddle." The waiter nodded and walked back up the aisle.

"Really, Jessie, this is fine," Ray said. "I'm having a great time."

"No! I haven't been to Green Animals in ages. I'd love for you to see it. And I'm never in Portsmouth. It's a perfect opportunity."

She smiled and placed her hand back in his.

"Who is Roger?" Ray asked.

"The conductor. An old family friend."

The train lurched to a stop at the bottom of a long road that ended abruptly where the asphalt met the rocky shoreline. A defunct, sloping boat launch poked up through the eddying waves. An old red truck was parked on a patch of gravel by the shoreline, and a lone fisherman sent a long cast into the water. A few befuddled patrons looked up nervously from their steak tartare appetizers.

"This must be us! Roger really is *such* a dear," Jessie said.

She stood up from the booth, smoothed out her dress, and, taking Ray's hand, led him down the aisle to the exit door, ignoring the incredulous looks of the train car passengers. As they stepped down onto the road, the train whistled and then continued its trundling journey down the tracks.

"It's just up this way," Jessie said, leading Ray up the road. "It's stunning at sunset."

Her white high-heeled shoes clicked against the pavement as they walked. After surmounting a brief incline in the road, they passed through a gap in an old stone wall and came to an immense Victorian manor. The grand estate stood at the head of a broad green lawn on a hill overlooking Narragansett Bay.

"I don't think we'll be able to go inside—I think they stop doing tours around five—but I'm sure they wouldn't mind us walking about the garden for a spell."

Meandering along a neatly maintained gravel pathway that curved behind the house, they passed under several green shrubberies that had been bent into graceful arches. They traipsed slowly along a path cut through a maze of bushes and trees. Colorful flowers burst from every corner. The vegetation was cultivated into geometric patterns, sharp edges cut into the sides of bushes and hedges groomed into precise dimensions. They followed the contrived paths in concentric circles through the lush garden, each turn revealing some new feat of horticulture.

"This is the best part," Jessie said, squeezing Ray's hand.

As they turned into the central ring of the garden, they came to an ornate stone fountain. Luminescent koi fish swam lazily under lily pads in the still water collected at the base of the sculpted limestone font.

"Look," Jessie said.

Ray's eyes followed where her finger pointed. At precise intervals around the fountain were several animals. Here was a camel, there an ostrich, a bear, an elephant, a reindeer. They were all the same shade of ivy, and the bushes that had grown them to life-size proportions had been cut into precise anatomical dimensions. The orange strokes of sunset glinted off the waxy ridges of the sculptures' leaves.

"Unbelievable," Ray said. "Has this always been out here?"

"Yes! I've always found it rather magical."

Ray wrapped his arm around her shoulders, and they waltzed slowly around the circle, pausing to admire the precision with which the sculptures had been cut. A crack of thunder boomed overhead as dark clouds rolled across the sky, obliterating the sun. A breeze blew in from the bay, and warm raindrops began pelting damp spots into their clothes and hair.

"Oh, I'm sorry. I thought we'd have enough sunlight to walk back along the railroad toward Newport. I didn't think it would rain. I don't see what we can do," Jessie said with a sigh.

The rain started falling harder. Within minutes, they were soaking wet. A white flash of lightning split the sky and, a few seconds later, another boom of thunder followed. They stared at each other helplessly for a moment before breaking into irrepressible laughter at their abrupt turn of fate, standing in a drenching downpour in evening wear while surrounded by unmoving green animals.

"Wait, look!" Ray cried, pointing toward the road.

The old red truck he'd seen parked by the shoreline was puttering slowly up the hill, a fishing rod poking up out of the bed. Holding Ray's blazer over their heads, they dashed toward the road, hollering and waving their arms. The truck halted, and the driver rolled down his window. He was a squat, dark man with a wispy black goatee and thick eyebrows. Poking his head through the window, Ray smelled gasoline, cigarette smoke, and squid bait.

"Are you heading toward Newport?" Ray asked.

"*Sí*, but only to Middletown," the man said.

"Would you give us a ride, please?"

The man ran his eyes over Ray's soaked outfit and the high-heeled shoes Jessie had removed and slung over her shoulder when they'd run to catch the car.

"You have cash?" he asked finally.

Ray yanked his wallet from his pocket and pressed several damp bills into the man's hand. The man counted the money slowly before leaning across the seat and unlocking the door. Ray helped Jessie into the middle passenger seat before clambering in beside her.

"*A donde?*" the man asked, shifting the vehicle back into drive and accelerating up the hill. Rain splashed in sheets against the windshield, and the old truck's wipers beat insufficiently against the torrent.

Ray glanced at Jessie, who was holding a hand up over her nose to keep from breathing in the stench of the fishing bait. Their eyes met, and she smiled, clamping her hand down to keep herself from laughing.

"*Al cine, por favor*," Ray said.

The driver nodded and twisted the radio knob until he landed on a grainy Spanish music station.

"What did you tell him?" Jessie whispered.

"I told him to take us to the movie theater. Sound okay? No reason a little rain has to spoil the night, does it?"

Jessie laughed and laid her head against his shoulder.

"I didn't know you spoke Spanish," she muttered, closing her eyes as the truck chugged down West Main Road.

It was still pouring rain when the truck pulled up to Island Cinemas 10.

"*Gracias*," Ray said, shaking the man's hand before stepping down from the truck.

"*Que gringos*," the man said, chuckling and shaking his head as he waved goodbye.

Taking shelter from the deluge under the cinema's awning, they watched the truck disappear from the parking lot.

"I don't think I've ever been to this theater," Jessie mused, stepping through the door that Ray held open for her.

"How is that possible?" Ray asked. "It's the only theater on the island!"

Jessie shrugged. "I've been to the Jane Pickens Theater. The one in Newport, you know?"

"Yeah, I know it," Ray said. "That artsy one, right? Where they show only, like, silent films and depressing documentaries?"

"They show normal movies too!" Jessie declared, laughing.

"Well, welcome to Island Cinemas 10," Ray said as they stepped up to the ticket booth.

To have grown up on Aquidneck Island was to have spent many a Friday night hanging around Island Cinemas. Before driver's licenses had been dispensed and before bars were even a distant possibility, the movie theater had been the de facto hangout spot for the island's youth. Carpools were coordinated, and a minivan would drop off a gaggle of gangly tweens long before the previews were projected onto the silver screen. This premature arrival was strategic, orchestrated so as to play the various arcade games that rose up out of the lobby's sticky reddish carpet like absurd Ozymandian monuments. Once a couple of prize bucks had been shot dead on the hunting game, two out of three races had been won on the car driving game, and a couple of dollars had been squandered on the infamous claw game, it would be time to buy some tickets with the crumpled wad of cash an indulgent parent had thrust into an expectant palm on its way out the door.

The undiscerning tastes of high schoolers typically led to repeat viewings of movies like *Transformers 2* or *Piranha 3D*, as the movie was not really the point. The point was feeling like an adult, released briefly into society and free to choose whatever snacks could be afforded with the little money that remained after splurging on a pair of 3D glasses, intoxicated by nothing more than suburbia's tepid thrills.

As they'd grown up, trips to Island Cinemas 10 became less frequent but more strategic. Ray and his comrades would go with the intent of seeing a movie for its own sake. They would drive themselves and stop at the Dollar Tree in the adjoining parking lot so as to sneak in cheaper packs of Swedish Fish and Skittles. They would arrive early not to play the arcade games but to smoke a joint in the parking lot. They had realized at some point that sneaking into the theater without paying was entirely feasible if they showed up a little late to the final showing, and maybe they'd even summoned the guts to do it once or twice in a moment of petty crime.

The theater itself was somewhat dingy. The floors were always sticky from spilled sodas, and the plastic armrests were coated in an eternal grime of popcorn butter. The movie itself occasionally petered out midway through and rarely started on time. The theater was rarely packed to capacity. In fact, if timed right, Ray and his friends, more often than not, would get an entire row for themselves. However shabbily appointed and unreliably staffed by stoned teenagers, Island Cinemas had an unforced charm that could not be replicated, a quiet, begrimed grace that, for Ray, was idyllic in its enduring familiarity.

"Two tickets for . . ."

"Ooh, *Baby Driver*. Let's see that. I've heard really good things," Jessie said.

Ray had seen the movie with Coyne the previous weekend, though he didn't say anything. He'd been too stoned to remember much of the plot, anyway. The ticket clerk, a slim boy with greasy hair and a faint mustache etched across his upper lip, accepted the bills from Ray's outstretched hand and slid the ticket stubs across the counter.

"It started about twenty minutes ago," the clerk mumbled.

"That's okay," Ray said. "We don't mind."

"Theater two. It'll be on your left."

Jessie slipped her shoes back on, and Ray draped his damp blazer over her shoulders. Arm in arm, they walked down the dimly lit hallway to the theater.

CHAPTER 18

A Picnic

It was the day after Coyne's birthday, and they all looked it, wearing the hangover in their slack faces. After starting the night at Genie's Hookah Lounge (where they'd tested both their tobacco tolerance and the limits of the lounge's BYOB policy), they'd stumbled downtown to the Boom Boom Room (where shorts were not allowed, they'd learned, upon being politely asked to leave).

"Twenty-two. What a worthless age," Coyne said. "Nothing changes except you get tired of blowing money on the legal drinks."

"Yeah, more fun when it was illegal," Ray agreed.

With Maya to his left and Coyne positioned strategically to his right, the trio walked along the old train tracks that skirted the edge of the St. Bede's campus. However ambivalent they'd been about the weekly church services they'd been compelled to attend throughout their tenure at the school, the sight of the old steeple poking out above the trees in the distance sent a swell of nostalgia through their chests. To their left, Narragansett Bay sparkled in the brilliance of the afternoon sun.

"Where'd you tell your mom you were going?" Ray asked Coyne.

It was a familiar question, both of them having spent years maneuvering around their nosy mothers' inquisitions. Coyne had had more success than Ray, though, somehow managing never to get caught doing much of anything. Meanwhile, Ray's mother possessed an uncanny ability to see through her son's falsehoods.

"I said I was going to the beach with you," he said.

"Not a lie, technically," Ray said, gesturing to the rocky shore.

They came to the old boathouse, and they paused to admire the squat conical structure with its chipping green paint and the bumpy cobblestone steps that led up to the medieval-looking padlock on the door. In high school, they'd occasionally snuck onto its weathered roof to smoke amateurly rolled joints after sundown. Lingering only briefly, they continued on their way, stepping from one rotting wooden slat to the next. Maya walked along the rusted rail, balancing with her arms held out at her sides.

"Do you think we're allowed to be here?" she asked.

"Sure. We're alums," Coyne said.

"Yeah, but it's not like we ever donate anything," Ray said.

"But we're *potential* donors. They expect us to cut big checks someday."

"Hey, did you hear back from that interview last week? The place you said you kind of liked?" Maya asked.

Coyne just shook his head. Now August, it had become a tender subject. His parents had been dogging him like everyone else's by that point in the summer, urging him to update cover letters, send out his résumé, meet with such and such family friend.

"At this point, I think I'll have to prostitute myself around Faneuil Hall if I ever want to move to Boston," he joked.

Despite his jocular tone, he still invoked Boston, Ray noted. That part of the equation was inevitable, apparently.

"You could always just stay in Newport. At least a little longer," Ray said. He hadn't told anyone about the internship offer yet. Not even his mother. He could still hardly believe it himself. He was worried about jinxing it, as though speaking the words out loud would make it disappear.

Only at night, lying in bed alone, would he allow himself to imagine his life as an uptown Boston lawyer. While he had little clue of the actual duties of the profession, he pictured himself walking along the sidewalk in a tailored suit, a slick leather briefcase swinging at his side. He and Jessie would kiss each other goodbye at the door on their way to their respective places of work, hurriedly making plans to meet at a tony restaurant in the North End for dinner.

"Fuck that. My parents are driving me crazy about finding a job," Coyne said, shaking his head. "I can't live there anymore."

"Just keep working at the marina till you find something," Maya suggested.

"No chance," Coyne said. He'd quickly become disenchanted with the marina job he'd accepted at the beginning of the summer, tying up yachts to the dock and filling them with immense quantities of gasoline while being barked at by some jawline with an expense account.

"Maybe you could sell shrooms to college kids," Ray joked, holding up the baggie and jostling its contents close to Coyne's face.

"Who did you get these from again?" Maya asked. She held the sandwich bag of dried mushrooms up to the sun.

"Gooch," Ray and Coyne replied in unison.

The day before, Ray had made the purchase at Purgatory Chasm. Showing up nearly thirty minutes late, Gooch had hopped off his moped and brandished the baggie, his sternum-length beard and rainbow-patterned pajama pants whipping in the breeze. He'd gone to St. Bede's with them for a few years before his long-expected expulsion. Still, the expulsion had evidently done little to dissuade him from providing the very service that had occasioned his premature excusal from the prep school.

"You bought drugs from a guy named Gooch?" she asked, skepticism rising in her voice.

"Only people with names like Gooch sell mushrooms," Ray explained. "And you know him too. Jay McNulty, that kid who got kicked out of St. Bede's our junior year."

"Oh, right," Maya said. "He sells shroom now? And goes by Gooch?"

"Yeah, he said they were quote, unquote, 'hella tight,' and that last time he had quote, unquote, 'insane visuals,'" Coyne said, laughing.

"Did you know he's going to work for Goldman Sachs?" Ray asked. "In New York. He told me yesterday."

Coyne halted, mouth agape.

"Are you kidding me? How the hell did that kid get a job at Goldman?"

"His dad is some big hedge fund guy in New York. He's just selling mushrooms for fun, I guess."

Coyne shook his head and kept walking.

Finally, they arrived at the spot they'd selected after much deliberation over drinks the night before. A dilapidated wooden picnic table sat on a sunlit patch of uncut wild grass atop a brief cliff overlooking the Narragansett. Two oak trees held hands above the glade, providing an awning with their intermingled branches.

Settling on a shady stretch of grass, they spread out the large pineapple-printed tapestry that Maya had brought from home. One at a time, they smeared peanut butter onto a few slices of sandwich bread. Folding the bread slices into shells, Ray distributed roughly equal portions of the dried, fibrous mushrooms. Folding the bread in half, they bit into the twiggy sandwich, fighting down the rough peanut butter–coated sprigs.

"You didn't want to invite the fabulous Jessie Biddle?" Maya cracked, shooting Ray a sidelong glance.

"Nah, I thought it would be weird," Ray said.

"Oh, what, you're embarrassed by us now?" Coyne joked.

"Ah, come on . . ." Ray said, laughing. "Mostly I didn't want to act all weird in front of her. You never know with these things. They say you're supposed to do them with people you trust, people you're, like, wicked comfortable around."

"Aw, that's kinda sweet, Ray," Maya said. Her voice was both mocking and sincere.

◇◇◇◇◇◇◇◇◇◇◇◇◇◇◇◇◇◇◇◇◇◇

"Are you guys feeling anything yet?" Coyne asked. He was lying on his back and watching the tree branches dance in the steady breeze overhead.

"No, not yet," Maya replied.

"Me neither," Ray said.

"Damn. Should we have bought more?" Coyne asked, anxiety rising in his voice.

"How long has it been?" Ray asked.

"Twenty minutes," Coyne retorted, as though he'd been counting off the individual seconds in his head the whole time.

"Let's give it some more time. Gooch said they take a little while to kick in. Twenty minutes isn't that long," Ray said. He adjusted his supine position, feeling the lush grass through the thin tapestry.

"How do you know? You've never done it before either!" Coyne snapped, propping himself up on his elbows.

"Relax, dude. Maya's about to diagnose you with acute anxiety disorder."

Maya laughed, and Coyne grumbled, but he resettled himself on the tapestry. Just when they'd closed their eyes, they heard heavy footsteps crunching against the earth behind them. Turning to look back toward the path, they saw Mr. Magnoli. He had served as their rather eccentric Latin teacher at St. Bede's. His chocolate Labrador came bounding up ahead of him and began sniffing them curiously, its tail beating the air. Mr. Magnoli squinted and then waved, walking in their direction.

"Shit, I knew we shouldn't have come here," Coyne muttered, holding a hand over his face.

"Just relax. It'll be fine. Just a quick hello and he'll be gone. Then we have this perfect spot to ourselves again," Maya counseled.

"Always good to see the class of 2013 hanging out together!" said Mr. Magnoli, a genuine smile appearing below his thick mustache.

They stood up off the tapestry and dusted the grass off their clothes and hair as best they could. One at a time, they each shook his stubby hand. Short and sturdily built, he coached the wrestling team in the winter. Wisps of gray hair had begun to sprout at his temples in the four years since they'd last seen him.

"How was your year?" Maya asked.

"Oh, you know, same old, same old," he said.

For better or for worse, boarding schools provided faculty and students alike with the opportunity to encounter one another in settings remote from the classrooms that usually occasion such interactions, humanizing each party in the eyes of the other. Just so, in addition to being responsible for their education, the faculty members also served as coaches, dorm parents, dance chaperones, bus drivers, and advisers for the students. The barrier that typically divides student and teacher diminishes fairly irrevocably once each party regularly sees the other in pajamas.

"Still declining those verbs?" Coyne asked.

The question sounded strangely silly to Ray. In the silence that followed, he clamped his jaw shut to keep from laughing out loud. A goofy smile worked its way across Maya's face, and the color rose in Coyne's cheeks.

"Er, ha, yes, of course! *Aqua* and *aquae* and all that. Got to keep our dead languages alive, as I always say," chortled Mr. Magnoli, looking quizzically from face to face.

"Anyway, sorry Cocoa here ruined your, er, picnic. Great to see you three!" he said, clipping a leash to Cocoa's collar and waving as he ambled away up the path.

Waiting until he disappeared into the trees, they collapsed to the ground in unrestrained peals of laughter that broke out from the depths of their stomachs.

"Still declining those verbs?" Maya mocked.

"Yeah, I don't know why the hell I said that," Coyne gasped between fits of laughter.

Eyes streaming, Ray gasped for breath. The salt smell of the sea wafted up to the glade and coursed through their lungs. Nerve endings broke loose from under their skin and connected to the swaying trees and the lapping waves and the ancient stones and the cackling seagulls and the clattering shells. The grass beneath their palms surged upward and into their atoms, meeting the sea breeze that lingered on their sun-drenched skin and wrapping them in a blissful embrace.

◇◇◇◇◇◇◇◇◇◇◇◇◇◇◇◇◇◇◇◇◇◇◇◇◇

The ocean was aquamarine gelatin. They held bits of seaweed in their hands as they floated, letting the cool saltwater drip in runnels down their arms, enjoying the creep of the briny liquid on their skin. The rocks under their bare feet felt pleasantly slick. Lying back, they submerged themselves in the green glimmer. In the water, they were wordless, each enjoying their own private euphoria. Coyne held a whelk shell to his ear, and Maya collected small gems of smooth sea glass in her palm. Ray bobbed in the gentle waves, watching a sailboat cruise idly by in the distance. His eyes lifted skyward, and he rose higher and higher until, looking down, he saw his body, a minute brushstroke in a vast landscape painting. He was smiling.

◇◇◇◇◇◇◇◇◇◇◇◇◇◇◇◇◇◇◇◇◇

Coyne suggested a joint. In his delicate fingers, he rolled a short, tight tube. Silently, seated on the picnic table and gazing at the ocean, they passed it back and forth. Their hair was matted and stiff, and their skin wore a pleasant crust of salt. The lush grass had dyed their feet the color of spinach. The endless sky gradually changed from long streaks of pale yellow to bursts of apricot-orange and grapefruit-pink.

◇◇◇◇◇◇◇◇◇◇◇◇◇◇◇◇◇◇◇◇◇

Taking advantage of his parents' absence (they were vacationing in Bermuda), Coyne fired up the grill on the patio, and Ray opened a cheap bottle of red wine. Along with the lamb chops that Maya had discovered buried in the depths of the freezer, they prepared a salad from the swollen tomatoes in Mrs. Coyne's garden. Bellies full and wine staining their teeth, they settled into the angular Adirondack chairs in the backyard and slipped into a lazy late-summer drunk.

"We should go to Hanging Rock tomorrow," Coyne suggested.

"I'm working tomorrow," Ray said.

"Ah, I forgot. Polo? Or the liquor store?" he asked.

"Polo. But you guys should come by the bar—I'll hook you up."

Dragonflies careened through the air overhead, chasing after the mosquitoes that had appeared with the onset of dusk. The Labradors nipped at the dragonflies when they got within reach, and a hummingbird hovered over the hollyhocks by the cellar door. Still barefoot, they felt the cool grass between their toes.

"Definitely! I haven't been to a polo match this summer yet, and I've been meaning to," Maya said.

"How have we not gone yet this summer? I hate that we always wait till August to do all our summer things," Coyne grumbled. "We gotta go before it's too late," he added. His swollen eyelids drooped low over his red eyes.

"Too late for what?" Maya asked.

He didn't say anything for a while, and Ray thought maybe he'd fallen asleep.

"I don't know," he sighed heavily, placing a fresh toothpick between his teeth.

CHAPTER 19

Lobstergate

In exchange for a few draughts of Stella Artois, Ray and Kirley were often rewarded with platters of food set aside for them by the young guys who catered the polo matches. Once, they'd even been gifted a whole rib eye steak, which, lacking utensils and fairly drunk, they'd eaten like cavemen, passing it back and forth with their hands and tearing off bites with their teeth. Too caught up in his own image to think of his employees' hunger, Fitz's negligence of Maslow's hierarchy of needs had compelled this secretive alliance with the caterers.

Every summer, around the middle of August, Newport Polo would host a resplendent lobster bake, a massive all-you-can-eat buffet in which any of the match's patrons were welcome to partake to their heart's content provided they had paid the four-hundred-dollar fee (which did not include the thirty-dollar general admission charge).

"Do you smell that?" Kirley asked, looking up from the soda can he'd been improving with a few fingers of Maker's Mark.

"Jesus, that smells good. That's gonna drive me crazy all night," Ray replied.

Mountains of lobster had been prepared for the occasion, and their sweet, fishy perfume rose in mellow clouds from the wood-fired grill that had been constructed behind the bar.

◇◇◇◇◇◇◇◇◇◇◇◇◇◇◇◇

Fingertips numb and coated in a sticky layer of citrus juice and grenadine, Ray and Kirley wiped ratty rags over the bar top one last time. The last car disappeared from the parking lot, and Kirley squirmed underneath the bar to unhook the keg from the draught. On their way to the employee parking lot, they noticed a small platter covered in foil sitting on one of the folding tables. Crinkled over the platter's bulbous contents, the metallic foil caught the yellow moonlight. To the two starved, drunken bartenders, it looked like a Christmas gift, wrapped in shimmering silver paper and waiting to be opened.

"What do you think?" Ray asked, his mouth already watering.

"Let's ask," Kirley said.

A few caterers lingered by the catering truck, smoking cigarettes as the last of the plates were rinsed and loaded into the vehicle.

"Hey, you guys mind if we grab this?" Ray asked. "We're starving over here."

One caterer shrugged and stubbed out his cigarette while another waved them on with his hand. To spare themselves the long walk across the fields to the employee lot, they found a golf cart, its keys still in the ignition. Ray tore open the tinfoil, and a plume of sweet steam blasted upward from the platter. Perching the small feast between them on the seat, they tore at the buttery lobster meat with their teeth, hurling shells and pink shards of claw off the sides of the cart. Faster and faster they drove, laughing hard and spiking the empty lobster husks to the ground with reckless abandon, washing it all down with sips of cold beer as they careened around the polo grounds in chaotic circles, leaving a trail of battered claws and pink tails in their wake.

Seeing no reason not to share their bounty, they brought the remaining lobster (there had been more than four pounds stuffed into the platter, to begin with) to the Finches' house later that night. The ever-present swarm of Finch relatives and in-laws were there, and on their way in to refresh drinks in the kitchen or on their way out to the patio carrying small plates of hors d'oeuvres, the partygoers would pause for a nibble of the creamy lobster meat that Ray had left prominently displayed on the kitchen island. (Of course, Mr. Finch did not partake, having eaten all the lobster he could stomach over the course of his childhood.) It was not until later in the evening, as the carousers returned from the bars drunk and appetitive, that every last claw would be cracked and every spindly red leg sucked of its juices.

The next day's hangover brought with it an unpleasant email that did little to improve their pounding headaches and roiling stomachs. Kirley read the message aloud over his pancakes at Atlantic Grille, much to the amusement of Ray, Coyne, Maya, Bane, Ella, McShane, and Finch, who were crammed into the booth beside him.

> *Dear Mr. Kenneth Kirley and Mr. Raymond Wilson-Domingo,*
>
> *Effective immediately, you are (both) hereby terminated as employees of Newport Polo. The reasoning behind this decision is no doubt obvious to you. Please know that we take Grand Theft Crustacea very seriously at Newport Polo. This decision brings us no joy. Also, effective immediately, you are (both) hereby banned from the Newport Polo grounds henceforth. Failure to comply will result in your immediate removal by Newport Polo security and the possible involvement of the Newport Police Department's Special Dinner's Unit. Please do not list your bartending stint at the Twisted Pony Bar on your résumé, and do not list Jerome Peppercorn Fitzwallace III as a reference.*
>
> *Signed,*
> *The Newport Polo Assoc.*

"Well Jesus Christ, think we struck a nerve of some kind?" Ray asked.

"*Grand Theft Crustacea?*" Coyne chuckled. "Is this a joke?"

"*Special Dinner's Unit?*" Maya crowed, snatching Kirley's phone and reading the email for herself.

"Know why they didn't call the police, though?" Kirley said. "Because Fitz doesn't pay taxes. Not one cent all summer long."

"That makes sense. No W-2s, always paid in cash," Ray noted.

"Exactly," Kirley said. "All the years I've worked there, I haven't received one check. Only cash. This stupid letter is all they'll do. Empty bluster. That's all it is. Empty, pompous bluster. I bet Fitz penned this bullshit while he was wasted last night. Probably really proud of it too."

Further details were supplied throughout the week. Other Newport Polo employees who had been loyal to their cause (that is, Kirley and Ray had slipped them free drinks on a regular basis) called them up, offering dramatic renderings of their own versions of the night's events and burning with questions for the lobster outlaws. Apparently, the lobster platter had been earmarked for Fitz, and he had planned to bring it to his own postmatch party later that night. Instead, his dozen or so guests had been disappointed to find mediocre delivery pizzas in place of the lobster banquet they'd been promised. It had been his daughter, Molly, who had witnessed the wild, lobster-flinging, four-wheeled bacchanal, identifying the culprits to her father with a delighted smile (according to a witness close to the source).

"Man, don't you think it's pretty messed up that he fired us over email like that? And you've worked for him for what, seven years now? Eight? And that's how he leaves it?" Ray said.

Kirley shook his head and said, "Fitz was always a twisted dude. That letter is all bullshit. Just pompous bullshit. And he knows it."

Still, they took a meek pride in having been ousted from the pretensions of the polo matches. Two feet of bar had always separated them from the Saturday evening hordes; the termination email simply articulated what they already felt to be true. And the extent of Fitz's pomposity had never been in doubt. At halftime, he would make a big show of riding his horse up to the bar, skipping the line and expecting the closest bartender to rush to deliver him a cranberry seltzer, never dismounting from his steed. During the game, panting and drenched in sweat, he would conspicuously douse his head with water as though he were Ali catching his breath between rounds in a prize fight. And long after the match had ended, he would keep his mud-streaked riding boots on, strutting about the grounds with his chest swelled.

Of course, even if the grounds for their termination were somewhat exaggerated, they granted that the firing in and of itself was entirely warranted. They'd been drinking on the job, stealing booze, showing up late and hungover, giving out free drinks, and smoking joints behind the Porta-Potties all summer long.

The summer was nearly over anyway. Kirley would be moving to Boston soon, having landed an accounting position with a big firm downtown. He'd been playing the stock market with the inheritance he'd received from his grandfather's passing the year prior and had had enough success not to need to work for several years, anyway, if he so chose. McShane had quit his valet job and was refusing all the caddying gigs that came his way, Coyne had quit the marina, Finch had quit his weekend shift at the Pearl, and Maya had quit working reception at the Ocean Cliff hotel. Ella had broken up with the older guy who had, up to that point, been funding her summer leisure, and even Bane had negotiated with his dad to reduce his hours at the construction sites.

They all wanted to enjoy the last month of the summer unimpeded by something so trivial as an hourly job. However much he might have wanted to, Ray couldn't quit working at the liquor store. As far as the internship with the judge went, he would not feel confident that the job was actually his until he was physically standing in the courthouse office. The pile of expensive LSAT prep books he'd bought a few weeks earlier were gathering dust on his bedside table. He'd feel guilty about abandoning Ron at the busiest point in the summer, anyway. Plus, the Campbell–Doheny wedding was fast approaching, and Ray would have regretted not seeing the order that he had checked and rechecked a hundred times through to its illustrious end. But he was becoming anxious for a change. The island was closing in around him, waves swallowing great chunks of shoreline and edging closer to his feet with each passing day. The internship was the raft on which he would make his escape.

CHAPTER 20

The Campbell-Doheny Wedding

The big day arrived with all the exclamation points that Ron's delivery message board inscription had promised since the order was first placed five months prior. But not at first. Even from his bedroom in the far reaches of the Fifth Ward, Ray sensed that Newport was on its toes, holding its breath. The weather was clear and sunny, the cloudless sky just begging to host a picturesque wedding. The aerial photographs that would be taken today would be sure to do the island's natural beauty justice. It wouldn't have surprised anyone to learn that either the Campbells or the Dohenys had paid off the gods for a day of sublime weather.

"You're up early. No drinking last night?" chimed his mother, glancing up from the *Providence Journal* only briefly before returning to her methodical scans of the real estate section.

Today being a Saturday, she would probably visit a few open houses. For years now, she and Ray's father had clung to a hope that they might find a nice, affordable home into which they could comfortably retire. With the focus of an air traffic controller, she studied the local real estate listings each day, searching for some modestly priced home in the greater

Newport area, perhaps somewhere off Green End Avenue or down near the Point. Middletown was probably more in their price range if they wanted someplace nicer than their current rental. But of course they lusted after the Newport zip code like everyone else.

"Yeah," Ray mumbled, pouring the last dregs of the coffee pot into a mug.

"I need the car today, *mijo*."

Ray groaned into his coffee mug.

"I may go see a few houses! Take the bus."

"I hate the bus."

"You'll survive. And try to remember everything you see at the wedding. I want details when you get back, okay? *Lo prometes?*"

"Sure," Ray grunted.

For the first time all summer, he'd gone to bed early the night before. He'd turned down an invitation to a bonfire on Bane's property in Tiverton, choosing instead to watch an old Indiana Jones movie for the hundredth time. The tape had become jammed in the VHS player at some point, and rather than getting rid of both the movie and the player, he and his brother had convinced their mother to keep the defunct technology together as a unit, so as to always have the film ready on demand. He'd fallen asleep soon afterward, clambering into the cramped lower level of the bunk bed that he and his brother had shared for years until Tony finally moved out. Occasionally, he'd hit his head on the top bunk when lurching up bleary-eyed from the lower level in the mornings, but there was nowhere that Ray slept better than in that narrow bottom bunk.

Fresh off his firing from the polo bar, the Campbell–Doheny delivery weighed heavily on his mind. It had struck him, lying in bed the night before, that any mistake had potentially seismic effects. Not only would he have Ron's ire to face, but Newport had been playing the blame game at a varsity caliber since the seventeenth century. And neither of the families—not the Campbells or the Dohenys, to be sure!—would ever admit fault should something go wrong. One way or another, any mistakes that resulted in a less than fabulous wedding would be pinned not on a drunken relative or an overly ambitious mother of the bride but on the vendors, caterers, waitstaff, flower arrangers, wedding planners, pianists, landscapers, valets, or ice sculptors who'd been hired on the implicit understanding that the event would be nothing short of perfect.

The reverent tone of the day had even found its way onto the RIPTA that afternoon. Not only was the frequently delayed bus miraculously on time, but it had also, in a further rarity, displayed an accurate account of its destination in the yellow, digitized lettering above the windshield. Furthermore, the winos managed to drink their cheap sherries at a leisurely pace, sipping as though they were not riding the public bus but relaxing on a yachting tour around the harbor. The ancient woman clutching the edge of her seat had replaced her usual cacophony of wailing sobs with intense, whispered intonations of the Hail Mary. From one finger to the next, her rosary trickled like a bike chain. Even the obese, sweat-streaked driver offered a pleasant hello this morning rather than his usual "In or out?" as Ray hopped aboard.

As the bus lurched off the main road and into the tight one-ways of Newport's downtown, the sensation intensified. The roads felt oddly empty. The usual hollering of fry chefs from back-alley kitchens had subsided to a soft, simmering hush. The tourists with their bike maps and sun visors, usually omnipresent downtown on Saturdays, were nowhere to be seen.

When Ray arrived twenty minutes early for his shift, Ron was standing on the loading dock waiting for him. Ron wore a tight grimace on his face as he fidgeted with the Campbell–Doheny receipt between his fingers, smudging the cheap blue ink.

"I need you to double-check the order," he said, speaking with the severity of an FBI agent conferring sensitive information.

Though Ray had checked the order at the start of each shift for the past three months, he nodded solemnly and took the wilted receipt from Ron's hand. On the delivery board, Ron had seen fit to circle the wedding reception again, as though the first two circles were simply not enough. All the other deliveries had been postponed. The wedding delivery was to go out at four-thirty sharp, where it would then be distributed among Rosecliff's three separate event bars by five. Guests would begin arriving fashionably thereafter.

Stepping into the walk-in cooler, Ray let the door clunk shut behind him. Though it wasn't terribly humid outside, the cold air perfumed with the tinny scent of beer cans and musty cardboard felt pleasant on his skin. He took a seat on an empty beer keg and set about checking over the order, using the seventeen-thousand-dollar receipt as a checklist. Should Ron's daughter make the surprising choice to forgo a private education and attend the University of Rhode Island, this sale alone could cover her freshman year at the current in-state tuition rate.

Two cases totaling twenty-four bottles of Kistler Vineyards chardonnay, check. Six cases totaling seventy-two bottles of Whispering Angel rosé, check. Four cases totaling forty-eight bottles of Simi sauvignon blanc, check. Six cases totaling thirty-six bottles of Dom Pérignon Champagne, check. Four cases of Sierra Nevada Pale Ale, four cases of Harpoon IPA, four cases of Newport Storm Summer Hefeweizen, and three kegs of Stella Artois, just in case people were thirsty. Check.

That did it for all the items that were to be delivered chilled. In the back room, just outside the walk-in, sat several thousand more dollars' worth of pinot noir, cabernet, scotch, whiskey, vodka, and gin. Additionally, there were a few wooden crates housing a miscellaneous collection of exquisite wines—vintages and varietals specially recommended by Ron—to be enjoyed by the immediate family once the majority of guests had cleared out. These selections were as rare as they were expensive, the cheapest bottle costing no less than twelve-hundred dollars.

When the time came, Ron helped Ray load the goods into the back of the battered van. Gently and with calculated precision, they set each crate into the trunk, fitting one box securely into the next like Lego pieces so that nothing would get crushed along the way.

"Okay. Drive slowly," Ron began. His eyes were wide as Kennedy half dollars and he stressed each syllable. "You know how to get there, right?"

When Ray had first started the job, he'd often gotten lost among the twisting back roads of Newport's most secluded neighborhoods. Prior to working at the liquor store, he'd never had reason to drive so deep into the city's sprawling collection of seaside homes.

"It's a giant baroque mansion, Ron. I think I'll find it," Ray said with a laugh. But upon catching the severe look in Ron's eyes, he added, "Rosecliff. I know where it is."

Ron gave him one more dubious eye-twitching glance before nodding and waving him away.

"Call me if you need anything. Or if there's any trouble at all, whatsoever," Ron muttered, backing away from the loading dock and into the air-conditioned back room. Sweat bled through his light dress shirt.

With MVY Radio crooning a mournful Cranberries track, the van grumbled along Bellevue Avenue. The van's dented, dusty appearance almost marred the avenue's beauty, with its picture-perfect manors and grandiose mansions tucked far behind medieval-looking stone walls and imposing iron gates. Ray had never driven such an expensive load, and each clink of the bottles behind him caused him to jump. Driving slowly and sitting rigidly on the duct-taped seat, his sweating hands choked the steering wheel, and he implored the shuddering old van to obey his orders.

It wasn't the first time that Ron had been contracted for a mansion wedding, though it was certainly the most anticipated and highest-profile event for which his services had been hired. By now, Ray was accustomed to using the vast estate's hidden service entrance, avoiding the long line of limousines and Land Rovers awaiting valet service. But today, even the service entrance was backed up, and Ray steered into line behind the flower deliveries, decorators, bakery vans, and caterers in their boxy black trucks with white cursive lettering scrawled on the sides.

In the packed parking lot, Ray, after some difficult maneuvering, managed to squeeze the van into a narrow space between two catering trucks. Grabbing a single case of chilled chardonnay, he trekked across the expansive lawn. He knew that it was best to get a sense of the venue before loading up a dolly with a stack of heavy wine cases, though he always made sure to take at least one box along for the reconnaissance. Forgo this calculation—as he had on several previous misadventures—and he could end up dragging a couple of hundred liquid pounds up staircases or across whole fields of acreage only to be told that the delivery was to be placed elsewhere. Case in hand, he made his way toward the event hall, where uniformed caterers and boutique flower arrangers scurried up and down the marble steps. At the edge of the parking lot, parked askew on the grass, was a sleek, cream-colored Jaguar Mark IX. Ray paused to admire its smooth, swooping curves and pristine tires. Even by Newport standards, it was a beautiful, unique car. Not one part of it looked like a machine, but rather a buttery liquid that had been blown into physical shape.

In the midst of the hubbub in the magnificent foyer, Ray noticed a clean-shaven man of about thirty with his shirt sleeves rolled up to the elbows arranging a punch bowl on a corner table. Bartenders were easy to recognize. Seeing Ray approach with the wine case weighing in his arms, they exchanged the quick, mutually respectful nod of two men toiling in different branches of the same industry, like a horseshoer meeting a cowboy.

"You can set those anywhere. I'll take care of them," the bartender said casually.

Plenty of bartenders, especially those hired for opulent Newport weddings, could get an inflated sense of self, referring to themselves as mixologists or cocktail artists. This one seemed grounded enough, though, taking the case from Ray's arms and setting it on the table.

"You'll be busy tonight," Ray said.

The bartender nodded and issued a low whistle through his teeth. With a wink, he tossed Ray a mango Smirnoff nip and held up a little bottle of his own. They clinked the miniature plastic bottles together and downed them in one gulp.

"First of many," the bartender said with another wink. "Only way I get through these things."

After Ray made a few booze-laden trips back and forth from the van to the ballroom, the bar was nearly stocked and the guests were beginning to arrive. Older couples were the first to show up, probably looking to score good seats and leave early with the foresight that age and decades spent on Newport's gala circuit had provided them. The last case of wine made its way to the bar, and the door swung shut on the now empty van. Now Ray would wait. Ron had instructed him to hang around inconspicuously for as long as possible, awaiting any unusual requests at the bar or watching for the bartender to run dry on a particular product.

Should either situation arise, Ray was expected to rush back to the store and add the bottle or case in question to the tab before returning to the wedding reception, smiling helpfully with the desired wine, beer, or spirit in hand.

Leaning against the marble facade of the mansion, Ray took in the stunning setting. A long silk carpet the color of cognac ran from the ballroom out to the lawn, reaching all the way up to the tastefully appointed stage where the ceremony would be held. Rows of delicate white folding chairs were arranged at perfectly spaced increments facing the podium. Sunflowers in massive vases were set at the corners of the stage, and bundles of white roses sat gracefully atop each circular table. Caterers circulated between the lawn and the ballroom carrying large platters of crab cakes and shooters of gazpacho. Two elegant swans had been corralled into a photogenic position in the bay beyond the cliffs. A photographer wearing chunky kneepads wandered along the edges of the lawn, pausing now and again to shoot a machine-gun riff of snaps from the massive camera that swung at his side. Emerald hummingbirds with long, transparent threads tied to their feet hovered in the air, tethered to an ornate flower centerpiece at the top of the marble staircase.

The ceremony itself, for all its splendor, was brief. Ray caught glimpses of it as he walked back and forth from the van to the ballroom where the reception would be held. A hunched old man supporting himself with an elegant cane had walked the bride down the central aisle that cut through the densely packed rows of chairs like a gap segmenting two front teeth. The bride was a squat woman with strawberry blond hair that had been arranged in an intricate crown atop her head. She clutched a large bouquet in her pudgy hands and teetered up the aisle on the smallest feet Ray had ever seen, which swished out from under her gown in choppy little kicks as she walked. The train of her dress was several yards long, and two small blond children had been tasked with holding its hem to help it negotiate the chairs lining the aisle. The groom—a stout, broad-shouldered man with ruddy cheeks, sharp blue eyes, and thinning brown hair that had been combed straight back over his head—was beaming. He had a small, leisurely gut that was almost hidden by his tailored suit. When the officiant gave the command, the bride and groom brought their lips together—a peck at first, then an honest-to-goodness smooch—and a loud burst of applause and cheers rose from the assembled crowd as the Campbells and the Dohenys were, at last, married. Ray slipped back to the bar as the attendees began standing and shuffling toward the reception.

The people filling the ballroom smiled and laughed, shaking hands with one another and whispering into each other's ears. The clientele of this crowd might as well have strolled in directly from Periwinkle Beach Club, so similar were their unhurried gaits and self-assured smiles. But tonight, they'd exchanged their faded polo shirts, understated swimwear, and pristine tennis whites for crisp monochrome suits and dark tuxedos on the men and elegant gowns on the women. Though Ray didn't recognize any of them individually, they looked familiar. To a certain extent, it no longer felt strange to him—or even particularly remarkable—to walk under the elaborate baroque arches of the mansion or to admire the sea from a spectacular grassy hilltop overlooking the Cliff Walk.

But then Ray saw faces that he actually did recognize, though not at first. Scanning the crowd, he saw Maya and Ella sipping prosecco in flowing gowns, posing for pictures with silver-haired men. That couldn't be Finch walking in with his parents, a buzzed hiccup in his footfalls—he'd been looking at apartments in Boston today, hadn't he? And there was Bane, standing with his hands in his pockets next to his father, who was deep in an animated discussion with another red-faced man. And surely that wasn't McShane shaking hands with a short, bald man by the door, for he had said that he'd be visiting family up in Brookline today. Kirley, in his pinstriped suit, stood by the bandstand, chatting up the guitarist. Could that really be Coyne, proffering his invitation to the prissy woman in the starchy dress checking in guests at the door? No, Coyne had mentioned that he hadn't been invited, hadn't he?

The bartender, whose name was Jake, handed Ray another Smirnoff nip, the fourth since he'd arrived. Behind the bar, they went relatively unnoticed, blending into the ornate ephemera that guests had come to expect at these events, as much a part of the decor as the large glass vases and polished silverware. The people who were connected to the hands that brought them hors d'oeuvres on silver platters or accepted their keys to valet park their cars formed the comforting background scenery of a well-funded life. Jessie floated across the lawn, charming the slacks off everyone in sight in her butter-yellow summer dress and white silent-film-era gloves. She wore an Audrey Hepburn smile that she might as well have picked up at Tiffany's, along with the gem dangling from her throat.

But Ray had expected her. Her claim to this world was unimpeachable. That was just it, though. His St. Bede's chums—it was their world too. At some point, he had deluded himself into thinking that it was his as well. It was an odd feeling, realizing something that he'd presumed always to know. Perhaps they thought they were protecting him, keeping him blissfully ignorant of an experience that could never be his, maintaining some distorted illusion of equilibrium. But in Newport, the people who worked on Saturdays could never be the same as the people enjoying those Saturdays.

Finch was the first to notice him, though not until his third trip to the bar.

"Holy shit! Ray! What's up, man?" he asked.

Words slurring out of the side of his mouth and eyes drooping toward his chin, he seemed to have forgotten that he'd lied to Ray about his plans for the evening.

"Not much," Ray said. He blamed the Smirnoff for making the words come out more warmly than he'd intended.

"Well, damn! I didn't know you were coming—Hey, Coyne! Coyne! Ray's here! Check it out!" he yelled across the room.

Glancing up from his conversation with a portly man who looked somewhat like an older version of himself, Coyne squinted toward the bar, orienting his functioning ear in the direction of Finch's bombastic voice. An ashen look crossed his face, and his eyes shifted to the floor. Collecting McShane (with some difficulty) away from the buffet table's offering of king crab legs, Coyne ambled slowly to the bar. Wiping his hands on his trousers, McShane followed close at his heels.

"Ray, hey, man. Listen, we didn't think—"

"Sorry, man, if we knew you were invited—"

"Yeah, we just didn't know if—"

"Miscommunication, you know how that goes . . ."

The excuses poured out like sand escaping from a shattered hourglass, but they sounded sincere enough.

"I wasn't invited. I'm working," Ray said, gesturing to the cases of wine and beer stacked up behind him.

Seeing their compatriots, Maya, Ella, Kirley, and Bane had by now joined the small crowd of St. Bede's alums, forming a close semicircle around the bar. Jake's hands fluttered away on the periphery, wiping down clean glasses and checking the corks of wine bottles that he knew to be tightly sealed and pretending not to notice the awkward silence that followed.

"Oh, well, you know . . ." Coyne started, his eyes shifting around the room, landing anywhere to avoid Ray's gaze.

"A round on us, man! If we're drinking, you're drinking. And you too, bartender!" Finch bellowed.

Shooting Ray a sidelong smirk, Jake poured out nine shots of whiskey and distributed them among the gathered party. The petite glasses were clinked together, followed by a collective groan as the burning liquor seared their throats.

"Keep it going!" Finch said, tossing a handful of twenties onto the table before Jake, either unaware that the bar was gratis or tipping generously.

With a curt nod, Jake gathered the bills into his back pocket and poured out another round. And then another. More twenties were thrown onto the table. Another round. Clink. Groans. Another round. Their ankles quaking in their narrow high-heeled shoes, Maya and Ella clomped away to sit on a bench overlooking the water, holding each other's arms for support. McShane placed another handful of bills on the table. The bartender looked from the cash to Ray, who shrugged. More whiskey was poured, splashing over the brim of the shot glasses. Clink. Groan. Ray looked up from the table, glancing over his friends' heads to the vista that was visible through the broad entryway. The oceanfront landscape transformed into an impressionistic blur, every shrub, face, bird, flower, and table denoted by blobs of color and shape. For Ray, though, the scene never lost its sense of harmony, though. Like a painting, it existed within a rigid frame, bordered by the smooth marble pillars of the entryway.

Evidently satisfied with their navigation of the uncomfortable situation, Ray's friends slapped him on the shoulder and retreated back into the blur of colors, rejoining the painting they'd left to console the viewer. Ray had been too busy at the liquor store to eat lunch. The whiskey shots cascaded in damp, burning gulps to the bottom of his empty stomach. Jazz riffs echoing from a chamber in the foyer seeped through pores in his skull. Ba-doom-doom-doom, ba-doom-doom-doom, ba-doom-doom-DOOM! The sound mixed with the wash of colors and motion, blurring Ray's vision and distorting his hearing. And yet, it was as though he was seeing it all for the first time. Red-painted lips smacked up and down between bites of crab cake or puckered to suck an oyster from its shell. Clean-shaven jaws powered up and down, and soft hands shook one another. Long pearl necklaces thudded against breastbones. The smell of fat cigars and crisp champagne. Disgust settled in Ray's stomach.

As Ray walked back across the lawn, the whiskey shots caught up to him, retarding his movements such that he actually had to think himself through each step. The sun was beginning to set, and faint charges of ruby light glinted off the whitecapped waves. The din and warmth of the wedding reception subsided into the cool navy-blue tones and hushed conversations of a late summer evening.

There was enough light that Ray was able to find the delivery van without much trouble. Pouring himself into the driver's seat, he felt grateful that Ron had opened his store so close to the mansions. The short drive was just a straight shot down Bellevue Avenue.

After a few tries stabbing at the ignition with the keys, Ray heard the engine moan to life. He eased the behemoth van out and away from the catering trucks that flanked him on either side. Negotiating the van onto the parking lot's main lane, however, he overcalculated, beginning the turn too early. His drunken foot misstepped, and he floored the accelerator rather than the brake.

He heard the crash before he could stomp on the brake pedal. With difficulty, Ray pushed the driver's side door open and half stepped, half fell out of the van.

A low but steady hissing sound was issuing from somewhere in the front of the van. Gathering himself to his feet, he ambled toward the sound, clutching the side of the van for support. A small crowd had formed a short distance away, a blurry semicircle of tuxedos, dinner jackets, and evening gowns. Perhaps the hissing sound was the whispers they exchanged, pointing in Ray's direction.

The van's front bumper, grill, and both headlights were crushed into a grotesque maw of bent metal and shattered fiberglass. The engine peered up from beneath the crinkled hood like a mussel partially pried from its shell. Everything happened in slow motion, dreamlike. The hissing sound appeared to be coming from the coolant, which was steadily escaping from the engine and forming a green puddle beneath Ray's feet. Once he finally lifted his head to see what he'd hit, though, he forgot all about the van.

It was the Jaguar, that perfect Grecian vase of a car, that he'd shattered. Its front half looked like a chew toy that some great dog had gnashed beyond recognition. The miniature silver jaguar that had been seen leaping off the tip of the car's hood mere hours before was now twisted so horribly in on itself that it was no more distinct than a paperweight.

A shout of agony drew Ray's stupefied attention to the crowd. A tall man sporting a curling mustache who looked to be in his early sixties had gone white in the face, staring not at Ray but at the Jaguar. A hand covered his gaping mouth, and his eyes bulged wildly.

Slowly, Ray took in the rest of the onlookers. A few faces he recognized from the polo grounds, a few from the liquor store, and still a few more from Periwinkle. Coyne, McShane, Kirley, and even Finch, drunk as he was, looked down at their shoes, peering up every now and then as others joined the crowd and let out little horrified gasps. There was Henry Blanchet, the adulterous liquor store patron, shaking his head slowly back and forth and staring dumbfounded at Ray. Hands already clasped to their mouths, Bane, Maya, and Ella made their way across the lawn. Appearing, as usual, from the ephemera, Jessie simply turned on her heel and waltzed away from the crowd, not looking back. Neither angry nor upset, she dropped him as easily as she had picked him up.

The crowd grew until surely all the remaining guests had formed into a crescent around the accident. Even a handful of caterers and florists lingered in the back of the assemblage. They stood on their tiptoes, enjoying a rare break from their obsequious toil. But now Ray recognized no one. The faces and jewelry and hair gel and makeup all morphed into one singular look of disgust. He could only summon the energy to stare dumbly back at them. He had, inadvertently, become the subject of the painting.

Without a word, he turned from the crowd. His oil-soaked shoes squelched against the gravel as he walked away. One foot after another, he made his slow, preposterous way down the long driveway and out onto Bellevue Avenue on his shuffling, ugly, drunken gait.

Snippets of their commentary joined the mosquitoes in buzzing about his ears.

"Well, I did see him drinking . . ."

"He works for Ron, doesn't he?"

"I've seen him around. A bit fringy if you ask me . . ."

"Isn't he Brazilian or something?"

"He wasn't invited. Of that, I'm *sure*."

CHAPTER 21

Low Tide

Though he had never been to the Celtica Pub (and knew nobody who had), its lack of popularity and its obscure location in the alleyways of the Newport Shipyard suited Ray's present desire for anonymity. This afternoon, though, the grimy bar hosted a considerable crowd of boisterous Irishmen. Ray supposed that he shouldn't have been surprised that the contingent of Irish folks who came to Newport every June, working odd seasonal jobs and sleeping five to a room in mouse-infested houses in hopes of experiencing an American summer, had claimed the Celtica as their go-to bar, given the name of the establishment and the intricate Celtic cross displayed prominently over the entryway.

One summer, Ray had worked with one of these Irish lads at the liquor store. This Gaelic fellow, Paul Murphy, had lasted only a short time on the job, though Ray had enjoyed his company, brief as it was. Before his firing (he'd skipped his shift to watch Hozier perform at Folk Fest), Paul had been living in a dilapidated summer rental on Dixon Street with several of his countrymen. He had made plain to Ray that his sole plan that summer was to spend all of the money he made on evenings out at the bars, reserving a small sum to cover his portion of the intricately divided rent. And this was precisely what he'd done. Though technically the apartment had only two bedrooms, they'd dragged in several couches and tables they'd found resting on the sidewalk next to steaming trash barrels and placed half-inflated air mattresses or beanbag chairs wherever the cramped floor space would allow.

In this way, Paul had paid only two hundred dollars a month for rent, leaving him with ample funds to party the summer away. Ray had visited the apartment once, and though he was no stranger to shabbily appointed college houses under the disastrous care of young men, the place had been, even to his tempered sensibility, shockingly derelict. Mice scurried about under the decaying furniture, chased by the stray cats that Paul had lured into the apartment for exactly this purpose. Pizza boxes were stacked nearly to the height of the ceiling, and beer bottles and empty handles of cheap vodka and tequila filled the sink and cluttered every available surface. Having forgotten to pay their electricity bill and never having owned a television in the first place, their daylight hours were spent playing cards and taking turns throwing Ping-Pong balls up into the lamp that hung from the center of the inutile ceiling fan. The Ping-Pong balls, Paul had explained, were left over from an America-themed party they'd hosted several weekends prior, where they'd played beer pong with red SOLO cups and listened to country music. Paul routinely talked about wanting to try heroin, just once, though he'd been fired before Ray had had a chance to ask him whether he'd yet fulfilled this quest.

As Ray sat sipping cheap vodka tonics on one of the Celtica's sticky barstools, the Irishmen's absurd European jargon split the air at irregular intervals. Their exuberant commentary was directed at a small television set propped on a corner of the bar, on which a grainy soccer match was playing out across the screen. Evidently they too had the day off.

"Come on, you goons! Crack on!"

"Christ! That keeper's acting the maggot now, ain't he?"

"This posh one thinks it's ballet, don't he? Oy, boyo! It's football we're playing here!"

Typically, Ray would be working on a Sunday, but no longer. It had been one of Ron's more memorable meltdowns—perhaps even his swan song. The call from the judge revoking the internship offer, explaining that Blanchet had told him what transpired at the wedding and that Ray's conduct was not agreeable with the responsibilities of the position, had paled in comparison to Ron's ire. Ray had just stood there and taken it, each word a mallet striking him deeper into the ground like a railroad spike. The mustachioed Jaguar owner happened to be a friend of Ron's and thus wouldn't be pressing charges, so Ray had taken the verbal flogging and the shower of vitriolic spit as his due. Good or bad, the nobility liked to keep their doings out of print—especially if their doings were being reported in the *Newport Daily News* police blotter, of all places. Even a passing mention that something had gone terribly awry at the perfect wedding would be to admit the unthinkable: vulnerability to the salacious follies that plagued the imperfect classes.

After he'd exhausted himself, red in the face and sweating profusely in the late August heat, Ron had waved Ray away with a flick of his jittering hand. Not wanting to reignite him with another apology, Ray had nodded and walked out of the store.

And then he had kept walking. Past the Blues Café, past Pelham East, past Speakeasy, past Gas Lamp. He knew he would recognize the kind of place he was looking for once he saw it. Anonymity was the key, and he had it so long as these hollering Irishmen filled the bar. Every time the ball was touched, a great shout went up and beer was spilled with the flinging of exasperated arms.

"He can't kick for shit!"

"I woulda netted that one!"

"They've lost it. It's all ova'!"

A hand clapping his shoulder disrupted Ray's staring contest with the bar straws. Turning around on the barstool, he saw Jonny grinning incredulously.

"Ray! What the hell are you doing down here, man?"

The muscles in Jonny's arms and chest strained against the faded gray U.S. Navy T-shirt he wore. And just as had been the case the last time Ray had seen him, at O'Brien's Pub, his hair seemed to have been freshly shorn, the neat high-and-tight buzz cut revealing his small ears.

"Thought I'd stop in for a drink. Never been here before," Ray said.

"I know a couple Navy guys who come here. It's a fun spot," Jonny said.

"They seem to like it," Ray said, nodding in the direction of the groaning crowd of men leaning over one another for a better view of the screen.

Jonny laughed and sat down on the stool beside Ray. As the bartender refilled their foggy glasses over the next hour, the awkwardness of the chance run-in melted away. The bartender, an older man with a shock of white hair and a small shamrock tattooed just below his left eye, seemed more interested in the game than in tracking their tabs, anyway. Ray asked about some of the other guys from the neighborhood.

"Sticking around here, mostly," Jonny said. "Same as me."

To Ray's ear, Jonny didn't seem to harbor any shred of regret about the prospect of sticking around the island. More like a simple resolve, a matter of practicality. Three drinks in, Jonny brought up fishing. It was the thing that had bonded them in the first place, way back in the sixth grade when he'd invited Ray to fish for skipjack bluefish from the dock near his grandfather's house in Bristol. For years they'd fished nearly every rocky crag along the island's coast, building campfires and staying out late. The tradition had ended once Ray was accepted to St. Bede's, fizzling at first and then dying completely. But there was no bitterness about the loss, and they'd remained in touch by dint of the island's compressed size, bumping into each other in line at Frosty Freez or catching each other in the lobby at Island Cinemas 10.

"We oughta go sometime," Jonny proclaimed, smiling warmly. "I was thinking about trying out a new spot, down at the bottom of Cory's Lane. I know some guy who pulled up a thirty-six-inch striper there last week."

"Definitely, man. That sounds really great."

And Ray meant it. The idea of fishing with Jonny again sounded nice, and the nostalgia was comforting. A group of beefy, neckless guys with severely short haircuts and anchor tattoos on their biceps were playing poker and throwing darts in the back corner of the bar. They called Jonny back to their table. He gave Ray a parting bro-hug before joining them.

"Good to see you, Ray. We'll go fishing sometime soon, yeah?"

"Absolutely. Take care, man."

Ray ordered another vodka tonic and tried to make sense of the game, though he couldn't even tell whether either or both of the teams were Irish. A woman's voice, close to his ear, caught his attention.

"Looks like my hideout has been discovered. You won't tell the Finches or any of that set you hang around with that you saw me here, will you? Of course you will—this is Newport. Can't say I blame you."

Rolling a thin red bar straw between her dry fingers, sky-blue nail polish chipping at the edges, the woman perched on a stool next to Ray. He'd been so absorbed in conversation with Jonny that he hadn't noticed her in the raucous bar. How long had she been there, he wondered? She looked familiar—and sounded familiar. Her words formed paragraphs in the air, unabashed and confident in tone. Unpretentious, Ray decided. But was she drunk? He couldn't tell. Draining her beer, she motioned to the bartender for another.

"Shouldn't be a problem. That's not really my 'set' anymore, anyway," he muttered in reply. He'd been receiving regular calls from Coyne, McShane, Maya, Kirley, Bane, Ella, and Finch, though he couldn't bear to answer them yet. He'd been using his voicemail as a shield against their concerned voices.

"Ah, yes. I heard about Mr. Toad's Wild Ride," she chuckled, looking him up and down. "Funny how gossipers will gossip to anyone about anything, isn't it? Never once imagining that others will do the same to them—or about them! But your stunt reached even my ears. Incidentally, it's one of the first bits of gossip I've heard since I moved here that hasn't been about me. A flair for the dramatic, yes?" she finished, gesturing to Ray with her frothing glass as though it were now his turn to speak.

"I suppose so. What is it that they say about you?"

"Oh, the usual, you know. I'm a nymphomaniacal lesbian gold digger murderess, or some variation thereof. Haven't you heard? I killed my husband so I could take his mansion and elope with the preteen I fell in love with at Burning Man."

Rolling her eyes, she lit a cigarette. She offered the pack to Ray, though he declined.

Suddenly Ray recognized her. She was the woman who had moved into Moon View. The woman who had once come into the liquor store like a whirlwind in search of a decent bottle of vodka. And that had been her, at the polo match, the thin woman wearing torn jeans and smoking a cigarette on the roof of her car. Her hair had been re-dyed an intense shade of blond, and her restless blue eyes jittered about the room. Tall and wiry, she sat with one long leg crossed over the other, one foot anchored on the stool while the other tapped absently in the air.

"You moved into Moon View."

Taking another drag on the cigarette, she nodded. The bartender gestured to a "NO SMOKING" sign behind the bar. Without missing a beat, she pulled two fifty-dollar bills out of her bra and slid them in the bartender's direction, barely meeting his eyeline. A stupefied look passed over the bartender's round face, and he paused, staring at the crumpled bills for a moment before shrugging and stuffing them into his pocket.

"So you do read the gossip column of the *Newport Mercury*. How nice," she replied, with an abrupt chuckle. "I'm kidding around—can't you tell? I'm Candy, by the way," she added, wiping the condensation from her hand on a cocktail napkin before extending it toward him. "Well, truthfully, I'm Catherine. But I go by Candy. I just think the East Coast is a bit too saturated with Catherines, don't you?"

Her hand felt bony and cold, but she gave him a firm, vigorous shake before picking the bar straw back up and rolling it around between her fingers again.

"Ray. Nice to meet you."

With a flick of her wrist and a pointed raising of her dark, undyed eyebrows, she summoned the bartender, who placed a fresh beer on the coaster in front of her and removed the empty glass.

"Well now, isn't this a perfect little pity party, the two of us?" Candy said, chuckling again.

"Yeah, this town can feel small," Ray said.

As the sentence left his lips, he became conscious of his own voice. It sounded so stiff and uninteresting to him when compared to Candy's loquacious patter, which echoed forth like written prose.

"Not just this town, kiddo. I've lived everywhere, Ray-buddy, and they're all the same. A place is as small as you make it. Stick around long enough, and you end up like these big old houses we have around here—known by everyone and slowly breaking down, becoming uglier with each winter."

Ray shifted on the rickety stool, feeling as though he'd forgotten his script at home.

"That sounds a bit deep for afternoon beer talk, now doesn't it?" Candy said, finally.

Clinking her empty glass against Ray's, she yanked another handful of bills out of her bra and set them on the bar top. For once, her eyes halted their jumpy dance, and she patted him on the shoulder, fixing him with a look of genuine sympathy.

"You ought to come by Moon View. It's about time I had a guest up at that big, empty place. And I might as well lean into the whole misfit spinster thing they've pinned me with here, don't you think? You'll be an excellent addition. So long as you don't mind a little gossip about how I've seduced you. But perhaps it'll be just the spin your story needs at the moment . . . How does Thursday sound, around three? I presume you're not working for that strange little man at that liquor store anymore. No? Excellent, see you then."

Winking to the bartender and waving over her shoulder to nobody in particular, she strutted out of the bar. Again, every loose object seemed to have been levitating so long as she was present, succumbing to gravity only once the door had slammed shut behind her.

◇◇◇◇◇◇◇◇◇◇◇◇◇◇◇◇◇◇◇◇◇◇

Tony's apartment was on the third floor of an old multiunit building on the corner of Broadway and Oak Street. A pawnshop and a cozy breakfast restaurant occupied the first floor. It had been hell maneuvering a couch up the narrow staircase back in May, their sweating palms straining as Ray and Tony, holding one end of the hefty couch apiece, negotiated its bulky edges over the banister and into the cramped apartment. Newport's Broadway district had begun to change over the past few years, morphing slowly from the city's seedier section to a chic up-and-coming neighborhood. Thai restaurants, record shops, vegan cafés, and craft coffee bars were popping up alongside the shabby liquor stores and tattoo parlors that had been there for decades.

"You want something to drink?" Tony asked. "All I've got is some cheap brandy."

Ray plopped down onto an armchair by the open window. Boisterous voices and the smell of cigarettes drifted up from the street.

"Just some water, thanks. Don't you have AC?"

Tony filled a glass from the tap and handed it to Ray before pouring himself a tumbler of brandy and seating himself on the couch.

"I bought a window unit but haven't gotten around to installing it. I'm barely here, anyway. Been working like crazy."

"Yeah, *Mamá* mentioned that. She was complaining about how you haven't been coming around for dinner."

"Bullshit! I was there three days ago!"

"I know, I know. You know how she is."

"Did she tell you about the referral program for barber school? The discounted rate?"

"Yeah," Ray said. "I don't know, man. I don't think the barber route is for me."

"Fair enough," Tony said. "We all know you're too smart for it. It's a good gig, though. The money is decent, you get to talk to different people, work with your hands. Guys walk into the shop all sheepish and leave the place feeling handsome. No kidding, man, give a guy a fresh haircut and he's got a spring in his step the rest of the day. Just think about it some more, okay? Could be fun to work together. And you need a haircut, by the way. You're starting to look like Serpico."

Ray pushed the thick mop of dark hair away from his face.

"Sure, I'll keep it in mind. Hey, you have any ice? I feel like I'm melting," Ray said.

"Nope," Tony said, scoffing. "Sorry, bro. If you want ice and AC you'll just have to go back to one of those palaces you're always hanging around."

"Yeah, well, I'm not expecting invitations anytime soon."

Tony nodded and took a long sip of brandy.

"I might've heard something about that. Not your finest moment?"

Ray shook his head and stared at the floor.

"How'd you hear about it?"

"One of my customers," Tony said, shrugging. "Old fat guy with a combover. He was having me dye his hair black. Said he wanted to look like Tom Cruise. You believe that? Anyway, apparently he was at the wedding. I think he said he was a caterer or a valet or something. He said some tan kid got wasted and crashed a car. Any of that ring a bell?"

"Unfortunately, yes," Ray groaned.

Getting up from the couch, Tony flicked on a fan by the window. The steel blades whirred quietly, blasting a tepid wind into the room.

"I'm only going to ask this once, okay?" Tony said, sitting back down on the couch. "Do you think you might have a drinking problem?"

"Yeah, the problem is all you have to drink is cheap brandy. Be serious, Tony. I'm not a drunk. I'm just in my twenties. Don't act like you weren't the same."

"I remember thinking like that," Tony said, smiling and glancing up and away at a fond memory. "But then you turn thirty and you realize that nothing has really changed. You're still you, just older. The hangovers are much worse, though."

"Great, something else to look forward to," Ray said. He used his T-shirt to wipe the sweat from his brow. "What I really need is a change of scenery. I'm sick of Newport. And I think it's sick of me."

"So that posh friend group of yours, it's all over? And that old-money blond girl you were telling me about, that's all done? Just because of that one day?"

"Yeah, maybe. To tell the truth, I never really belonged with that group anyway," Ray said. "I guess it had to end sometime."

Tony drained the tumbler and sat staring at the bottom of the glass for a long moment. He ran a hand through his neatly cropped dark hair and looked up at Ray, his eyes slightly narrowed.

"You want to know what I think? I think you kind of like not fully belonging to that crowd. I bet you think it gives you some kind of credibility, some kind of perspective that they're all lacking, right? You'll join them on their yachts, but you're not a poser so long as you maintain a quiet, unspoken hostility to everything they represent. You're the outsider on the inside. They're the insulated tribe, and you're the intrepid anthropologist. They're simple, but you're complex. You see things as they really are, while they're running around with monogrammed wool over their eyes. They may be rich, but you're authentic, right?"

Ray stared at his brother, his mouth slightly agape. The voices outside were getting louder now, the sidewalks filling with crowds bustling to and from the restaurants and bars. Cars honked peevishly at one another, angling for the few parking spots that lined the street. For a second he was angry, hunched over his knees with the blood boiling in his ears. But the anger quickly subsided, leaving a shameful ache in his stomach and an acrid taste on his tongue. He sighed and collapsed heavily back into the chair.

"Jesus," Ray said, finally. "I'll take that brandy now, if you don't mind."

Laughing, Tony went to the kitchen. He grabbed the bottle from its perch on top of the refrigerator and poured out a generous glass for Ray.

CHAPTER 22

Moon View

It felt strange to Ray to be driving to a house on Ocean Drive without a collection of wine cases clattering behind him. And where before these massive estates had simply formed the scenic backdrop of sunset drives with his friends, today one of them had become his destination. Of course, the way Candy had invited him had been so flighty and casual that he half expected her to have forgotten about it altogether. Maybe she wouldn't even be home.

But when he got to the top of the twisting hill overlooking Brenton Point, there she was, smoking a cigarette on the mansion's vast granite porch. The Bane construction trucks were gone, the brilliantly restored facade the only indication that they'd been there at all. For all Mr. Bane's flaws, impeccable restoration jobs like this one left little doubt as to the quality of his company's work. The mansion looked magnificent, transformed from the crippled state it had been in at the beginning of the summer to the superlative work of architecture it was now, all while retaining an ancient dignity that could not be purchased at any price.

"I like your car," she joked, nodding in the direction of the yellow moped he'd rented again.

Though his mother hadn't yet heard anything about the mishap at the Campbell–Doheny wedding, she had forbidden him from borrowing the Volvo, distrustful of his vague answers about why he'd quit his job at the liquor store—especially since this news had come on the heels of his (equally dubiously received) disclosure that he'd quit the lucrative polo match bartending gig. His refusal to provide anything beyond monosyllabic details about the wedding itself, something she'd been looking forward to seeing through his eyes, had only incensed her further.

"I like your giraffe," he said.

The preposterously large animal stood at one corner of the property, perhaps an acre away from the mansion's granite steps. Reaching its elegant neck up to its full height, it wrapped its thick purple tongue around a branch of one of the many trees that grew just beyond the limestone walls marking the boundaries of the estate. In a slow, effortless motion, the leaves were stripped from the branch and pulled into the giraffe's mouth, followed by a low, reverberating munching noise that could be heard from the steps.

"Ah, yes. That's Rupert. The fulfillment of a childhood dream. People ought to do it more often," she said, staring lovingly at the giraffe. "When I was a little girl—maybe nine or ten years old—my grandfather promised me that he'd buy me a giraffe for my birthday one day. But of course, he never did, the old bastard. So when I caught wind that Rupert here wasn't getting along with his fellow giraffes over at the zoo—Roger Williams Park Zoo, I'm sure you've been, haven't you? Over in Providence? Oh, well, of course you haven't. Nobody ever leaves this island, do they? Not even to see a panda. Well, long story short, I offered to take him off their hands. It seems neither of us is terribly fond of our own species. I'm having a barn built for him, right here on the property—for the winter, you see."

Candy stood up as she spoke, and Ray followed her through a large, brand-new oak door that she left open behind them as they entered the foyer. Her loose pajama bottoms swished as she walked, and she wore a T-shirt with crusted blue paint on the sleeves. Long strands of hair had come loose from the messy bun atop her head, and they whipped about her face as she moved through the house. She brushed them away with absentminded flicks of her hand. In a crisp collared shirt, Ray felt overdressed. It was strange to think of people living regular lives in these extravagant mansions, waking late, burning toast, spilling coffee, clogging the shower drain. But Candy seemed as though she would have been as comfortable in a trailer park as she was here in this four-story granite edifice.

Through the high-ceilinged foyer, she led him into a long hallway where several massive portraits leaned against the wall, yet to be hung. In the next room, they passed under a grand spiral staircase. Ray paused beneath a shimmering diamond chandelier, ogling it momentarily before hurrying to catch up with Candy. Her bare feet bounced purposefully across the marble floor.

A large set of French doors opened onto the back patio, which had been constructed atop a wide, raised ledge of polished slate overlooking the bay. The view was undisturbed by trees or roads. Rather, the grassy knoll upon which the house sat seemed to end just where the ocean began, the horizon line merging green to blue in a stunning trick of the eye. From where they sat, lodged comfortably in sturdy iron patio chairs, there wasn't the slightest suggestion that the limestone wall and a stretch of rocky beach would have stopped them from walking straight out into the water at the end of the lawn.

At some point prior to Ray's arrival, Candy had set out two glasses of bubbling liquid on a small table between the chairs. The drinks were garnished with sprigs of mint and slices of lemon, which bobbed drowsily among several ice cubes.

Raising her glass to Ray in salutation, Candy took a long sip. Ray followed suit, savoring the crisp burn of the gin and tonic.

"You must be sick of views like this," she said.

An osprey skirted low across the water, its reflection rippling along the calm surface of the bay.

"Not at all," Ray replied.

"Really? When I was your age, all I wanted to do was go someplace loud—a big city or something. I used to come here as a girl, and I hated it. I hated the quiet," she mused, taking another long sip.

"You came here? Before you moved here?"

"Oh, yes. Every summer until I thought I'd blow my brains out. I nearly did once, actually. Then my mother never made me come here again. She basically pretended I wasn't in the family after that. The arrangement suited us both, I think. The old bird's dead now, of course, along with every other one of the East Coast Ridgemonts. Pretentious, isn't it? The way we amass such large families of such societally ordained prominence that we see fit to claim entire regions of the country in our name," she scoffed, pausing only to light a cigarette.

The cool drink settled in Ray's bones, and he reclined against the rigid, sloping back of the patio chair. Its metalwork arms, hot to the touch at first, now felt pleasant against his skin.

"Let me know when you tire of my self-loathing," she said with a short, staccato snort of laughter.

"So . . . you're a Ridgemont then?"

"Look at you, catching the good gossip. *A* Ridgemont. That's very good, yes. Not just Ridgemont but *a* Ridgemont. Not Candy Ridgemont but *the* Catherine Ridgemont. That's the tone they use, too, isn't it? You've been around Ocean Drive for a while now, haven't you?"

The timbre of her voice was pleasantly hoarse, like a veteran rock singer, and she chuckled as she spoke.

"Well, it's just that, you know, everyone talks about how you divorced some rich guy. I don't think anyone knows that *you* are actually the Ridgemont in the matter," Ray said.

He could hear the defensiveness in his voice and wished that he could speak with her same eloquence.

"None of that's true. Well, the Ridgemont part is true, of course. But the fact is, I've divorced three rich guys, not one. Ha! If only the Newport talking heads knew about the first two. The way they'd glom on to *that* tidbit! It's like buzzards to a stricken deer around here, isn't it?"

Were it not for the cocktail or the cigarette, the words might have just kept flowing from her mouth and into the air. Perhaps that was why she kept these props so close at hand, Ray thought.

"Well, why don't you tell them? That you're the Ridgemont, I mean, not about the other divorces. It might get them off your back, at least a little," Ray suggested.

Surely the remedy was as simple as confronting these masked gossipers with the truth, Ray thought, picturing Candy standing on a stage outside the Redwood Library with a microphone and her birth certificate and a sign that read "I AM ONE OF YOU."

"Why? Well, because it's all bullshit, Ray-buddy, if you'll be so kind as to pardon my French. It's just a name. That's all it is. Sure, Ridgemont means a little something in this bizarre little incestuous town. Maybe it even means something up the coast in Cape Cod and down a little to New York. But beyond that, nobody cares about the Ridgemonts. It's true! It's just a name, a word. I lived for three years in pleasant obscurity down in New Orleans. Now *there's* a city. Besides, I want to be the kind of person who doesn't rely on my name, don't you? Though of course, I do. Or I have, at least. Ha."

Afraid of disappointing her with a dull answer, he turned her questions over in his mind, trying fruitlessly to articulate something equally cutting or insightful.

"Yeah, I guess not."

Exhaling a light cloud of smoke, she cocked an eyebrow at him, waiting to see if he'd say more.

"New Orleans, yeah. You oughta check it out sometime. Colorful place," she continued when he was unforthcoming.

"So why'd you come back?"

For once, she was slow to respond, staring out at the horizon and blowing neat ringlets of smoke.

"Because I wanted to. And I wanted to be able to do the things that I wanted to do without fear of people disparaging my character simply because I had a name that attracted their lurid interests. Sticks and stones, and all that. And this place," she said, gesturing to the veritable castle behind her, "well, I hated it when I was growing up. But I'd have hated more to see it sold off just because I was afraid of a few bastards talking about me over martinis. Plus, I mean, Jesus, look at this place, would you? And me hiding out in New Orleans. It was too ridiculous to bear, even for me."

"Well, this place is gorgeous," Ray said.

"It had better be for what those Bane people charged," Candy scoffed, her eyes never leaving the sea. "That man. Do you know him? *Asshole*. Not a word I throw around casually, mind you."

For a long moment, they sat in silence, punctuated only by the clinking of ice cubes as they brought the drinks to their lips. The giraffe gamboled a short distance across the yard, its hooves thudding against the manicured grass.

"So what's next for you, Mr. Ray? And don't say Boston, or I'm sure I'll have a conniption," she said finally.

"Actually, I'm gonna be heading out to California."

While searching his wallet for loose change at the laundromat the day before, Ray had discovered the business card that the vintner had handed him at the liquor store. It felt like so long ago now, though it had only been a few months. He didn't expect the man to pick up when he called. But he had, and after a brief conversation, arrangements were made. He'd be living on the vineyard, spending his days learning about the fermentation process, from harvesting the grapes from ancient vines to storing the wine in casks and, eventually, bottling the product for sale. He'd bought a one-way ticket on his phone, right there in the laundromat. He was running away, he knew. The West Coast's promise of anonymity had a definite appeal, the opportunity to be a nobody from some obscure little island on the other side of the country for a while.

"Ah, moving to California to find yourself, is that it? Have yourself a little memoir-worthy experience, right? Manifest destiny, and all that? Sure. Not terribly original. It's about as cliché as getting a nose ring in your twenties—which I did, by the way—but it works. California's a pit," she said, waving her hand as though shooing away a fly. "But so are most places worth being."

◇◇◇◇◇◇◇◇◇◇◇◇◇◇◇◇◇◇◇◇

Deciding not to return the moped right away, Ray drove down the long, swooping curves of Ocean Drive to Reject's Beach. It was nearly empty but for a few college kids smoking a joint on the seawall and an older man wading in the gently lapping waves. Intent on watching the sunset, Ray plopped down onto the sand. The granules felt cool and soft between his fingers. The tractors humming along Periwinkle beach, just next door, were sweeping the sand clear of seaweed, depositing the great dark clumps of sea flora into a growing pile on Reject's side of the rope divider.

Ray had turned twenty-three a few days earlier. In a surprise arrangement by his mother, his friends had stopped by for a sumptuous feast of pernil, black beans and rice, tostones, and guava pastelitos. Tony was there too, with his new girlfriend, and, in a further surprise, his father had taken a week's leave to join the festivities. His mother had prepared far too much food and by the time the meal was over it was all anyone could do to move from their chairs. Though it had been a little awkward with his friends at first, everyone tiptoeing around his delicate mood, soon enough they were ribbing him about the accident as though it had been nothing more than yet another drunken anecdote that they would recall in increasingly dramatic detail for years to come.

Tomorrow would be September first. Coyne would be going to work for his uncle in Quincy and Bane for his dad at the company's Boston office, both of them unsurprised by how things had turned out but both also somewhat melancholy about the odd constraints of privilege. Kirley and Finch would be moving into an apartment in Southie together, making the most of their new lease by moving in on the first of the month. By this point in the summer, they were tired of their parents, anyway. McShane would stick around through Labor Day weekend, but then he too would be donning a suit and occupying a desk in Boston's financial district. Maya had already left for her medical school orientation, and Ella had plans to move in with a new boyfriend in Back Bay. Though ultimately their lives would remain the same—and though they would return to Newport for many summers to come—September was coming for them too.

But tonight, sitting on the sand and not moving even when the tide began to lick at his buried toes, Ray welcomed the end of August. The summer had left a sick feeling in his stomach, like when he'd eaten too much birthday cake as a kid. September had to come so that June could come again. They were reliant upon each other—not weakened by their dependence but strengthened by their resolute consistency.

His bare feet rooted in the sand, he stayed until long after the college kids had left the beach, giggling as they walked past him. The old man gave him a polite nod as he exited the water, leaving a wet trail on the sand behind him like a snail. Ray stayed on the beach until the sky went dark, the sun replaced by the bright glow of the moon.

THE END

Acknowledgments

I am so grateful to my parents, Michael and Laureen Bonin, and my siblings, Drake and Sydell, for their continued support of my creative pursuits. Furthermore, no succinct dedication line is sufficient to demonstrate just how much I value the support of my partner, Julia Thompson. I am forever grateful to my wonderful (and often debaucherous) friends: Starky, Lowis, Justin, Sheerin, Medley, Knowlan, and Pray—thank you all for inspiring the characters printed on the pages herein, and for simply being inspiring people yourselves. When your parents inevitably ask questions about our summer escapades on Aquidneck Island, be sure to remind them that *Glass Bottle Season* is a work of fiction. I would also like to thank Ryan Smernoff and Todd Bottorff at Turner Publishing/Keylight for believing in this novel and for working so hard to prepare it for publication. Finally, I would like to thank Rhode Island itself, for reasons obvious to anyone who has become acquainted with its shores and its people.

About the Author

FLETCHER MICHAEL is a writer from Rhode Island. He holds a BA from Salve Regina University and an MA in English Literature from Catholic University of America. Prior to attending graduate school, Fletcher taught English in Taiwan and worked at an art gallery and television studio in Manhattan. His work has been published in *Literary Imagination*, *Mobius Magazine*, *Meat for Tea: The Valley Review*, *Points in Case*, *Slackjaw*, *Jane Austen's Wastebasket*, and *The Lindenwood Review*. His debut novel, *Vulture*, was published in 2022. The fruits of his writing efforts can be found here: byfletch.wordpress.com.